THE
Ugly Duchess

Center Point
Large Print

Also by Eloisa James and available from
Center Point Large Print:

The Duke is Mine

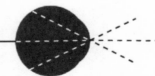

**This Large Print Book carries the
Seal of Approval of N.A.V.H.**

THE
Ugly Duchess

Eloisa James

CENTER POINT LARGE PRINT
THORNDIKE, MAINE

This Center Point Large Print edition
is published in the year 2012 by arrangement with
Avon Books, an imprint of HarperCollins Publishers.

The text of this Large Print edition is unabridged.
In other aspects, this book may vary
from the original edition.
Printed in the United States of America
on permanent paper.
Set in 16-point Times New Roman type.

ISBN: 978-1-61173-608-3

Library of Congress Cataloging-in-Publication Data

James, Eloisa.
The ugly duchess / Eloisa James. — Center Point Large Print ed.
p. cm.
ISBN 978-1-61173-608-3 (lib. bdg. : alk. paper)
1. Duchies—Fiction. 2. Dowry—Fiction. 3. Marital conflict—Fiction.
4. Man-woman relationships—Fiction. 5. Large type books. I. Title.
PS3560.A3796U35 2012
813′.54—dc23
2012034487

This book is dedicated to the wonderful poet and storyteller Hans Christian Andersen. His plots have given me obvious inspiration, as in this version of his fairy story *The Ugly Duckling*, but more than that, his ability to weave together joy and philosophical thought inspires every novel I write.

Acknowledgments

My books are like small children; they take a whole village to get them to a literate state. I want to offer my heartfelt thanks to my village: my editor, Carrie Feron; my agent, Kim Witherspoon; my website designers, Wax Creative; and my personal team: Kim Castillo, Franzeca Drouin, and Anne Connell.

Part One

Before

One

"You'll have to marry her. I don't care if you think of her as a sister: from now on, she's the Golden Fleece to you."

James Ryburn, Earl of Islay, and heir to the Duchy of Ashbrook, opened his mouth to say something, but a mixture of fury and disbelief choked the words.

His father turned and walked toward the far wall of the library, acting as if he'd said nothing particularly out of the ordinary. "We need her fortune to repair the Staffordshire estate and pay a few debts, or we're going to lose it all, this town house included."

"What have you done?" James spat the words. A terrible feeling of dread was spreading through his limbs.

Ashbrook pivoted. "Don't you *dare* speak to me in that tone!"

James took a deep breath before answering. One of his resolutions was to master his temper before turning twenty—and that birthday was a mere three weeks away. "Excuse me, Father," he managed. "Exactly how did the estate come to be

9

in such precarious straits? If you don't mind my asking."

"I do mind your asking." The duke stared back at his only son, his long, aquiline nose quivering with anger. James came by his temper naturally: he had inherited it directly from his irascible, reckless father.

"In that case, I will bid you good day," James said, keeping his tone even.

"Not unless you're going downstairs to make eyes at that girl. I turned down an offer for her hand this week from Briscott, who's such a simpleton that I didn't feel I need tell her mother. But you know damn well her father left the decision over who marries the girl to her mother—"

"I have no knowledge of the contents of Mr. Saxby's will," James stated. "And I fail to see why that particular provision should cause you such annoyance."

"Because we need her damned fortune," Ashbrook raged, walking to the fireplace and giving the unlit logs a kick. "You must convince Theodora that you're in love with her, or her mother will never agree to the match. Just last week, Mrs. Saxby inquired about a few of my investments in a manner that I did not appreciate. Doesn't know a woman's place."

"I will do nothing of the sort."

"You will do exactly as I instruct you."

"You're instructing me to woo a young lady whom I've been raised to treat as a *sister.*"

"Hogwash! You may have rubbed noses a few times as children, but that shouldn't stop you from sleeping with her."

"I cannot."

For the first time the duke looked a trifle sympathetic. "Theodora is no beauty. But all women are the same in the—"

"Do *not* say that," James snapped. "I am already appalled; I do not wish to be disgusted as well."

His father's eyes narrowed and a rusty color rose in his cheeks, a certain sign of danger. Sure enough, Ashbrook's voice emerged as a bellow. "I don't care if the chit is as ugly as sin, you'll take her. And you'll make her fall in love with you. Otherwise, you will have no country house to inherit. None!"

"What have you done?" James repeated through clenched teeth.

"Lost it," his father shouted back, his eyes bulging a little. "Lost it, and that's all you need to know!"

"I will not do it." James stood up.

A china ornament flew past his shoulder and crashed against the wall. James barely flinched. By now he was inured to these violent fits of temper; he had grown up ducking everything from books to marble statues.

11

"You will, or I'll bloody well disinherit you and name Pinkler-Ryburn my heir!"

James's hand dropped and he turned, on the verge of losing his temper. While he'd never had the impulse to throw objects at the wall—or at his family—his ability to fire cutting remarks was equally destructive. He took another deep breath. "While I would hesitate to instruct you on the legal system, *Father,* I can assure you that it is impossible to disinherit a legitimate son."

"I'll tell the House of Lords that you're no child of mine," the duke bellowed. Veins bulged on his forehead and his cheeks had ripened from red to purple. "I'll tell 'em that your mother was a light-heeled wench and that I've discovered you're nothing but a bastard."

At the insult to his mother, James's fragile control snapped altogether. "You may be a craven, dim-witted gamester, but you will *not* tar my mother with sorry excuses designed to cover up your own idiocy!"

"How dare you!" screamed the duke. His whole face had assumed the color of a cockscomb.

"I say only what every person in this kingdom knows," James said, the words exploding from his mouth. "You're an idiot. I have a good idea what happened to the estate; I just wanted to see whether you had the balls to admit it. And you don't. No surprise there. You mortgaged every piece of non-entailed land attached to the estate, at least those you didn't sell outright—and pissed all the money away on the Exchange. You invested in one ridiculous scheme after another. The canal you built that wasn't even a league from another canal? What in God's name were you thinking?"

"I didn't know that until it was too late! My associates deceived me. A duke doesn't go out and inspect the place where a canal is supposed to be built. He has to trust others, and I've always had the devil's own luck."

"I would have at least visited the proposed canal before I sank thousands of pounds into a waterway with no hope of traffic."

"You impudent jack-boy! How dare you!" The duke's hand tightened around a silver candlestick standing on the mantelpiece.

"Throw that, and I'll leave you in this room to wallow in your own fear. You want me to marry a girl who thinks I'm her brother in order to get her fortune . . . so that you—*you*—can lose it? Do you know what they call you behind your back, Father? Surely you've heard it. The Dam'Fool Duke!"

They were both breathing heavily, but his father was puffing like a bull, the purple stain on his cheeks vivid against his white neck cloth.

The duke's fingers flexed once again around the piece of silver.

"Throw that candlestick and I'll throw you across the room," James said, adding, "Your Grace."

The duke's hand fell to his side and he turned his shoulder away, staring at the far wall. "And what if I lost it?" he muttered, belligerence underscoring his confession. "The fact is that I did lose it. I lost it all. The canal was one thing, but I thought the vineyards were a sure thing. How could I possibly guess that England is a breeding ground for black rot?"

"You imbecile!" James spat and turned on his heel to go.

"The Staffordshire estate's been in our family for six generations. You must save it. Your mother would have been devastated to see the estate sold. And what of her grave . . . have you thought of that? The graveyard adjoins the chapel, you know."

James's heart was beating savagely in his throat. It took him a moment to come up with a response that didn't include curling his hands around his father's neck. "That is low, even from you," he said finally.

The duke paid no heed to his rejoinder. "Are you going to allow your mother's corpse to be sold?"

"I will consider wooing some other heiress," James said finally. "But I will not marry Daisy." Theodora Saxby—known to James alone as Daisy—was his dearest friend, his childhood companion. "She deserves better than me, better than anyone from this benighted family."

There was silence behind him. A terrible,

warped silence that . . . James turned. "You didn't. Even you . . . *couldn't.*"

"I thought I would be able to replace it in a matter of weeks," his father said, the color leaving his cheeks suddenly so that he looked positively used up.

James's legs felt so weak that he had to lean against the door. "How much of her fortune is gone?"

"Enough." Ashbrook dropped his eyes, at last showing some sign of shame. "If she marries anyone else, I'll . . . I'll face trial. I don't know if they can put dukes in the dock. The House of Lords, I suppose. But it won't be pretty."

"Oh, they can put dukes on trial, all right," James said heavily. "You embezzled the dowry of a girl entrusted to your care since the time she was a mere infant. Her mother was married to your dearest friend. Saxby asked you *on his deathbed* to care for his daughter."

"And I did," her father replied, but without his usual bluster. "Brought her up as my own."

"You brought her up as my sister," James said flatly. He forced himself to cross the room and sit down. "And all the time you were stealing from her."

"Not all the time," his father protested. "Just in the last year. Or so. The majority of her fortune is in funds, and I couldn't touch that. I just . . . I just borrowed from . . . well, I just borrowed some.

I'm deuced unlucky, and that's a fact. I was absolutely sure it wouldn't come to this."

"Unlucky?" James repeated, his voice liquid with disgust.

"Now the girl is getting a proposal or two, I don't have the time to make it up. You've got to take her. It's not just that the estate and this town house will have to go; after the scandal, the name won't be worth anything, either. Even if I pay off what I borrowed from her by selling the estate, the whole wouldn't cover my debts."

James didn't reply. The only words going through his head were flatly blasphemous.

"It was easier when your mother was alive," the duke said, after a minute or two. "She helped, you know. She had a level head on her shoulders."

James couldn't bring himself to answer that, either. His mother had died nine years earlier, so in under a decade his father had managed to impoverish an estate stretching from Scotland to Staffordshire to London. And he had embezzled Daisy's fortune.

"You'll make her love you," his father said encouragingly, dropping into a chair opposite James. "She already adores you; she always has. We've been lucky so far in that poor Theodora is as ugly as a stick. The only men who've asked for her hand have been such obvious fortune hunters that her mother wouldn't even consider them. But that'll change as the season wears on. She's a taking little piece, once you get to know her."

James ground his teeth. "She will never love me in that way. She thinks of me as her brother, as her friend. And she has no resemblance whatsoever to a *stick*."

"Don't be a fool. You've got my profile." A glimmer of vanity underscored his words. "Your mother always said that I was the most handsome man of my generation."

James bit back a remark that would do nothing to help the situation. He was experiencing an overwhelming wave of nausea. "We could tell Daisy what happened. What you did. She'll understand."

His father snorted. "Do you think her mother will understand? My old friend Saxby didn't know what he was getting into when he married that woman. She's a termagant, a positive tartar."

In the seventeen years since Mrs. Saxby and her infant daughter had joined the duke's household, she and Ashbrook had managed to maintain sufficiently cordial relations—primarily because His Grace had never thrown anything in the widow's direction. But James knew instantly that his father was right. If Daisy's mother got even a hint that her daughter's guardian had misappropriated her inheritance, a fleet of solicitors would be battering on the town house door before evening fell. Bile drove James's stomach into his throat at the thought.

His father, on the other hand, was cheering up. He

had the sort of mind that flitted from one subject to another; his rages were ferocious but short-lived. "A few posies, maybe a poem, and Theodora will fall into your hand as sweetly as a ripe plum. After all, it's not as if the girl gets much flattery. Tell her she's beautiful, and she'll be at your feet."

"I cannot do that," James stated, not even bothering to imagine himself saying such a thing. It wasn't a matter of not wishing to spout such inanities to Daisy herself; he loathed situations where he found himself fumbling with language and stumbling around the ballroom. The season was three weeks old, but he hadn't attended a single ball.

His father misinterpreted his refusal. "Of course, you'll have to lie about it, but that's the kind of lie a gentleman can't avoid. She may not be the prettiest girl on the market—and certainly not as delectable as that opera dancer I saw you with the other night—but it wouldn't get you anywhere to point out the truth." He actually gave a little chuckle at the thought.

James heard him only dimly; he was concentrating on not throwing up as he tried to think through the dilemma before him.

The duke continued, amusing himself by laying out the distinction between mistresses and wives. "In compensation, you can keep a mistress who's twice as beautiful as your wife. It'll provide an interesting contrast."

It occurred to James, not for the first time, that there was no human being in the world he loathed as much as his father. "If I marry Daisy, I will not take a mistress," he said, still thinking frantically, trying to come up with a way out. "I would never do that to her."

"Well, I expect you'll change your mind about that after a few years of marriage, but to each his own." The duke's voice was as strong and cheerful as ever. "Well? Not much to think about, is there? It's bad luck and all that rot, but I can't see that either of us has much choice about it. The good thing is that a man can always perform in the bedroom, even if he doesn't want to."

The only thing James wanted at that moment was to get out of the room, away from his disgusting excuse for a parent. But he had lost the battle, and he forced himself to lay out the rules for surrender. "I will only do this on one condition." His voice sounded unfamiliar to his own ears, as if a stranger spoke the words.

"Anything, my boy, anything! I know I'm asking for a sacrifice. As I said, we can admit amongst ourselves that little Theodora is not the beauty of the bunch."

"The day I marry her, you sign the entire estate over to me—the Staffordshire house and its lands, this town house, the island in Scotland."

The duke's mouth fell open. *"What?"*

"The entire estate," James repeated. "I will pay

you an allowance, and no one need know except for the solicitors. But I will *not* be responsible for you and your harebrained schemes. I will never again take responsibility for any debts you might incur—nor for any theft. The next time around, you'll go to prison."

"That's absurd," his father spluttered. "I couldn't—you couldn't possibly—no!"

"Then make your good-byes to Staffordshire," James said. "You might want to pay a special visit to my mother's grave, if you're so certain she would have been distressed at the sale of the house, let alone the churchyard."

His father opened his mouth, but James raised a hand.

"If I were to let you keep the estate, you'd fling Daisy's inheritance after that which you've already lost. There would be nothing left within two years, and I will have betrayed my closest friend for no reason."

"Your closest friend, eh?" His father was instantly diverted into another train of thought. "I've never had a woman as a friend, but Theodora looks like a man, of course, and—"

"Father!"

The duke harrumphed. "Can't say I like the way you've taken to interrupting me. I suppose if I agree to this ridiculous scheme of yours I can expect to look forward to daily humiliation."

It was an implicit concession.

"You see," his father said, a smile spreading across his face now that the conversation was over, "it all came well. Your mother always said that, you know. 'All's well that ends well.' "

James couldn't stop himself from asking one more thing, though, God knows, he already knew the answer. "Don't you care in the least about what you're doing to me—and to Daisy?"

A hint of red crept back into his father's cheeks. "The girl couldn't do better than to marry you!"

"Daisy will marry me believing that I'm in love with her, and I'm not. She deserves to be wooed and genuinely adored by her husband."

"Love and marriage shouldn't be mentioned in the same breath," his father said dismissively. But his eyes slid away from James's.

"And you've done the same to me. Love and marriage may not come together all that often, but I will have no chance at all. What's more, I will begin my marriage with a lie that will destroy it if Daisy ever finds out. Do you realize that? If she learns that I betrayed her in such a callous way . . . not only my marriage, but our friendship, will be over."

"If you really think she'll fly into a temper, you'd better get an heir on her in the first few months," his father said with the air of someone offering practical advice. "A woman scorned, and all that. If she's disgruntled enough, I suppose she might run off with another man. But if you already

21

have an heir—and a spare, if you can—you could let her go."

"My wife will *never* run off with another man." That growled out of James's chest from a place he didn't even know existed.

His father heaved himself out of his chair. "You as much as called me a fool; well, I'll do the same for you. No man in his right mind thinks that marriage is a matter of billing and cooing. Your mother and I were married for the right reasons, to do with family obligations and financial negotiations. We did what was necessary to have you and left it there. Your mother couldn't face the effort needed for a spare, but we didn't waste any tears over it. You were always a healthy boy." Then he added, "Barring that time you almost went blind, of course. We would have tried for another, if worse came to worst."

James pushed himself to his feet, hearing his father's voice dimly through a tangle of hideous thoughts that he couldn't bring himself to spit out.

"Neither of us raised you to have such rubbishing romantic views," the duke tossed over his shoulder as he left the room.

Having reached the age of nineteen years, James had thought he understood his place in life. He'd learned the most important lessons: how to ride a horse, hold his liquor, and defend himself in a duel.

No one had ever taught him—and he had never

imagined the necessity of learning—how to betray the one person whom you truly cared for in life. The only person who genuinely loved you. How to break that person's heart, whether it be tomorrow, or five years, or ten years in the future.

Because Daisy would learn the truth someday. He knew it with a bone-deep certainty: somehow, she would discover that he had pretended to fall in love so that she would marry him . . . and she would never forgive him.

Two

Theodora Saxby, known to James as Daisy, but to herself as Theo, was trying very hard not to think about Lady Corning's ball, which had been held the night before. But, as is often the case when one tries to avoid a topic, the only thing her mind saw fit to review was a scene from said ball.

The girls she had overheard chattering about her resemblance to a boy weren't even being particularly unkind. They weren't saying it *to* her, after all. And she wouldn't have minded their comments so much if she didn't have the distinct impression that the gentlemen at the ball agreed with them.

But what could she possibly do about it? She stared despairingly into her glass. Her mother's fear of just that assessment—though Mama refused to acknowledge it—had led to Theo's hair being turned to ringlets with a curling iron. The gown she'd worn, like everything else in her wardrobe, was white and frilly and altogether feminine. It was picked out in pearls and touches of pink, a combination that (in her opinion) did nothing but emphasize the decidedly *un*feminine cast of her profile.

She loathed her profile almost as much as she loathed the dress. If she didn't have to worry about people mistaking her for a boy—not that they really did, but they couldn't stop remarking on the resemblance; at any rate, if she didn't have to worry about that—she would never again wear pink. Or pearls. There was something dreadfully banal about the way pearls shimmered.

For a moment she distracted herself by mentally ripping her dress apart, stripping it of its ruffles and pearls and tiny sleeves. Given a choice, she would dress in plum-colored corded silk and sleek her hair away from her face without a single flyaway curl. Her only hair adornment would be an enormous feather—a black one—arching backward so it brushed her shoulder. If her sleeves were elbow-length, she could trim them with a narrow edging of black fur. Or perhaps swans-down, with the same at the neck. Or she could put a feather trim at the neck; the white would look shocking against the plum velvet.

That led to the idea that she could put a ruff at the neck and trim that with a narrow strip of swansdown. It would be even better if the sleeves weren't opaque fabric but nearly transparent, like that new Indian silk her friend Lucinda had been wearing the previous night, and she would have them quite wide, so they billowed and then gathered tight at the elbow. Or perhaps the wrist would be more dramatic. . . .

She could see herself entering a ballroom in that costume. No one would titter about whether she looked like a girl or a boy. She would pause for a moment on the top of the steps, gathering everyone's gaze, and then she would snap open her fan. . . . No, fans were tiresomely overdone. She'd have to come up with something new.

The first man who asked her to dance, addressing her as Miss Saxby, would be treated to her slightly weary yet amused smile. "Call me Theo," she would say, and all the matrons would be so scandalized they would squeak about nothing else the whole night long.

Theo was key: the name played to all those infatuations men formed on each other, the way their closest relationships were with their friends rather than with their wives. She'd seen it with James. When he was thirteen he had positively worshipped the captain of the cricket team at Eton. It stood to reason that if she wore her hair sleeked back, along with a gown that faintly resembled a cricket uniform, all those men who had once adored their captains would be at her feet.

25

She was so caught up in a vision of herself in a severely tailored jacket resembling the Etonian morning coat that at first she didn't even hear the pounding on her door. But an insistent *"Daisy!"* finally broke through her trance, and she pushed herself up from the settee and opened the bedchamber door.

"Oh hello, James," she said, unable to muster much enthusiasm at the sight of him. The last thing one wants to see when in a melancholic fit is a friend who refuses to attend balls even when he knows perfectly well that all three weeks of her first season had been horrific. He had no idea what it was like. How could he? He was devastatingly handsome, rather charming when he wasn't being a beast, and a future duke, to boot. This embarrassment of riches really wasn't fair. "I didn't realize it was you."

"How could you not realize it was me?" James demanded, pushing open the door and crowding her backward, now that he knew she was decent. "I'm the only person in the world who calls you Daisy. Let me in, will you?"

Theo sighed and moved back. "Do you suppose you could try harder to call me Theo? I must have asked you a hundred times already. I don't want to be Theodora, or Dora, or Daisy, either."

James flung himself into a chair and ran a hand through his hair. From the look of it, he'd been in an ill humor all morning, because half his hair was standing straight up. It was lovely hair, heavy and thick. Sometimes it looked black, but when sunlight caught it there were deep mahogany strands, too. More reasons to resent James. Her own hair had nothing subtle about it. It was thick, too, but an unfashionable yellowy-brown mixture.

"No," he said flatly. "You're Daisy to me, and Daisy suits you."

"It doesn't suit me," she retorted. "Daisies are pretty and fresh, and I'm neither."

"You are pretty," he said mechanically, not even bothering to glance at her.

She rolled her eyes, but really, there was no reason to press the point. James never looked at her close enough to notice whether she'd turned out pretty . . . why should he? Being only two years apart, they'd shared the nursery practically from birth, which meant he had clear memories of her running about in a diaper, being smacked by Nurse Wiggan for being smart.

"How was last night?" he asked abruptly.

"Terrible."

"Trevelyan didn't make an appearance?"

"Geoffrey was indeed there," Theo said gloomily. "He just never looked at me. He danced twice—*twice*—with the cow-eyed Claribel. I can't stand her, and I can't believe he can either, which means he's just looking for a fortune. But if he *is,* then why doesn't he dance with me? My

27

inheritance must be twice as large as hers. Do you think he doesn't know? And if so," she said without stopping for breath, "can you think of some way of bringing it up that wouldn't be terribly obvious?"

"Absolutely," James said. "I can hear that conversation now. 'So, Trevelyan, you flat-footed looby, did you know that Theodora's inheritance comes to thousands of pounds a year? And by the way, what about those matched grays you just bought?' "

"You could think of a more adroit way to bring it up," Theo said, though she couldn't imagine it herself. "Geoffrey isn't flat-footed. He's as graceful as a leaf. You should have seen him dancing with cretinous Claribel."

James frowned. "Is she the one who was brought up in India?"

"Yes. I can't understand why some helpful tiger didn't gobble her up. All those plump curves . . . she would have made a lovely Sunday treat."

"Tsk, tsk," James said, a glimmer of laughter coming into his eyes for the first time. "Young ladies in search of husbands should be docile and sweet. You keep coming out with these appallingly malicious little remarks. If you don't behave, all those matrons will declare you unfit, and then you'll be in a pickle."

"I suppose that's part of my problem."

"What's the other part?"

"I'm not feminine or dainty, nor even deliciously curvy. No one seems to notice me."

"And you hate that," James said with a grin.

"Well, I do," she said. "I don't mind admitting it. I think I could attract a great many men if I were simply allowed to be myself. But pink ruffles and pearl trim make me look more mannish than ever. And I *feel* ugly, which is the worst thing of all."

"I don't think you look like a man," James said, finally inspecting her from head to foot.

"You know that opera dancer you've been squiring about?"

"You're not supposed to know about Bella!"

"Why on earth not? Mama and I were in Oxford Street when you passed in an open carriage, so Mama explained everything. She even knew that your mistress is an opera dancer. I have to say, James, I think it's amazing that you got yourself a mistress whom everyone knows about, even people like my mother."

"I can't believe Mrs. Saxby told you that rot."

"What? She's not an opera dancer?"

He scowled. "You're supposed to pretend that women like that don't exist."

"Don't be thick, James. Ladies know all about mistresses. And it isn't as if you're married. If you carry on like that once you *are* married, I'm going to be terrifically nasty to you. I'll definitely tell your wife. So beware. I don't approve."

"Of Bella, or of matrimony?"

"Of married men who run about London with voluptuous women with hair the color of flax and morals that are just as lax."

She paused for a moment, but James just rolled his eyes. "It's not easy to rhyme extempore, you know," she told him.

He obviously didn't care, so she returned to the subject. "It's all very well now, but you'll have to give up Bella when you marry. Or whatever her replacement's name is by then."

"I don't want to get married," James said. There was a kind of grinding tension in his voice that made Theo look at him more closely.

"You've been quarreling with your father, haven't you?"

He nodded.

"In the library?"

He nodded again.

"Did he try to brain you with that silver candlestick?" she asked. "Cramble told me that he was going to put it away, but I noticed it was still there yesterday."

"He demolished a porcelain shepherdess."

"Oh, that's all right. Cramble bought a whole collection of them in Haymarket and strewed them all around the house in obvious places hoping your father would snatch those as opposed to anything of value. He will be quite pleased to see that his plan is working. So what were you rowing about?"

"He wants me to marry."

"Really?" Theo felt a not altogether pleasant pang of surprise. Of course James had to marry . . . someday. But at the moment she rather liked him as he was: hers. Well, hers and Bella's. "You're too young," she said protectively.

"*You* are only seventeen and you're looking for a husband."

"But that's just the right age for a woman to marry. Mama didn't let me debut until this year precisely because of that. Men should be far older than nineteen. I expect thirty or one-and-thirty is about right. What's more, you're young for your age," she added.

James narrowed his eyes. "I am not."

"You are," she said smugly. "I saw how you were flitting about with Bella, showing her off as if she were a new coat. You probably set her up in some sort of appalling little house draped in blush-colored satin."

His scowl was truly ferocious, which, rather than alarming her, merely gave Theo confirmation. "At the very least, she could have chosen some shade of blue. Women with yellow hair always think that pink shades will flatter their skin. Whereas a blue, say a cerulean or even violet, would be far more pleasing."

"I'll let her know. You do realize, Daisy, that you're not supposed to mention women like Bella in polite company, let alone offer advice on how they should design their nests?"

31

"When did you become *polite* company? Do *not* call me Daisy," Theo retorted. "Whom are you thinking of marrying?" She did not like uttering that question. She had something of a possessive bent when it came to James.

"I have no one in mind." But the corner of his mouth twitched.

"You're lying!" she cried, pouncing on it. "You *do* have someone in mind! Who is she?"

He sighed. "There's no one."

"Since you haven't been to a single ball this year, I cannot imagine whom you could have fixed your eye on. Did you go to any balls last year, when I was still confined to the schoolroom? Of course, *I* should play an important part in choosing your betrothed," Theo said, getting into the spirit of it. "I know you better than anyone else. She'll have to be musical, given what a beautiful voice you have."

"I am *not* interested in anyone who can sing." James's eyes flashed at her in a way that Theo secretly rather liked. Most of the time he was just the funny, wry "brother" she'd had her whole life, but occasionally he turned electric with fury and she saw him in a whole different light. Like a man, she decided. Odd thought.

She waved her hands. "For goodness' sake, James, calm down. I must have mistaken the sure sign that you were fibbing." She grinned at him. "Do you think I would tease you about your choice? I, who blurted out my adoration of Geoffrey? At least you don't have to worry about being entirely overlooked by your beloved. You're quite good looking; the girls don't know you well enough to guess at your faults; you sing like an angel when someone can coax you into it; and you shall have a title someday. They would have fallen about hoping to dance with you last night and I could have watched it from the side."

"I loathe balls," James said, but he wasn't really paying attention. He was trying to puzzle something out; she recognized the look.

"She's not *married,* is she?" Theo asked.

"Married? Who's married?"

"The woman who has fixed your attention!"

"There isn't anyone." The edge of his mouth didn't curl, so he was probably telling the truth.

"Petra Abbot-Sheffield has a lovely singing voice," Theo said thoughtfully.

"I hate singing."

Theo knew that, but she thought he would surely grow out of it. When James sang "Lives again our glorious king!" in church she found herself shivering all over at the pure beauty of it, the way his voice swooped up to the rafters and then settled into an angel's trumpet for "Where, O death, is now thy sting?" Whenever he sang she thought of bright green leaves in late spring. "Isn't it interesting that I think in colors," she asked now, "and you think in music?"

33

"Not at all, because I do not think about music."

"Well, you *should* think in music," Theo revised. "Given your voice." But he was obviously in a serious temper, and she had learned over the years that the best tactic was not to engage when he was peevish.

"I wish I had your advantages." She dropped onto her bed and drew up her knees so she could hug them against her chest. "If I were you, Geoffrey would be at my feet."

"I doubt it. He wouldn't want a wife who has to shave twice a day."

"You know what I meant. All I need is for people to start paying attention to me," Theo said, rocking back and forth a little bit. "If I just had even the smallest audience, I could be funny. You know I could, James. I could talk circles about Claribel. I just need one proper suitor, someone who's not a fortune hunter. Someone who would . . ." An idea popped into her head, fully formed and beautiful.

"James!"

"What?" He raised his head.

For a moment, looking at him, she almost dropped her idea. His eyes were positively tragic, and there were hollows in his cheeks, as if he hadn't eaten enough lately. He looked exhausted. "Are you all right? What on earth did you do last night? You look like a drunkard who spent a night in a back alley."

"I'm fine."

One had to suppose he had spent the previous evening drowning in cognac. Her mother was of the opinion that gentlemen pickled themselves in the stuff by age thirty as a matter of course. "I have an idea," she said, returning to her point. "But it would mean that you'd have to delay your plan to marry for the immediate present."

"I have no such plan. I don't wish to get married, no matter what my father says about it." James could be maddeningly sullen when he wished. It had gotten better since he was fifteen, but not that much better. "Do you know what I hate most in the world?"

"I'm sure you'll say your father, but you don't really mean it."

"Besides him. I hate feeling guilty."

"Who on earth makes you feel guilty? You're the perfect scion of the house of Ashbrook."

He ran a hand through his hair again. "That's just what everyone thinks. Sometimes I would kill to go away, where they've never heard of earls and *noblesse oblige* and all the rest of it. Where a man could be judged on who he is, rather than on his title and the rest of that tomfoolery."

Theo frowned at him. "I don't see where the guilt comes in."

"I'll never be good enough." He got up and strode to the side of the room to look out the window.

"You're being absurd! Everyone loves you, including me, and if that doesn't mean something, I don't know what does. I know you better than anyone in the world, and if I say you're good enough, then you are."

He turned around, and she found to her relief that he had a lopsided smile on his face. "Daisy, do you suppose you'll try to take over the House of Parliament someday?"

"They should be so lucky!" she retorted. "But seriously, James, will you at least listen to my plan?"

"To conquer the world?"

"To conquer Geoffrey, which is much more important. If you would pretend to woo me, just long enough so that I would be noticed, it would mean the world to me. You never come to balls, and if you began to escort me, then everyone would be asking why, and before we knew it, I would find myself talking to Geoffrey about something . . . and then I could charm him into overlooking my profile and he would be mine." She sat back, triumphant. "Isn't that a brilliant plan?"

James's eyes narrowed. "It has some advantages."

"Such as?"

"Father would think I was wooing you and leave me alone for a bit."

Theo clapped. "Perfect! I'm absolutely certain that Geoffrey will talk to you. Wasn't he head boy in your last year at Eton?"

36

"Yes, and because of that I can tell you straight out that Trevelyan would make an uncomfortable husband. He's far too clever for his own good. And he has a nasty way of making jokes about people."

"That's what I like about him."

"Not to mention the fact that he's ugly as sin," James added.

"He isn't! He's deliciously tall and his eyes are bronzy-brown colored. They make me think of—"

"Do not tell me," James said with an expression of utter revulsion. "I don't want to know."

"Of morning chocolate," Theo said, ignoring him. "Or Tib's eyes when he was a puppy."

"Tib is a dog," James said, displaying a talent for the obvious. "You think the love of your life looks like a ten-year-old obese *dog?*" He assumed a mockingly thoughtful attitude. "You're right! Trevelyan does have a doggy look about him! Why didn't I notice that?"

Demonstrating that she had not spent seventeen years in the Duke of Ashbrook's household for nothing, Theo threw one of her slippers straight at James's head. It skimmed his ear, which led to an ungraceful (and rather juvenile) scene in which he chased her around the bedchamber. When he caught her, he snatched her around the waist, bent her forward, and rubbed his knuckles into her skull while she howled in protest.

It was a scene that Theo's bedroom, and indeed,

many other chambers on various Ashbrook estates, had seen many a time.

But even as Theo howled and kicked at his ankles, James had the sudden realization that he was holding a fragrant bundle of woman. That those were *breasts* against his arm. That Daisy's rounded bottom was grinding against him and it felt . . .

His hands flew apart without conscious volition, and she fell to the ground with an audible thud. There was true annoyance in her voice as she rose, rubbing her knee.

"What's the matter with you?" she scolded. "You've never let me fall before."

"We shouldn't play such games. We're—You're soon to be a married woman, after all."

Theo narrowed her eyes.

"And my arm is sore," James added quickly, feeling his cheeks warm. He hated lying. And he particularly hated lying to Daisy.

"You look fine to me," she said, giving him a sweeping glance. "I don't see an injury that warrants your dropping me on the floor like a teacup."

It wasn't until James practically ran from the room that Theo sank onto the bed and thought about what she *had* seen.

She'd seen that particular bulge in men's breeches before. It was a shock to see it on *James,* though. She didn't think of him in those terms.

But then, all of a sudden, she did.

Three

Eight hours later . . .

"Theodora, darling, are you ready?" Mrs. Saxby entered Theo's room in a headlong trot. Theo often thought of her dear mama as being like an ostrich, all neck and long legs in constant motion.

At the moment that neck was much in evidence, as diamonds glittered all over it.

"Tell me how I look," her mother demanded.

"Like St. Paul's at Christmas," Theo said, giving her a kiss. "All twinkly and pretty, as if you wore a necklace of stars."

Her mother turned a little pink. "I am wearing quite a lot of diamonds, aren't I? But the countess's ball comes only once a year. One should definitely put one's best foot forward."

"Or best diamonds, as the case may be," Theo agreed.

"Let me look at you, darling," her mother said, drawing back. "That dress is quite pretty."

"I loathe pretty," Theo said, knowing this opinion carried no weight. " 'Pretty' is terrible on me, Mama."

"I think you look absolutely lovely," her mother replied, honesty shining from her whole face. "Like the prettiest, sweetest girl in the whole of London."

"You don't think that you might be the slightest bit blinded by your maternal sensibilities?" Theo asked, submitting to a fragrant hug.

"Not at all. Not a bit."

"Last night I overheard two girls remarking on how much I look like a boy," Theo said, probing the memory like a sore tooth. "And let's not even entertain the idea that I'm *sweet,* Mama."

Her mother scowled. "That's absurd. How can anyone possibly think such a thing? They're probably blind, like poor Genevieve Heppler. Her mother will not allow her to wear her spectacles, and last night she blundered straight into me."

"They think it because I *do* look like a boy," Theo retorted. But she didn't expect agreement, and she didn't get it. "At any rate," she said, "James and I have hatched a scheme that will get me noticed by the utterly delicious Geoffrey."

For some reason, Mrs. Saxby did not think that young Lord Geoffrey Trevelyan was as perfect as Theo knew him to be. But, then, she hadn't spent much of the last three weeks examining him as closely as Theo had—albeit from afar, since they'd exchanged scarcely a word.

"James will pretend to woo me," Theo explained, turning to the mirror and patting the ringlets that had taken her maid a good hour to concoct.

Mrs. Saxby's mouth fell inelegantly open. "He will *what?*"

"Pretend—just pretend, obviously—to woo me. His father has determined it's time he looked for a wife. But James doesn't want to. You know how he hates even making an appearance at a ball, let alone engaging in polite conversation with a lady. But if it looks as if he's squiring me around the ballroom, not only will the duke be appeased, but everyone will take note, because James never comes to events like these. And that means they will notice *me*."

"They'll take note all right," her mother said.

"Once they are actually looking at me, I can attract Geoffrey's attention," Theo said. The scheme sounded rather foolish once she said it aloud. A man like Lord Geoffrey Trevelyan probably didn't care to have a horse-faced girl like herself making clever remarks at him.

But her mother looked rather surprisingly amenable. Then a frown crossed her face and she asked, quite sharply, "Whose idea was this?"

"Mine," Theo admitted. "I don't think James wanted to, but I didn't give him the chance to refuse. Besides, it is the perfect solution to the duke's demand that he marry. He's far too young, don't you think, Mama? He's not even twenty."

"I don't know about that," her mother said. "In terms of maturity, he's already at least a decade older than his father. And from what I hear, he'd better marry a girl with a fortune so that he can repair the estate once Ashbrook falls over in an

41

apoplectic fit. I expect that's why the duke is pushing him onto the market."

"You're always telling me not to make cutting remarks," Theo said. "Just listen to yourself, Mama. Do I really have to wear these pearls? I detest pearls."

"Young ladies wear pearls. What are you doing, darling?"

Theo looked up from her writing desk. "I'm amending my list. Just in case I *ever* get to dress as I wish."

"Something about pearls?"

"Yes. I've added two rules in the last day or so. *Pearls are for swine.*"

"And debutantes," her mother added. "What's the other one?"

"You won't like this one," Theo observed. *"Etonians merit consideration."*

"I don't dislike it. But I think rank is a better judge of a man than education. Besides that, there are schools other than Eton, my dear."

"Mama! This list has nothing to do with possible husbands; it only reflects how I shall dress when I have the chance to be myself. In short, once I am married. The Etonian morning coat is altogether delicious. I don't care a bit about the bodies inside it, unless one of them is mine."

"I hope I don't live to see you dress like a schoolboy," her mother said, shuddering visibly. "I don't like to even imagine it."

42

"Don't you remember the hopeless adoration James had for the captain of the cricket team after his first term? There's a great deal of glamour to be had by looking like a schoolboy, if I can figure out how to harness it. At least it would stop girls from being so *blasted* sympathetic about my profile."

"Here is my advice," her mother said, turning from the mirror. "Every time you detect even the faintest hint of sympathy from one of those empty-headed little chits, reach up and touch your grandmother's pearls. You may detest them, Theodora, but they are worth as much as most girls' dowries. There's much to be said for unentailed personal property when it comes to attractiveness."

"If I get near Geoffrey, I'll be sure to direct his attention to them. Maybe I will draw the string through my teeth, just to make sure he sees it." She came up behind her mother and gave her a hug. "I don't know why I couldn't have turned out to be as pretty as you are, Mama."

"You *are*—"

Theo interrupted her. "Hush. I have a long nose and chin and I look remarkably mannish. But I can live with it, or at least, I could if I didn't have to wear so many white ruffles that I look like a pail of foaming milk."

Her mother smiled at her in the glass. "There isn't a seventeen-year-old young lady in all

43

London who doesn't long to wear colors in the evening. It will happen soon enough."

"Once I'm Lady Geoffrey Trevelyan," Theo said with a giggle.

Four

When the ducal carriage drew up before Devonshire House, Theo hopped out after her mother, followed by an obedient, if morose, James. They all paused at the doorway to the ballroom for a good moment after they'd been announced, but to Theo's disappointment, no one seemed to notice that she was accompanied by the most elusive matrimonial catch of the year.

Not that anyone would have thought there was a possibility of catching James until this very moment.

"A sad crush," Mrs. Saxby said disapprovingly, surveying the floor. "The countess obviously did not prune the invitation list. I shall retire upstairs to play a round or two of piquet."

This was a development that Theo had both hoped and planned for. "James will escort me home," she said instantly. "I doubt he will agree to stay very long. We have to ease him into polite society."

44

In fact, James had already begun tugging at his neck cloth. "It's infernally hot in here. I shall remain a half hour at the most."

Theo's mother took one final look at the thronged room and departed for an upstairs sitting room, where she could play piquet with her friends all evening.

"Back up!" Theo hissed at James, as soon as her mother was well out of sight.

"What?"

Theo pulled him into the entrance hall. "Now that Mama's gone, I need a moment." She hauled him down the corridor and turned in at the first open door she saw, which turned out to be a nicely appointed sitting room with—thankfully—a glass over the mantelpiece. She removed her pearls and dropped them in James's pocket.

"They will ruin the line of my coat," he protested.

"As if you care! Mama says they are worth more than a dowry, so please endeavor not to lose them."

He grimaced, but gave in. Then she gave the pink ruffle around her neckline a sharp tug and—as she had strategically loosened its stitches earlier that afternoon—it came obediently away from her gown.

"I say, what are you doing?" James asked, rather alarmed. "You can't wear a bodice as low as that. You haven't anything covering your—yourself."

"Why can't I? It's not nearly as low as some

women out there are wearing. And they have bosoms like ostrich eggs compared to mine. I don't have much to show, so I might as well display what I have."

"You are certainly doing that," he said, his voice betraying a certain fascination.

Theo glanced up. "It's just a bosom, James."

He frowned, stepped back, and coughed.

"A very nice one, mind," she said, giving him a naughty smile. "Definitely one of my better features." With one tug, the pink ruffle was stripped off her left wrist, quickly followed by that on the right. Then she pulled the pins out of her carefully arranged curls and let her hair fall about her shoulders. Taking a band of copper-colored lace from her reticule, she wound it through her hair, pulled it back from her forehead, and secured it on top of her head with the pins so that it wouldn't fall down. It formed a rather disheveled chignon, but the contrast between her hair and the copper lace was definitely interesting.

"You look different," James said, narrowing his eyes at her reflection in the glass.

"I look better," Theo told him, with the confidence of someone who had practiced hair-plus-lace twisting five times that afternoon. "Do you think he'll like it?"

James was looking at her neckline again. "Who?"

"Geoffrey, of course!" Theo said. "Really,

46

James, do try to keep up." She glanced at herself in the glass. Without the horrid pink ruffles, her gown had a certain sophistication. Plus, her breasts did look delectable, if she said so herself.

"Oh! I forgot." She dug in her reticule and pulled out a brooch that had also belonged to her grandmother but was far more evocative than the pearls. It was heavy gold, in the shape of a rose, with a garnet pendant dangling below.

"What are you doing with that?" James asked. "I don't think that sort of jewelry is meant for gowns like yours."

"Like what?"

"Your dress is made out of that light stuff," he said. "Practically transparent."

"The silk net is covering a plain muslin," Theo told him. "This net is embroidered with curlicues and by far the best aspect of this wretched gown."

He peered a little closer. "Does your mother know you aren't wearing a chemise?"

"Of course I'm wearing a chemise!" Theo stated untruthfully. She fastened the piece just under her bosom, attached to the ribbon circling the gown's high waist. "Besides, my undergarments are none of your business, James."

"They are when I can see the whole line of your leg," he said, scowling. "Your mother won't like it."

"Do you like it—and obviously, here I mean you as an exemplar of your sex?"

"Must you talk like that?" he complained. But he obediently glanced at Theo's gown. She pushed her leg forward in such a way that its shape could be glimpsed—only glimpsed, mind you—through the silk net and its underskirt.

"It looks dashed odd," James said bluntly. "And so does that jewel you have hanging just below your bosom. People will think that you're deliberately trying to draw attention to that area."

"I am," she said with satisfaction. The garnet added a flash of color that complemented her hair ribbon. What's more, any gentlemen who missed her cleavage on the first glance would be encouraged to take another look.

Not to mention the fact that James was the most handsome man at the ball and some of his allure would rub off on her. She wound her arm through his. "I'm ready to make my entrance."

"Your mother will kill you. Or me," he added, even more unhappily.

"You ogled me a moment ago."

"I did not!" He made a fairly good stab at offended astonishment.

"Yes, you did," Theo retorted. "And frankly, James, if you ogle, other men will as well. Let's go back to the ballroom. I'm ready to find Geoffrey."

"Do you see him anywhere?" she hissed a moment later, smiling and nodding at Lady Bower, who seemed distinctly intrigued by the sight of James at Theo's side. Of course, she would be: she had three marriageable daughters.

"Who?" James said absentmindedly. He was pulling at his neck cloth again. "I think I'm going to suffocate. I don't think I can take even a half hour of this."

"Geoffrey!" she whispered, pinching his arm. "Remember? That's why you're here. You have to introduce me."

James frowned down at her. "I thought you already knew him."

"But he has never paid any attention to me," Theo said with remarkable patience, to her mind. "I already told you that."

James snorted. "That's right. I'm supposed to turn the conversation around to dowries and then announce that yours is bigger than—"

"Hush!" She pinched him again, so sharply that he winced. "I'm counting on you not to botch this up."

"I won't."

His eyes looked a little haunted. "It's not *so* terrible being here, is it?" Theo asked, rather startled by the strain in his face. "I know you don't like balls, James. If you just take me to Geoffrey, I promise to leave directly afterwards."

They stopped to let pass a herd of people making their way to the refreshments table. "I believe you are making a mistake," he said.

"About Geoffrey?"

James nodded. "I had to live with Trevelyan at

49

Eton, and I wouldn't want to repeat the experience or wish it on you."

"It's different if you're married, silly!" Theo said. She could just see herself and Geoffrey sitting opposite each other at the breakfast table, reading the papers. He was so clever, and he would appreciate her wit the way no one else did, including James and her own mother.

"Marriage would be even worse," James said. The crowd in front of them cleared, and they moved further into the ballroom. "At least I could wallop him when he was particularly pestilent."

"My marriage is nothing for you to worry about. Just please keep an eye out for him, will you? I'm not quite tall enough to see over people's heads."

"All right, I see Trevelyan," James said, drawing her to an opening in the crowd and motioning in the general direction of Theo's quarry. "He's with Claribel."

"Naturally," Theo said with a groan.

"She's dashed pretty."

"Flirt with her!" she commanded, struck by the idea. "You could do worse than marry her, you know."

"You want me to marry cretinous Claribel?" James said, in a not-very-effective whisper.

"I suppose not." Theo had just caught sight of Geoffrey, and she found herself clinging to James's arm in a sudden bout of nerves.

Lord Geoffrey Trevelyan had light brown hair

that he wore tousled in a style known as the Titus, and his clothes were always elegant, though not overly fastidious. But it was his face that fascinated Theo. It was narrow and sardonic, and the edges of his eyes slightly tilted up. You could take one glance and know that his lordship had graduated from Cambridge with a double first in philosophy and history.

He was just the right sort of man for Theo—not so handsome that she would always be aware that her husband was far better looking than she. (She actually felt a mild pity for whomever James married; that woman would forever remain in his shade.)

As it happened, Geoffrey was standing at the center of a knot of beautiful people. To a one, they had high cheekbones, deep bottom lips, and finely shaped noses. Even worse, they looked abominably clever, all except Claribel, of course.

Her stomach sank down to her knees, and for a moment she tried to hold James back. But just at that moment the group caught sight of him, and their faces lit up like tradesmen's wives seeing the queen.

There were even a few who greeted her.

Geoffrey was one of them. "Miss Saxby," he said, bowing.

Theo's heart was pounding in her throat from pure excitement. "Lord Geoffrey," she said, dropping a curtsy.

51

"Oh, Miss Saxby," Lady Claribel Sennock said in her high, piping voice. "You look lovely. Come meet my cousin, Lady Althea Renwitt."

"We've met," Althea said with perfect indifference, her eyes skating over Theo's bodice and then, without subtlety, riveting on James.

Watching her simper and hold out her hand to be kissed, Theo decided that there was nothing more rapacious than a young lady in the midst of a huddle of eligible gentlemen. Althea was like a fox with a clutch of hen's eggs.

"Is *he* your escort for this evening?" Claribel whispered. "How lucky you are to have grown up with him."

Theo really wished that Claribel was more of a beast; it would be easier to dislike her. Instead she was like tepid milk at bedtime. "James is very dear to me," Theo said, trying to sound romantically inclined.

Just then Geoffrey made some sort of joke about the deposed King of Imeretia, who had been visiting the English court for the last fortnight, and everyone laughed. Theo turned, resolved to be as witty as he was, no matter the subject. James, of course, was right in the middle of the group, entirely at ease.

It would be very easy to resent James. Wherever he went, people liked, if not loved, him, and he didn't even bother to be witty.

"In truth," Geoffrey was saying, "Her Royal

Highness is by all accounts discreet, of admirable temper, and guilty of not a single vice."

"When someone is said to have no vices," Theo said, before she could lose her courage, "it generally turns out that they have as many sins as hairs on their head."

"You think that the Princess of Imeretia has that many sins?" Geoffrey drawled. "Do tell us more, Miss Saxby."

Theo was aware that the entire group was listening, and her heartbeat grew even faster, though she managed to keep her expression casual. "Avarice is one of the seven deadly sins, and Her Highness bathes, it is said, in a solid silver bathtub," she said with a careless wave of her fan. "She has a private quartet that lulls her to sleep on restless nights. And surely you have noticed that she has a lover? Baron Grébert, the man with drooping mustaches and too much hair. He looks like a lion pretending to be a lion-tamer."

Claribel tittered nervously, but Geoffrey's eyebrow shot up and he looked at Theo more closely, a little smile curling his lips.

"And Her Highness," he asked. "How would you describe her?"

"A fox terrier in skirts," Theo said.

Geoffrey threw back his head and laughed, and all the other young men echoed him. Except James. He scowled, because he never liked it

53

when she was malicious, even when the malice was funny.

"I think I'm rather afraid of you," Geoffrey said. His eyes were warm and admiring.

"Yes, you should be," James stated.

"Lord Islay, you know Miss Saxby better than anyone," Claribel put in with a girlish squeal. "Surely she is not dangerous!"

Claribel was so dim that Theo thought there was a good chance she wasn't even joking.

"Theodora has a tongue as sharp as a cracked mirror," James said.

"Pish. I have sweet moments!" Theo said, flirting with Geoffrey over the edge of her fan.

"Yes, and they're about as convincing as Marie Antoinette pretending to be a shepherdess," James retorted. "It's bloody hot in here." He yanked at his neck cloth again, this time managing to untie it.

"Perhaps you should take yourself off, Islay," Geoffrey murmured. "You are looking conspicuously ungroomed; it quite reminds me of school, and not in a good way, either. Miss Saxby, that is a remarkable pendant."

Theo met his eyes just as he raised his from her cleavage—a moment they both enjoyed. "A gift from my grandmother," she murmured.

"The same grandmother who turned Theodora into an heiress," James said with the air of someone getting an unpleasant duty over with. "Well, I think it's time to leave, *darling*."

Geoffrey's eyebrow shot up at this, and he took a step back.

"Oh, but James," Theo said, "I'm not ready to leave." She smiled at Geoffrey, but she could see James's face from the corner of her eye. He looked as if he was going to explode, and she hastily decided that perhaps she had made sufficient inroads on Geoffrey's attentions for one evening.

She had the feeling that he would look for her the next night, and the one afterward.

Feeling magnanimous, Theo dropped a curtsy in the general direction of Claribel and the unpleasant Althea, and allowed James to tow her away.

James strode through the crowded ballroom like one of those Greek gods in a bad mood.

Theo trotted along beside, feeling too happy to protest.

Five

"I think that went very well," Theo said, once they were in the carriage on the way home.

"No, it did not," James said shortly.

"How can you say that? Geoffrey was quite taken with me!"

"He might have been taken with your bubbies."

"Bubbies? *Bubbies?* James, you really shouldn't be using that sort of slang around me," Theo said with some delight. "Bubbies. I love that word."

He leaned forward, and she realized with a start that he was furious. "Don't *'James'* me. You could not have been more obvious flirting with Trevelyan."

"That's true. I meant to be obvious."

"Well, do you want to know something? You don't belong with your darling Geoffrey. Not at all."

"Why not?"

"His tongue is even more spiteful than yours. He used to poke at me, just for fun, and if I had paid him any mind, he could have proved a pain in the ass."

Theo broke into a laugh. "You, upset?"

"I said, *if* I paid him any mind. You're not me, Theo. *You* would listen to him, and he would cut you to pieces."

"He will love me," Theo explained. "I shall quite enjoy watching him dissect our fellow man, but because he will love me, I'll be out of bounds."

"Nothing and no one is out of bounds for Trevelyan. I've heard him make jokes about his own mother. To be utterly frank, Daisy, he's the kind of man who is most himself when he is dressed as a woman."

"What!"

"Just what I said." James leaned back and looked at her with an insufferably smug expression. "I know him and you don't."

"Are you saying that he's interested in *men?*"

"Is there anything you don't dare to say aloud?" James yelped. "No, I am not! I'm just saying that he's an odd bird, that's all. Very odd. Not for you. I won't let you marry him."

"*You* won't let me marry him? *You?*" Theo was incensed. "Well, let me remind you that you have absolutely nothing to do with whom I marry. Nothing!"

James narrowed his eyes. "We'll see about that."

"There is nothing to see," she snapped. "If I want Geoffrey, I'll marry him."

"Not unless you want to share your silk stockings."

Theo gasped. "You're being unspeakably rude, and you should apologize. I don't know why you would say such a thing of Geoffrey."

"Because it's the truth. I lived with him. Only when he put on skirts—which he did at the slightest pretext—did he stop being so nervy that he bit at someone every five minutes. But go ahead. I gather you think you know him best."

"I *do* know Geoffrey best. You may have played at charades when you were at school. But he's grown up now, even if you haven't."

"Right. It's all my fault."

"Not your fault," Theo said. "But I think I understand men a bit better than you do, James. After all, you're still thinking of Geoffrey as a boy. I see him with a woman's eyes."

James scowled at her. "Woman's eyes! Piffle."

"If you accompany me just one more time," Theo coaxed him, "just to the royal musicale tomorrow night, after that I'm certain I will not need the attention I get from dragging you with me. Geoffrey has noticed me now, you see. One more encounter will be enough."

"For what? True love?"

"Perhaps," Theo said, thinking of the way Geoffrey's mouth curved up on one side and not the other. "Maybe."

"You wouldn't know true love if it hit you on the side of the head," James said, folding his arms over his chest.

"Well, you are no more of an expert. Don't tell me that you feel true love for Bella, because I know perfectly well you don't. You are infatuated with those enormous *bubbies* that she was displaying to everyone on Oxford Street."

"Look here," James said, looking a bit alarmed. "You mustn't start using that word. It's not polite."

"Bubbies!" Theo repeated, just stopping herself from sticking out her tongue at him. She was seventeen, after all. She had to act like a lady. "I know what you see in Bella," she contented herself with saying. "And it isn't love."

"Bella's attributes are not a matter for our conversation," James retorted.

Theo laughed. "Then her pretty face? I don't think so!"

"No more!"

"Who's going to talk to me about this sort of thing, if not you?" she said, relaxing back into the corner.

"Not me."

"Too late. You're the closest thing I have to a brother," Theo said, feeling a little sleepy. "Can you wake me up when we're home?"

James sat rigidly in his own corner and stared at her. Even with the dim lantern that lit the carriage he could see the line of her thigh. Not to mention her bubbies, breasts, whatever.

Trevelyan had certainly noticed them. James had to stop himself at the ball from reaching over and jerking the man's head out of Daisy's décolletage.

She would not marry Trevelyan. Not under any circumstances.

Even—even if he really did have to marry her himself to prevent it.

Six

The next evening
Carlton House
Residence of the Prince of Wales

To Theo's extreme annoyance, James not only didn't accompany her to the Prince of Wales's private musicale, but also didn't bother to show up until it was almost time for supper.

"Where have you been? You were supposed to be here hours ago," she hissed at him, pulling him away from the group to the other side of the drawing room, out of earshot. "Claribel has turned herself into a plaster and applied herself to Geoffrey; he's hardly had a moment to breathe, let alone notice I am in the room."

"Well, I'm here now," James said.

Theo took a closer look. He wore a beautiful indigo coat with dark green velvet lapels, entirely appropriate for a private musicale hosted by the Prince of Wales. But there was something about his face, and his eyes . . .

"You're tipsy!" she exclaimed, with some delight. "I've never seen you three sheets to the wind. Are you about to cast up your accounts, or will you just sway gently all night? You look like a hollyhock that someone forgot to stake."

"I never sway!" He sounded indignant.

"You're swaying now. For goodness' sake, look at that," she cried, nodding toward Claribel, who was leaning on Geoffrey's arm. "You'd think they were already betrothed. Or that she was as bosky as you are. I don't suppose you got a chance to mention my dowry to Geoffrey at White's this afternoon?"

"Funny, that," James said. "Trevelyan wasn't at the club, or in my carriage . . . wait . . . because he was here making sheep's eyes at Lady Claribel. How in bloody hell do you think I had the chance to drop your inheritance into the nonexistent conversation I've had with him? Besides, I mentioned it yesterday. That's good enough."

"*He's* not making sheep's eyes; *she* is. Oh well, it's probably better, since you're drunk anyway and would make a hash of it."

"What's better?" James said, looking more than a little owlish.

Theo looked up at him and felt a wave of affection. "I *do* adore you, James. You know that, don't you?"

"Don't say that I'm like a brother to you. Because I'm not your brother, and you should keep that in mind. We should both keep that in mind. That is, we're not siblings, even though we may feel like siblings. Sometimes."

"Perhaps you should take my arm," Theo suggested. "You'll be embarrassed tomorrow if you fall at the royal slippers like a chopped tree."

"Just back up a trifle," James said, looking distinctly inebriated. "I'll lean against the wall and pretend I'm speaking to you for a minute. I may have drunk a bit more cognac than was ad . . . ad . . . advisable. Is my father here?"

"Certainly he is," Theo said. "And he's peeved that you didn't come home to escort us here. You're lucky he hasn't seen you yet."

They stood to one side of Carlton House's music room. Most of the company was grouped in straight-backed chairs, listening raptly to the command performance of the evening. No one seemed to have noticed the two of them at the other end of the room.

"That fellow is pounding the keys in a way that will give everyone a headache," James complained, too loudly. "He sounds as awful as you used to, back when your mother still thought you might have a musical bone in your body."

"You mustn't say such a thing! That's Johann Baptist *Cramer*," Theo exclaimed. But she instantly realized there was no point in being shocked that James didn't recognize the celebrated pianist. He would never willingly sit through an evening of music.

If she didn't do something, he would create a scene. She took his hand and pulled him around the far side of a tall Chinese screen carved in lotus blossoms; at least anyone casually turning about wouldn't see him collapsing into an inebriated heap. Then she backed against the wall, tugging him over to her.

James swayed gently toward her, bracing himself by putting his hands against the wall, one on either side of her, creating a little cave that smelled like the best cognac and the outdoors, with just a note of soap.

"Just give me a moment until my head clears," he murmured. "What on earth are you thinking? You have the most peculiar look on your face."

"I'm smelling you," Theo said. "I never realized how nice you smell, James."

"Huh." James didn't seem to know what to make of that, but at least he didn't seem quite as wobbly as he had a few seconds ago.

"Perhaps we should find you a cup of tea," she suggested. For some reason—could it be that odd encounter they had had in her bedchamber the day before?—she was having some trouble thinking of James as casually as she ought. He was hopelessly beautiful. He had all the elegance of his father, but his jaw was measurably stronger, and his eyes were steady—even though he was tipsy. Just then his face came much closer.

"Are you about to fall over?" she squeaked.

But he wasn't.

Instead, he did the one thing that she had never imagined James doing: he kissed her. His lips came even closer, and then they touched hers.

His lips were very soft, Theo thought dimly.

That surprised her, though it shouldn't have. It was her first kiss, after all. Yet it was so unlike the kisses she had imagined.

She had imagined kisses as a delicate brushing of one pair of lips against another. But what was happening now was nothing like that. It wasn't the part about his lips, but that he put his tongue straight into her mouth, which was strange and yet intimate at the same time. In fact, the whole kiss was like that: a mix of the James she knew and a James she didn't know at all, a wild James. A manly James. It was all odd, and yet her knees went weak and she found her arms twining themselves around his neck.

James stood back from the wall, wrapped an arm around her waist, and pulled her against his chest. "Kiss me back," he demanded, low and fierce.

"How drunk are you?" Theo asked. "What are you doing?"

"You're my Daisy," he said, staring down at her. His voice was unsteady, his breathing harsh.

His eyes burned with an emotion that she didn't recognize, but it sent an instant thrill through her whole body. She started to speak, but he bent his head again and silently demanded that she kiss him back. The problem was that she wasn't sure how. At the same time, she rather desperately wanted to do whatever he asked, so she touched his tongue with her own. She expected it to be revolting, but instead . . .

Dimly, she knew that she should have laughed, or pushed him away, or called for help. Her mother—not to mention the Prince of Wales himself!—was only a matter of feet away, on the other side of the screen.

She should slap him, really. That's what a well-bred young lady would do after being grabbed by an inebriated gentleman and kissed in public. Or in private, for that matter.

But she wanted more of the taste of James, more of the melting fire that was sweeping her body, more of the irresistible longing that made her move closer and closer to him.

"That's it," he said, his voice a thread of sound.

Giddy heat seared what little logic Theo had left. She took his face in her hands. She could kiss the way he wanted. It wasn't really about tongues. It was a matter of *possessing* him. The way he was possessing her.

Once she realized that, kissing him was easy. Her tongue tumbled over his, and her fingers clenched his hair, knowing that the same flame that touched her singed him.

James made a kind of inarticulate noise, almost a groan, and pulled her closer. The sound of his growl was so heady that Theo shivered all down her body, a direct response to his tight grip and the sensual touch of his tongue. She had never thought of herself as particularly feminine—no girl who grew up with such pronounced features could do so—but in James's arms she suddenly felt feminine, not in a delicate way, but in a wild, erotic way.

It was intoxicating. It made her tremble with desire, from an almost savage feeling of wanting more of him. She pressed closer and felt her breasts flatten against his chest; he made that sound deep in his throat again. And then he *bit* her lip.

She gasped and—

Found herself reeling backward, thanks to a hand pulling her free as if she were a dog in a fight. To her profound dismay, it was her mother. "James Ryburn, what in the name of heaven do you think you're doing?" Mrs. Saxby demanded.

Theo stood still, breathless, her eyes fixed on James, feeling as if he'd somehow passed his intoxication on to her.

"And you, Theodora," her mother cried, rounding on her, "what in God's name do you think that you're doing? Have I taught you *nothing?*"

A deep, cultivated voice said in a rather amused fashion, "They don't call it the marriage mart for nothing, Mrs. Saxby. Looks like your girl will be the first of the season to tie the knot."

James made a choking noise and Theo turned around, only to find a group of fascinated spectators that included the Prince of Wales, Lord Geoffrey Trevelyan, and the despised Claribel, who for once was not ogling Geoffrey but had a look of stark envy on her face.

Theo looked at James and saw confusion in his face at the same moment that she realized that her lips felt puffy and her hair was falling around her shoulders. She must look like one of those ravished maidens in a bad melodrama.

But she had to say something. "I—We were just—"

James interrupted, his voice overriding hers. He no longer sounded tipsy. "I love Daisy. I am going to marry Daisy."

Theo's mouth fell open. James was glaring at her mother, his voice grating a little. "You want to marry her to another man, but she's *mine,* she's always been mine."

Theo drew in a breath, and he swung to her. "Do you remember when I had an eye inflammation when I was twelve and you were ten? And you read to me all that summer in a darkened room because my eyes were weak?"

She nodded, looking up at him in a daze, aware of their audience, and yet trying to ignore them.

"I didn't know it, but you were mine," he said, staring down at her almost as if he hated her.

"But I came out three weeks ago," she whispered, her words falling into the utterly still drawing room. "You didn't go to a single event until last night."

"I thought you were just dancing," he said, his

voice ragged. "I didn't think about it seriously. But if you are going to marry anyone, Daisy, it will be me. I don't want you to even think about other men." He shot a virulent look at Geoffrey, who fell back a step.

James turned back to Theo. A flash of uncertainty crossed his eyes. "I know you have other . . ."

"I do not know what I was thinking," Theo said slowly, feeling a tremendous sense of *rightness* settle about her shoulders like a warm blanket. She reached out and took his hand in hers—his familiar, utterly dear hand. "You're right. You are the only one."

"Well," her mother said firmly, from somewhere behind her. "I'm sure we can all agree that that was a *most* romantic proposal. But I think that's enough for the night."

Theo didn't move. Her oldest friend, her near-brother—that person was gone. Instead there was a desirable, powerful man looking down at her. And the look in his eye made her flush straight down to her toes.

"It isn't enough," James growled, his eyes fixed on hers. "She has not accepted. Daisy?"

"Yes," she said, her voice breathless and trembling in a fashion that she despised when other girls used it. "Yes, I will."

"I suppose that's settled," the Duke of Ashbrook said from behind James, the cheerful approval in his voice making them both look up. "Very convenient, what? My son marrying my ward. Keeps it all in the family, so to speak. Mind you, it wouldn't be proper unless it was a real love match."

Mrs. Saxby said briskly, "I certainly agree with you."

"But it looks as if we haven't much to say about it," the duke continued.

James met his father's eyes, and his heart dropped into his shoes. He had lost his head, and what's more, he lost it in service to the devil.

He had never experienced a kiss like that, never thought to feel such a searing wave of possessive passion in his life. But he had done it only because his bombastic, embezzling father had demanded it. That kiss . . . that kiss happened because he had been ordered to do it.

He felt like the dirt under his own shoe. And the aching pain in his heart said something even worse: that he had warped what could have been—*would* have been—one of the most precious moments of his life. He would give anything to have entered into that kiss with a pure heart and a clean conscience.

Mrs. Saxby drew Theo away, and his father came up to slap him on the back with a stream of inconsequential, patently false remarks directed at the people gaping at them. "I had no idea he was looking in that direction," he told the prince. "I suppose parents are always the last to know. But Son"—this with a tone of genial disapproval—"I hope I've trained you better than to snatch a lady and kiss her in public. A gentleman doesn't go about declaring himself in that sort of manner."

"Indeed," Geoffrey Trevelyan chimed in. He waved his hand with that dilettantish, amused air that Theo appreciated and James loathed. "Wouldn't have thought you had it in you, Islay. All that ardor and whatnot."

The reminder that Theo had wanted Geoffrey crashed into James's mind like a great wave. He turned to look at her, but she was gone.

The next few minutes passed like some sort of dizzy nightmare. James found himself bowing to the prince, who was genially cheerful about the whole thing. "Passions of the heart, what ho! They say polite society doesn't have passion, but I've always disagreed." And he threw a lustful glance at Mrs. Fitzherbert, standing to his right.

James flinched, and bowed his way out of the room. His father's effusive congratulations spilled out the moment they were in their carriage.

"I had no idea you'd go straight for the prize like that!" Ashbrook bellowed. "Proud of you! I'm proud of you! You're as randy as I am, and you used it to perfection. I would never have thought of doing it myself. She looked at you as if you were King Arthur and Lancelot rolled into one."

"Do not ever speak about my future wife in such a manner," James hissed.

"No doubt you're feeling short-tempered. It must be a shock. Yesterday you were a carefree bachelor, squiring that luscious young opera dancer about the town, and now you're on the verge of being leg-shackled."

James ground his teeth but remained silent.

His father burbled on but kept coming back to James's adroit brilliance in compromising Theo in front of the Prince.

As they rounded the corner of their street, James felt his control snap. He reached out and grabbed his father's neck cloth, crushing the elegant concoction of starch and linen topped by the duke's weak chin. "You will never say a word about this night to me, ever again. Do you understand?"

"No reason to be so violent about it," the duke said. "Not the proper attitude for a son, may I point that out?"

"I consider myself to be addressing not a father but an embezzler," James said, his voice icy. But at the same time he knew that for all he blamed his father, it was *he* who was the real villain. *He* had betrayed Daisy.

"Well," Ashbrook huffed. "I don't see why you would wish to characterize my ill luck in such a harsh fashion, but I assure you that I have no mind to discuss this night with you. I merely wanted to offer my congratulations. The fact that I expressed a need for help, and you responded within the day, doing precisely what I asked you to . . . well, it makes up for many of life's smaller blows."

And then he sat back and beamed at his son and heir until the carriage door opened.

James waited until his father descended before leaning forward to empty his stomach onto his own shoes, not that there was anything in his stomach but cognac and bitterness.

Seven

June 14, 1809

The wedding of James Ryburn, Earl of Islay, future Duke of Ashbrook, to a little-known heiress, Miss Theodora Saxby, drew the kind of breathless attention usually reserved for royal nuptials. The scandal rags, in particular, had latched onto the story of a true love match.

The account of Miss Saxby's care of James during his childhood illness had been told, retold, and embellished until, by a fortnight before the wedding day, most of London believed she had read to him on his deathbed, and her voice alone kept him from drifting into an eternal sleep.

By one week before the wedding, the young Miss Saxby had actually revived James as he swooned into that "dark night from which there can be no recovery" (as the *Morning Chronicle* put it).

And the wedding itself promised to be as lavish as that of a princess. Not only had it been orchestrated in a matter of mere months, but no expense had been spared. The Duke of Ashbrook had declared that nothing was too good for the wedding of his ward to his only son and heir.

On the grand day itself, Miss Saxby was delivered to St. Paul's in a lavishly gilded open carriage that made its way through crowded streets, most of London having turned out in hopes of catching a glimpse of the bride.

Reporters for London's papers, from the august *Times* to rags like *Tittle-Tattle*, were clustered together by the door of the cathedral. As the carriage approached, they crowded forward, pressing against the barricade erected to keep out hoi polloi.

"The bride," scribbled Timothy Heath, a young reporter for the *Morning Chronicle*, *"looked like a French confection, her skirts a veritable cloud of silk and satin. She wore flowers in her hair and held a bouquet in her hands as well."* He paused. Miss Saxby wasn't a pretty girl, which made it all a bit difficult. *"The future duchess,"* he finally wrote, *"has a profile that is worthy of the peerage. Her features speak to the generations of Englishmen and women who have stood shoulder-to-shoulder with our monarchs."*

The reporter from *Tittle-Tattle* had a simpler and considerably more brutal summary. "She's an ugly duchess and I'll be damned if she's ever going to turn into a swan," he exclaimed, watching as the Duke of Ashbrook held out his hand to help his ward from the carriage.

Although he was likely speaking to himself, every reporter in the vicinity heard him and rejoiced. *Tittle-Tattle* put out a special evening edition whose headline screamed, "The Ugly Duchess!" Editors all over London took one look at that catchy précis and swapped their morning headline for a version of *Tittle-Tattle*'s.

All the young ladies who had sighed over James's broad shoulders and handsome face giggled into their morning tea. And all the gentlemen who had ever contemplated dancing with Miss Saxby felt virtuously satisfied that they hadn't lowered their standards in exchange for her dowry.

The received idea that James was wildly in love with his "ugly duchess" turned overnight to a ridiculous myth that no one believed. Obviously the Earl of Islay had married for money: there could be no other explanation. And what the press declared to be fact, England believed.

"I'm that surprised," a young opera dancer named Bella confided to another member of the corps the morning after the nuptials. She had found herself the recipient of a large emerald and a formal good-bye a few months earlier. "I would never have picked him for the sort who'd go all sober when he got married, especially if he was marrying a woman like *that*."

She pointed to an illustration in their favorite theatrical gossip page, which had dashed out a quick approximation of an "ugly duchess." It was more of a caricature than a portrait, with a few scattered feathers showing under her bonnet.

"He'll be back," her friend Rosie replied. Rosie was more cynical, and wiser. "Give him six months."

Bella tossed her curls. "I shan't wait six months for anyone. There are gentlemen lined up at the door waiting for *me,* I'll have you know."

"Well, I feel sorry for her," Rosie said. "She's being called ugly in every paper in London. She's bound to find out. And when one of *them*"—by which Rosie meant the gently born—"gets a nickname like that, they have it for life."

Staring at her reflection in the glass, Bella adjusted the emerald necklace and thought about how her pink and cream loveliness must provide a terrible contrast with James's new bride. "I'm sorry for him. I heard she hasn't any curves. He loved my apple-dumplings, if you know what I mean."

"She hasn't," Rosie confirmed. "I got a good look when she got out of the carriage. She's as thin as a clothespin, and flat down the front. You know Magis down in the box office? He reckons she is a man, and it's all a big hoax."

Bella shook her head. "This emerald says it's no hoax."

At precisely the same time, in a very different part of London, Theo woke the morning after her wedding, feeling confused. The wedding itself was a blur of smiling faces . . . the grave eyes of the bishop . . . the moment she heard James's strong voice promise to be hers *til death do us part,* the moment when she herself said *I do* and saw a lightning-quick smile touch his lips.

Later, after they had returned home, her maid, Amélie, had divested her of the despised puff of lace and silk that her mother had identified as the perfect fairy-tale gown—and which twelve seamstresses had worked on day and night for a month in order to finish—and put her in a sheer pink negligee. With ruffles.

Her new father-in-law had vacated the matrimonial chambers, and she had undressed in the bedchamber belonging to the former duchess, a room so large that it could contain her former bedroom three times over.

And then James had entered from the duke's— now his—bedchamber next door, looking rather pale and stern around the mouth.

After that the night had been a blur of nervousness and flashes of desire and just plain awkwardness. It wasn't exactly what she had expected, but what had she expected? When it was over, James had kissed her, very precisely, on her brow. And that was the first time she realized that if *she* had felt a little dizzy at various points, her new husband appeared to be remarkably collected. Not at all as hungry as he'd been before, at the musicale, when they were merely kissing.

Before she could say a word, he had quietly closed the door between their adjoining rooms.

Of course, his departure was to be expected. She knew that no one but the poor actually slept together in the same bed: it was unhygienic, and led to restless sleep. Not only that, but one of her governesses had briskly told her that men smelled like goats in the morning and that if a woman didn't put a door between herself and horrors of that nature, she might find herself pressed under an evil-smelling male body.

It didn't sound nice when she first heard it, and it didn't sound nice now. Perhaps it was all right, then, that James slept in his own room. But did he have to leave so quickly? While she was still feeling as if she could barely remember the day of the week?

Then it occurred to her that he might well have retired because after he achieved satiety, for want of a better word, the evidence was left on her sheets. Who wants to sleep on soiled sheets? Not she. Maybe in the future she would visit his room and then retire to her own clean bed.

That idea made her smile, even though she was now aware that her body seemed to have some new twinges in place where there had been no twinges before. Luckily, her mother had been thorough in explaining what happened in the marital bed.

It was all the way she had described, more or less. Her mother had said that a husband touches his wife down there, for example, but James hadn't. And she'd implied—though she didn't say it directly—that a wife might do the same for her husband. But since James hadn't . . .

They had kissed for quite a long time, and then he rubbed her breasts, and he braced himself over her (a happy tingle coursed up her legs at the memory), and finally he pushed inside, which wasn't all that comfortable. After that, it was over quickly.

She did like it, almost all of it, particularly the part where he kissed her so urgently that they were both moaning, because that made her feel like a bit of paper about to go up in flames.

Though she hadn't, of course.

And now she was a married woman on the very first morning of her married life. Which meant, among other things, that she would never wear a string of pearls, or a ruffle, or a white dimity gown again in her life.

Amélie had carefully draped Theo's monstrosity of a wedding dress over a chair. She climbed out of bed and wandered over to take a look. It was the last, the very last, piece of clothing that her mother would have the pleasure of choosing for her. *That,* if nothing else, deserved a celebration. With a grin, Theo pushed open the tall windows looking down onto the formal garden that stretched behind the Duke of Ashbrook's town house, and snatched up the gown.

At that moment there was a brisk knock, and the door between her and James's bedchambers opened. He was fully dressed in his riding habit, complete with boots and a whip, and she was barefoot in her negligee, her hair loose and billowing down her back.

"What on earth are you doing?" he asked, nodding at the wedding gown in her arms.

"Throwing this horror out the window."

He reached her shoulder just in time to watch it fall. The top layer caught a little wind on the way down. "I hope that wasn't a symbolic representation of your attitude toward our marriage?"

"Even if it were, it's too late," Theo said. "You're too heavy for me to tip out the window. Just look at that. It looks like a drunken meringue." The dress settled with a flourish of lace on top of the boxwood hedge below.

"I suppose there's no call to wear such a thing

more than once," James commented, a familiar note of wry amusement in his voice.

Theo felt a wash of relief. If they could just go back to being *themselves,* to being comfortable together rather than all this . . . this hotness and awkward feelings, it would be so much more agreeable to be married.

"I intend to change the way I dress," she said, grinning at him. "I may throw everything I own out this window."

"Right," James said. He sounded utterly uninterested.

"Including the garment I'm wearing at the moment," she said with distaste.

At that his face brightened a little. "Do you intend to toss your negligee this minute? I could help you disrobe."

Theo grinned at him. "Fancy a look at your bride in the daylight, do you?"

But he had a little frown between his brows. Theo had to stop herself from reaching up to soothe his forehead. "What's the matter?" she asked instead.

"Nothing." The corner of his mouth twitched, so she reached out a finger and touched him there, just enough to make it clear that she knew his expressions so well that lying to her was of no use. Then she leaned back against the windowsill and crossed her arms, waiting.

"I was wondering if you could spend a few

hours with me and Mr. Reede, the estate manager, before luncheon."

"Of course. How can I help?"

"My father has turned over the estate to me. After my ride, I'm going with Reede to the docks, as we have a ship there, but we should be back in an hour or two."

"Your father did what?" Theo repeated, scarcely believing her own ears.

James nodded.

"How in the bloody hell did you talk him into that?" she demanded.

A ghost of a smile touched his lips. "I asked your mother to insist on it in the marriage contract. She understood absolutely; she'd heard about various rash investments of his."

"But you never said anything about that to me! Nor did my mother!"

"I had made Father promise that I would inherit the estate on my marriage, rather than on his death. But I wasn't sure he would actually follow through unless it was legal. Your mother was entirely in agreement, so she played along."

Theo nodded. "And she specified that you had to bring me into conversation about the estate."

"No, she said nothing of the sort. I had the papers drawn up so that you and I are both executors."

This time Theo's mouth actually fell open. "You did *what?*"

"It's entailed, of course. You cannot sell it, any more than I can."

"This was my mother's idea?"

"No. Actually, she wasn't enthusiastic, and my father was apoplectic, to put it mildly. But I forced it." A gleam of satisfaction shone in his eyes. "You know I'm hopeless when it comes to numbers and the like, Daisy. But you're not. We can think together about what's to be done. We used to come up with all sorts of ideas, remember?"

Theo gaped at him. She'd never heard of an estate administered by a woman. Well, at least by a woman who wasn't a widow.

"I'm at my best out-of-doors," James continued doggedly, "and if you tell me to pick the best horse in a race, I can do it with a fair degree of accuracy. If you think we should improve the breeding stock of the sheep on the estate, I can certainly do that. But sitting in the library and listening to a string of numbers? I'll go mad."

"I'm happy to come," Theo said. She felt almost as if she were going to cry. "I'm just—I'm so *honored* that you wish me to help."

"No reason to be," James said, a trifle sharply. "You might as well know now that my father's nearly driven the estate into the ground. It's your inheritance that has to get it solvent again. So it's only fair that you be part of it all."

Theo blinked at that revelation but pushed the thought away for the moment. "I don't think there are many men who think as you do," she said a little mistily. "As long as you know that I didn't learn double-entry bookkeeping or anything truly useful from my governesses."

"You can learn. From what my father has told me, my mother ran the estate while she was alive, and she wouldn't have had any training, either. And I'll be there, Daisy. I just don't want to do it without you."

"All right," Theo said. She felt a burst of happiness so acute that she couldn't say another word.

But her new husband merely stood there, looking rather awkward. Finally he said, "Was last night acceptable? You aren't injured, are you?"

"James, you're turning pink!" Theo exclaimed.

"I am not."

"You really must stop fibbing," she observed. "I can see through you every time. And to your question, yes, it was surprisingly nice. Although I have thought of one thing we should do differently."

He instantly looked wary. "What?"

"I shall come to your bedchamber, rather than you coming to mine."

"Oh."

"How often does one do this marital business?" Theo asked, with some curiosity. James looked rather staggeringly delicious. In fact, she could quite imagine kissing him at that very moment. But, of course, one didn't do that sort of thing spontaneously, and certainly not during the day.

"As often as one wants," James replied. His cheeks were undeniably rosy now.

She dropped into a chair. "I realize that I do have a question about last night." She waved her hand at the chair opposite. "Please sit down."

He sat, if with obvious reluctance.

It was strangely wanton to sit opposite a man—her *husband*—while wearing nothing more than a light silk negligee. Early morning sunlight streamed over her shoulder and played on her hair, and even though her hair was an odd color, it always looked best in natural light, so she pulled it forward over her shoulder.

"Last night was the first time I made love to anyone," she announced, rather unnecessarily, but she wanted to make the point.

"I know that."

"I would like to know how many women you have made love to."

James stiffened. "More than enough."

"How many?"

"Why do you want to know?"

"Because I just *do*. It's my right to know, as your wife."

"Nonsense. No one tells his wife that sort of thing. You shouldn't even ask. It's not proper."

Theo crossed her arms again. She'd noticed that

it made her breasts plump up. "Why won't you tell me?"

"Because it's not proper," James repeated, starting up from his chair. His eyes were fiery, and Theo felt a glow of excitement. She loved it when James lost his temper, even though she hated it when his father did. He bent over her, bracing his arms on her chair. "Why do you want to know? Was there something about last night that made you feel that my experience was insufficient?"

Enthralled by his darkening eyes, Theo fought the desire to pull him closer. Or break into laughter. "How would I know if last night was insufficient?" she said, choking back a giggle.

One hand closed around her neck with slow deliberation. "You'll probably be the death of me." A thumb nudged up her chin. "Were you satisfied last night, Daisy?"

She scowled at him and shook her head, dislodging his hand. *"Theo."*

"How can I not think of you as Daisy when your hair is all about your face like the petals of a flower?" He crouched down on his heels before her chair and picked up a thick curl. "It's glossy, like sunshine."

"I prefer to be addressed as Theo," she told him, once again. "And it was very nice last night, thank you. I asked about others because I want to know something about you that no other person knows."

James was looking at the lock of hair he held

85

with as much concentration as if he held strands of gold, but at that he met her eyes. "You know everything about me."

"No, I don't."

"You're the only one who knows me," he said quietly. "All there is to know about me that matters, Daisy—I mean, Theo. I'm rotten with figures. I'm good with animals. I detest my father. I can't control my temper, and I hate the fact I inherited that trait from him. I'm possessive. I'm intolerable—you've said that many times."

"You love your father, too," Theo pointed out, "however much you rage against him. And I still want to know the answer to my question."

"If I tell you, may I have a lock of hair?"

"Goodness, how romantic," Theo breathed, a thrill going straight to her toes. But a pang of common sense intruded. "If you cut one from the back, where it won't show."

James pulled out a penknife and moved behind her. "Not too much," she entreated him, pulling her hair up and then letting it fall down the chair back. "Amélie will be terribly cross if I have a bald spot."

He ran his hands through her hair and then said, quietly, "You were the second, Daisy. And the last."

The smile on Theo's face came straight from her heart, but she thought the brevity of his list was probably not a matter for celebration, to his mind at least, so she said nothing. She tilted her head back and saw that he had cut off a thick lock of her hair. "What on earth are you going to do with that? I'm dazzled by this sentimental streak of yours, James." She reached up toward him. "What about a good morning kiss, then? For the one person who knows you best and still signed on to a lifetime of tolerating intolerableness?"

His eyes were still dark and troubled, but he leaned over and dropped an upside-down kiss, a soft and sweet one, on her lips.

"Actually, I'd prefer the other kind." She felt her heartbeat start a tattoo in her throat.

"The other kind," James said slowly. He drew the lock of hair through his fingers, then put it on a side table and drew her to her feet. "One kiss. Then I must make my way downstairs."

For all that, he took her mouth slowly, as if they had all day to do nothing but taste each other, come together like silk and velvet.

At some point the door opened, and a maid squeaked something. The door closed again, and still they kissed.

James's mouth kept sliding to her jaw, to an eyebrow, to an ear, always coming back, taking her mouth again. Theo began a rambling sort of monologue, a shivering, breathy series of comments that made little sense, until she found herself saying, "I cannot believe I didn't know I felt like this . . . What would have happened if you hadn't realized in time, James? What if I had managed to entice Geoffrey to the altar?"

He pulled his mouth away. By now she was clinging to him, trying to fit all the curves of her body to the hard places in his, trying to climb up him like a cat, her breath coming in little sobs.

But he thrust her away, putting the chair between them for good measure. "James," she said, her voice threaded with desire.

"Don't." His voice was hoarse too, but there was something strange in his expression, a kind of agonized rage in his eyes.

"What on earth is the matter?" Theo asked, suddenly aware that there really was something the matter; James wasn't simply in an odd mood.

"Nothing," he said, with patent falsehood. "I must meet the estate manager. I don't want the man to think that the whole family is cut along my father's pattern. He sometimes keeps Reede waiting for days after summoning him."

"Of course," Theo replied. "Still, I know you, James. There's something really wrong, isn't there? Please tell me. What is it?"

But he turned and fled, and she spoke to the closed door.

Eight

Amélie's horrified cry at discovering the wedding dress serving as a perch for a pair of London sparrows was matched by her despair as Theo tossed dress after dress behind her on the bed.

At the end of it, Theo had almost nothing to wear, but she had a growing sense of excitement.

When she finally managed to dress in one of the few gowns left to her name, she wandered down to breakfast. James had not yet returned from his trip to the wharf, and no one else was at home. "Where is His Grace?" she asked Cramble, allowing a footman to spoon scrambled eggs onto her plate.

"The duke went to the races in Newmarket and won't be home until tomorrow."

"And my mother?"

"Mrs. Saxby left early this morning for Scotland; I believe she is paying a visit to her sister."

"Of course! I entirely forgot," Theo said. "Yes, I would like two pieces of that ham, thank you. Cramble, would you please send a footman to Madame Le Courbier and inform her that I will pay a visit this afternoon? And since I am alone, I would love to see a newspaper."

"Only the *Morning Chronicle* has been delivered, Lady Islay. I shall bring it to you immediately."

Theo almost didn't catch his answer, lost as she was in the surprising pleasure of being addressed by James's title. She never thought of James as the Earl of Islay, but of course he was. Then the butler's comment dawned on her. "No other papers? How very peculiar. Couldn't you send someone out for them, Cramble?"

"I am very sorry, my lady," he said. "I am afraid I am unable to spare anyone from the household at the moment."

"Perhaps this afternoon," Theo said. "Surely *Town Topics* will be delivered at some point?"

"I shall ascertain," Cramble replied discouragingly.

Theo began to think about the whole vexing question of the estate. She had no problem believing that her new father-in-law had lost a great deal of the estate's fortunes. He was an irascible, gambling fool, and even if she hadn't reached that conclusion herself, her mother had said so, forcibly, at least once a day for as long as she could remember.

Still, she was rather surprised that Ashbrook had agreed to give over the reins to James. He must have been pushed to the wall, which suggested the estate was in truly bad straits.

Once James and the estate manager returned from their errand, she joined them in the library to find that the meeting had an air of crisis. James had clearly been tugging at his hair, as his short

Brutus looked much more disarranged than was fashionable. The estate manager, Mr. Reede, looked both aggrieved and defensive.

"Gentlemen," Theo said, walking into the room. "Mr. Reede, how kind of you to join us."

"It's his bloody *job*," James snapped, "and if he'd been doing his job a bit more keenly, we might not be in the straits we are."

"Begging your lordship's forgiveness," Mr. Reede said, "but may I remind you that I had no authority to stop His Grace from any of the decisions that you disparage."

"Right," Theo said, seating herself beside James and trying not to think about how much she liked feeling the brush of his shoulder against hers. "How bad is it?"

"It's hellish," James stated. "My father has managed to come near to bankrupting the entire estate. He's sold everything that he could put his hands on, and only the entail has saved the rest from disappearing into his pockets."

Theo put a hand on his arm. "Then it's an excellent thing that you have assumed control, James. Remember those ideas we used to have for making the Staffordshire estate self-sustaining? We have a chance to put them into practice."

He cast her a look that was half despair and half exasperation. "We were *children,* Daisy. We had stupid, quixotic ideas that were probably about as practical as my father's wretched plans."

It was clear to her that James was on the verge of combustion. "Mr. Reede, could you give me a précis of what is left in the estate, and what debts are encumbered thereto?" Theo asked.

Mr. Reede blinked at her, clearly startled.

"I told you," James said to him with a hollow laugh.

Mr. Reede found his tongue. "The Staffordshire estate is entailed, of course, as is this town house and the island in Scotland."

"Island?"

"Islay," James put in. "No one has visited it in years; I gather it's nothing more than a heap of rock."

"I'm afraid that there are debts against the country estate totaling thirty-two thousand pounds," Mr. Reede said.

"What about income from the sheep farm, and the rest?"

"The income is approximately the amount that has been agreed upon as His Grace's annual allowance. There are also debts against the town house totaling five thousand pounds."

"And against the island?" Theo asked.

"No one would lend him money against it," James said. "It has nothing but a meadow and a hut."

"His Grace does own a ship that has, in the past, made successful runs to the East Indies for spices. Lord Islay and I spent the morning at the *Percival*, which has been dry-docked as a result of non-payment of customs fees."

"I thought ships were generally named after women," Theo said.

"His Grace named the vessel after himself. With fines," Mr. Reede said, moving smoothly on, "the duties attached to the *Percival* added up to eight thousand pounds. We secured payment and the ship is no longer impounded. His Grace had continued to pay the crew's wages, but the captain left for a better post." Mr. Reede turned over a page in his ledger.

"We're up to forty-five thousand pounds in debt," Theo said. "That really *is* rather a lot."

"There is a small firm of weavers located in Cheapside," Mr. Reede said. "Ryburn Weavers has made a steady profit of around three thousand pounds per annum."

"Why didn't the duke sell it?"

"I believe he forgot about its existence," Mr. Reede said, adding rather hesitantly, "I used the income to pay for the staff wages in the various houses, as well as the crew of the *Percival*."

"So naturally you did not remind him of the existence of the weavers," Theo said admiringly. "That was exceptionally shrewd of you. Thank you, Mr. Reede."

She elbowed James, and he muttered something. But he started up from the table as if he could no longer bear to sit, and began ranging about the room, running his hands through his hair.

Theo ignored him for the time being and turned back to Mr. Reede. "My preference would be to pay down the debt from my dowry, and then work toward a goal of making the estate self-sustaining. Is that possible, in your estimation?"

"I have often thought," Reede offered, "if a reasonable investment were made in the sheep farm, we could bring the income up twenty percent within a short period of time, say two to three years."

"I would be more comfortable if we received income from various sources. One thing that Lord Islay and I discussed in the past was the possibility of building a ceramics business. Wedgwood has had remarkable success using Staffordshire clay, and half our estate seems to be clay. I find Wedgwood's patterns stultifyingly boring. I'm sure that we could do better."

"It would take a considerable outlay to establish a profitable concern. My guess is that you would have to try to lure someone away from Wedgwood." Mr. Reede cast a nervous glance at James, who was staring out the window, his shoulders tight.

"I'll explain any plans we might make to my husband," Theo said.

"Just do whatever you want," James said, not turning to face them. "I'm useless at this stage." He had never been happy with facts and figures, but once they were tramping around the estate, he would probably have a hundred ideas about how to increase the wheat harvest.

And once they got the ceramics business up and running, Theo had no doubt that he could handle any contingency. He had a true gift for talking to laborers, likely because he envied their lot.

"What do you think about the idea of establishing a ceramics industry on the estate, Mr. Reede?"

The estate manager glanced over his shoulder again. James had one arm up against the window, and he was leaning his forehead against it, the very portrait of despair. "In conjunction with improvements to the sheep farm, I think that would serve very well indeed, my lady."

Nine

By the time the meeting was drawing to a close, James felt like jumping out the library window and running into the street, screaming. He was an idiot who would never be able to manage his own estate because he couldn't bear thinking or talking about numbers. As Reede prosed on, his entire body tensed with the fervent wish to get the hell out of the library.

So it had been Daisy—Daisy, whom he had betrayed—who spent two hours going over figures, coming up with idea after idea to repair their finances. At one point he had sat down at the table again, but the numbers had flowed past him as relentlessly as when he paced the room.

It wasn't that he couldn't do mathematics or accounting; he'd learned both in school. But his concentration constantly slipped in the face of such calculations, and he found himself thinking not about selling horses for profit but about the ways he planned to repair the stables. Daisy and Reede talked about the tons of hay produced by the south field compared to the west, and whether the disparity had to do with runoff from the stream; his only contribution was the comment that scything the west field was difficult because it was on the slope of a hill.

He knew *that* only because he had joined the workers on the estate the previous summer, reveling in the simplicity of learning to lean into the sweep of the scythe, the pleasure of a day spent doing physical labor, even the ache of his muscles at bedtime.

The truth of it was that he was a fool who was really only good for scything, because if he didn't get into the fresh air and exercise hard every day, he couldn't control his bloody, bloody temper. And he'd be damned if he ended up endangering his household with airborne china statuettes.

Even so, he could have lived with the brutal

truth of his own ineptitude. After all, Daisy—Theo—had made fun of him for years, and her cheerful affection had always smoothed over the fact that he would rather hang himself than attend an opera.

The only time he had sat still long enough to listen to a book being read aloud (let alone read one to himself) was during the bout of ophthalmia, when the doctors banished him to a dark room, threatening that he'd go blind. Even then, he suspected that he would have been up and running about, and be damned with his eyesight, except that Daisy made him laugh, and petted him, and fed him. When Daisy read him Shakespeare, he was fascinated. When he tried to read it to himself, the words jumbled on the page and his mind slipped off to other things.

Finally all the bookkeeping and talking and planning were over, and Daisy said good-bye to Mr. Reede in the prettiest manner possible, James grimly standing at her side in the entryway. Then she pulled him back into the library.

"What?" he said flatly. "I must go for a ride, Daisy. I didn't have time earlier, and my head is pounding." He still couldn't believe that he had a wife. Let alone that the wife was Daisy. His Daisy. He reached out and ran a finger down her face. "You have the most beautiful bones of any woman I've ever seen. Like a Russian princess, I think."

She liked that; he could read it in her eyes. "Kiss me," she said. "*That* kind of kiss."

He kissed her.

The damned thing about it was that James had discovered that he actually meant all those things he had said in front of the Prince of Wales that night back in March. Daisy was *his,* and he *was* possessive, and he *did* want her more than anything or anyone in the world.

But now it would never be pure or true between them. And so he kissed her with such a mixture of lust and despair that he fancied he could taste his own misery, so he tore himself away with a muttered comment about his headache.

After riding his horse too fast—which took care of his headache, but not his heartache—he had luncheon in his club and then returned to the house. But rather than enter that blasted library, he fell onto his bed, staring up at the canopy, unable to think or move or even sleep.

His valet, Bairley, appeared after a few hours and inquired about supper. Apparently her ladyship was paying a visit to a modiste and had not yet returned.

"Later," James said dully. He was in the grip of the kind of guilt and despair that murderers presumably feel. More than anything, he longed to knock his father against the wall with a leveler to the jaw: for ruining his marriage, his love for Daisy, his future. His whole body vibrated with hatred for the man who had so selfishly and carelessly ruined their lives.

Some time later, his valet knocked softly and entered the room again.

James pushed himself upright. "I suppose it's time to dress for supper."

"Yes, your lordship. I have your bath ready. But Mr. Cramble thought you should know . . . ," Bairley began and then seemed to lose steam.

"What is the problem?" James asked. "Has my father returned from the races?"

"No, your lordship. It's the papers."

"What about them?"

"Mr. Cramble told her ladyship at breakfast that most of them had not been delivered, though he did put them in the library for you to read."

"Right. I didn't get to them. Why on earth did Cramble say such a thing to my wife?"

"It was because of what they wrote about your wedding, that is, about Lady Islay. He meant to show them to you as soon as he had a chance."

James shook his head. "What in God's name did the papers say about my wife? Why were they bothering with our wedding?"

"It was the wedding of the season," Bairley said reproachfully. "The descriptions of the ceremony and reception are quite laudatory. The gilded coach and footmen in cloth-of-gold were universally admired."

"I feel as though I'm pulling teeth here, Bairley," James said, stripping off his waistcoat. "Have you chosen something I should put on for the evening?"

"Mr. Cramble thought he would send a meal to her ladyship's room," Bairley said, stammering a bit. "And you might dine with her there, private-like. When you ring for it, that is."

His valet's English was generally better than James's own, so that colloquial "private-like" was a sign that something truly was wrong. A flare of anger ignited by fear swept over James. "What in the bloody hell are you getting at, Bairley?" he said sharply.

"The papers are all calling her the 'Ugly Duchess,'" his valet replied miserably.

"What?"

"The 'ugly duchess,' a play on that fairy tale 'The Ugly Duckling.' My lord, please keep your voice down. Her ladyship is next door. She retired to her room directly after returning from the modiste."

"When you say the 'papers,' which ones do you mean, precisely?" James pulled off his shirt and tossed it on the bed. Daisy must be devastated. They were all blasted liars. He'd kill the scribblers himself. He'd have the presses shut down by the next morrow. He discovered his fingers were shaking slightly with rage.

"All of the dailies," Bairley replied. "All except

the *Morning Chronicle*, which said that she had the profile of a king."

"That's all right," James said, deciding to spare the *Morning Chronicle*. He tore open his breeches and a button skipped across the floor.

Bairley scurried after it.

"I'll have a retraction and apology from every one of them tomorrow morning," James said through clenched teeth, "or by God I'll torch their buildings myself. There's some power in a dukedom yet, and I'll use every iota of it to destroy them."

"Yes, your lordship," his valet said, having found the button. He turned to pull evening clothing from the wardrobe and lay it carefully on the bed. "Unfortunately, her maid reports that her ladyship saw the papers when she visited the modiste today. It's not only the papers—there are prints in the stationers' windows already. They did them overnight because of all the excitement about the wedding."

"Oh, for—" James broke off. "Lady Islay went out and saw all that, and now she's . . . where?"

"Next door," Bairley said. "She went straight to her chamber, her face white as a winding sheet, that's what Mr. Cramble said."

"Where's her mother?"

"Mrs. Saxby left early this morning for Scotland, before the papers were delivered."

101

James threw his breeches and smalls on the bed. "I'll have a quick bath and then pay a visit to my wife. Tell Cramble that I want no one interrupting us until I ring. Not even her maid," he said to Bairley over his shoulder. Five minutes later he pulled on a dressing gown and headed for the door to Daisy's room.

Ten

Theo was in the grip of a desolation so vast that it swallowed any tears she might have felt like shedding. On the way to the modiste's in Piccadilly, she had caught sight of a cluster of people around a new print in Hatchards window, but it would never have occurred to her that the print had anything to do with her.

Until she was on the way home and the carriage drew to a halt in front of yet another stationery store—and she saw the illustration. Though she only knew the extent of it after sending a grooms-man into the store to buy the papers, the same papers that the butler swore hadn't been delivered.

She would never have imagined that anyone could be so cruel. Let alone ten or twenty someones, or however many had written all those articles, and edited them, and approved them. And then there were the people who stayed up all night etching her likeness wearing that horrendous dress. But of course it wasn't the dress.

She had only to turn her head to see her face in the glass. It was angular, with the high cheekbones that James liked so much. But she also had a straight nose, and a strong chin, and something indefinable about the cast of her profile, and it all added up to . . . to an ugly duchess, that's what it added up to.

When the adjoining bedchamber door burst open, Theo didn't even look up. "I'd rather you left me alone at the moment," she said, swallowing a lump in her throat even though she wasn't crying. "I'm absolutely fine. I haven't shed a tear over those silly articles. Just nonsense, that's all."

Of course, James didn't obey her. From the corner of her eye, Theo caught a blur of movement, and suddenly she was tucked against his chest and he was sitting down. "I'm too big to sit in your lap," she gasped, realizing that his dressing gown had fallen open and the chest in question was quite bare. "And you are not properly attired."

James ignored that as well. "They're all insolent bastards and I'm going to chop their printing presses into shards tomorrow morning." His voice vibrated with anger, an emotion that he was exceptionally good at.

"Destroying the presses won't help now," Theo said. But she leaned her head against his bare chest and let him rage on. It was definitely comforting. James, like her mother, truly didn't see her the way the rest of the world did.

He actually saw her as a *daisy,* for goodness' sake. A daisy. Theo didn't care to think overmuch about her profile, but she had concluded long ago that the best adjective that could be applied to it was *severe.*

There was no such thing as a severe daisy.

"Do you suppose I could be carrying a child?" she asked when he paused for breath.

James made an odd sound, somewhere between a gulp and a cough. "What does that have to do with anything? I certainly hope not. I'm not ready for fatherhood. Just look at what a miserable job my father has done of it. I may never be ready."

"I know we're young," Theo said. "But if I were carrying a child, my figure would change. I would have more in front. Maybe we should try again tonight."

James frowned down at her. "You mean you want to develop that bovine look that some women have? *Udders?*"

His shudder was obviously genuine and highly satisfactory. "This is the perfect size," he added, putting a hand directly on her breast. "Just right for a man's hand. My hand."

Theo was wearing a walking dress that flattened what little she had in the front, but even so, James's hand seemed to curve around her breast quite nicely. She felt somewhat calmer, until it all flooded back into her head. "I don't think I can ever leave this house again. Everywhere I go people will be calling me *the ugly duchess,* you just know they will. Even if they don't say it to my face, they'll be thinking it. I cannot bear it. I don't have the courage."

His hand tightened on her breast for a moment and then he wrapped his arms around her again. "They're all idiots," he said into her hair. "You *are* beautiful."

"I'm not," Theo said miserably. "But it's nice of you to say so."

"I'm not just saying it!" He was at a near bellow again.

"Remember how you resolved to control your temper now you've turned the grand age of twenty?"

"Any man alive would be enraged by this kind of lying insult to his wife. Tomorrow I'm going into the office of each one of those rags that call themselves newspapers, and I shall put my hands around the neck of the proprietor, and—"

Theo put a hand over his mouth. "There's no stopping it, James. The illustrations are everywhere. I saw people all around Hatchards, gawking at the window. And on the way home, I realized that a portrait of me in that ghastly dress is in the front of every store. I'm stuck with the label. *For life.*"

"Nonsense," James said, more quietly. "Lots of

people acquire unpleasant nicknames that are soon forgotten. Richard Gray was known as Little Dick for a while. And Perry Dabbes—Lord Fentwick, now—was Periwinkle. Then everyone forgot about it."

"Apparently, they didn't," Theo pointed out. "You remembered both of those names without hesitating. And what's more, I bet there are lots of men who think Periwinkle every time they see Lord Fentwick." She hesitated. "Is that a reference to the size of his male organ?"

"I'm afraid so."

"I should think small would be a benefit. I'm certain most women would prefer it. They should boast about those nicknames."

A little laugh exploded from his mouth. "Am I to take it that you're sore from last night?"

"Yes," Theo admitted. "I wish you had a periwinkle."

"I'm glad I don't, even though I *am* sorry if I hurt you in any way, Daisy."

"My point is that no matter the size of their organ, at least they're not ugly. It's the worst thing you can say about a woman."

James's arms tightened again. "You are not ugly, Daisy. Do you think that I'm ugly?"

She glanced up at him. "You are breathtakingly handsome, and you know it. I'm very irritated just by the sight of you."

"I may know it, but I don't give a damn," he

said. "Still, a man's got some pride. Why on earth do you think that *I* would marry an ugly woman?"

Theo thought of saying *Because you just did,* but she choked back the words. She didn't really want to convince him that she was ugly. He and her mother were the only people in the world who idealized her this way. It was comforting to have a few people blind to reality.

"I would never marry an ugly woman," James continued with the superb confidence that came from being born not only handsome, but the heir to a dukedom as well. "I have some pride, you know. I married you because you are delectable, and beautiful, and also because you don't look like all those other girls."

Theo sniffed. She hadn't cried over the prints, but James was making her feel like crying now. "What do you mean when you say that I don't look like the other girls?"

He frowned. "All pink and puffy."

"But that's what Bella looked like," Theo objected. Then she stiffened. "Bella *is* part of your past, is she not?"

"I said good-bye to Bella the morning after I proposed to you. I gave her an emerald, though I wouldn't have done it if I'd known how Father played ducks and drakes with the estate." He was stroking her hair the way you might soothe an agitated cat.

"Oh, that's all right," Theo said, feeling a swell

of generosity. "I'm sure she doesn't have an easy life. But I have to say that she doesn't bear the slightest resemblance to me, James."

"A mistress is one thing," James said stubbornly. "A wife is quite another. I couldn't bear having all that pinkness around every day. And besides . . ." His hand slid from her shoulder back to her breast. "I didn't care for her bosom, to tell the truth. A man could suffocate if he wasn't careful."

Theo gave him a cracked bit of a laugh. "Must you do that?" she asked after a while as he continued to caress her breast. "It's making me feel rather odd."

"Why don't you remove your clothes and we can make each other feel odd?" he suggested.

"James! People don't do that sort of thing at this hour."

"It's almost evening," he said, glancing outside. "And I'm pretty sure that people do it all day long if they're lucky enough not to live with a passel of servants."

"Do you wish you didn't have servants?"

He rubbed a thumb across her nipple, and even through the layers of cloth she felt it so keenly that she actually jerked. "Do you like that?"

"I suppose," she said uncertainly.

"I wish I'd been born a laborer," James said suddenly, and quite ferociously. "I would be able to do just as I wish, and marry whom I want, and work in the outdoors and *never* have to spend hours with a man like Reede. Let alone have him look at me as if I were a veritable idiot. Which I am."

"You are *not,*" Theo cried. "You know perfectly well that you could have had a first at Oxford if you'd cared to stay past a year."

"Except I'd have jumped in a lake with stones in my pockets first."

"That's irrelevant. My point is that you were the top of your class at Eton, when you could be bothered."

"Thank God that's over."

His hand started moving again, which Theo had to admit she rather liked. In fact, she was actually considering removing her gown, scandalous though it would be. "So you would truly like to be a laborer?"

"Yes."

"You did choose your own wife," Theo said softly. "You shocked everyone with your declaration."

His hand tightened for a moment. "Yes. I suppose I don't feel that I'm ready for marriage. If I have to get married, I wouldn't want anyone but you."

"Well, I would hate being a laborer's wife, so I'm glad you were born to be a duke. It would be so exhausting to cook and clean and lay fires all day, and then just wake up and do precisely the same the next day. I would rather be planning a ceramics factory. And what did you think of my idea for having Ryburn Weavers specialize in re-creating the kind of figured fabric they wove in the time of Queen Elizabeth?"

"I think it is brilliant. I suppose what I most want is to be outdoors, and not suffocating in ridiculous neck cloths. I loathe starch."

"We are so different," Theo exclaimed. Even though it was something she'd known practically her whole life, it struck her anew. "I love thinking about clothing, and judicious use of starch can have such a gorgeous effect. Madame Le Courbier—that's my modiste—and I came up with a wonderful plan to use blue starch to stiffen some fine pleats. She's putting them at the wrists and the neck of a walking dress of cherry-colored twilled sarcenet with cord trim that will make it resemble the uniform of the Queen's Household Cavalry."

"I don't recall any pleats on their tunics," James drawled. He had tipped Theo forward, away from him, and now she realized that he was deftly unbuttoning her gown in the back.

"James, we can't possibly do this," she said, twisting about to look at him over her shoulder.

"What are we doing? I fancy sitting around with my wife while neither of us has any clothes on. You know there are religions where people behave like that all the time. 'The Family of Love,' I think one of them is called. My cousin was telling me about it in the club the other day."

"Not your cousin Pink," Theo said, allowing him to continue unbuttoning, because no matter how calm her tone was, her heart sped up at the very idea of sitting unclothed on James's lap.

"He prefers Pinkler-Ryburn," he replied, undoing the last button and pushing her gown forward, down her arms.

Theo pulled the gown farther down so that she could free her arms. "I really can't bear him."

"I can't imagine why. After all, he's as interested in fashion as you are."

"No, he's not. He's just a heedless follower of other people's ideas. He looks absurd. At the wedding his collar was so high that he couldn't turn his head at all. And did you see the absurd coat he was wearing? It was lined in pink satin, and he kept fidgeting with it to make sure that everyone saw inside."

"He's a macaroni, but he isn't a bad fellow once you get to know him," James said. "Why aren't you wearing one of those corset thingies?"

"I don't need to," Theo said with a flash of pride. "They're meant to keep in one's stomach, but I don't have one."

"You have one," James said, easing her back against him. He slid his hand down over her chemise, from her neck, over her breasts. "Right here." His hand slid a little lower. "Like a path leading right to where a man most wants to be."

Theo squirmed, half wanting his hand to slide

111

lower, half wanting to jump from his lap. "I have an idea," she said, rather breathlessly.

"What?" His hand slid a little lower.

"Well, the ugly duckling turned into a swan, didn't she?"

James stopped what he was doing. But then he lifted her up and tugged her gown straight down to the floor. "How does this chemise come off?"

"There are just two buttons," she said, lifting her hair to show him.

"Tell me about the swan," he said, pulling her back down onto his lap.

"I can't believe we're doing this," Theo mumbled. She changed the subject. "I've been thinking about ideas for months, actually, ever since I debuted and Mama made me wear all those white ruffles."

"Like the gown you threw out the window." Nimble fingers brushed her hair to the side, leaving warm sparks wherever they touched her skin.

"Yes, like my wedding gown," Theo said, bending her head forward. "Are you really unbuttoning my chemise?" It was a stupid question; she could feel his fingers at her neck.

"Yes."

"But Amélie might enter any moment," she said, rather panicked. "It must be time to dress for supper."

"I told my valet to keep them all away until we ring. We will be dining here."

"Oh." The very idea of eating with James in such an intimate setting—though surely they would dress again—made her breath quicken. "I intend to develop my own set of rules for fashion," she said, changing the subject. "The opposite of your cousin Pink. He merely imitates whatever the other fops are doing."

"Rules sound good," James said agreeably. He had the yoke of her chemise undone and was starting to slide it forward, off her shoulders.

Theo had a moment of panic, and then let him do it. He plucked her up and then pulled the chemise free. Without a word he nestled her back against his chest, quite as if she wasn't almost entirely naked but for her lacy little drawers.

"That's a very pretty garment," he said, with a distinct note of masculine satisfaction as he ran a finger along the lace trim.

"I designed it myself," Theo said. "It's made of knotted silk. That's double-edged lace."

"What *are* your rules?" he asked in her ear just as one of his hands settled on her bare knee.

He didn't seem to be looking at the lace, but Theo couldn't think very clearly. She was too fascinated by the contrast of James's sun-darkened hand on her white knee. In that moment, she actually felt rather pink and white, at least compared to his brownness. "Here's one: *Look to the Greeks.*"

"Don't," James said. "They have an awful lot of

facial hair as a rule, Daisy. Besides, you're married to me now. You shouldn't look at any other men."

There was a note of hot possession in his voice that made her feel ridiculously joyful. "It's not about *men,*" she said with a giggle. "I was thinking of Greek gowns." She felt even more naked because James was still covered by his dressing gown except for where it gaped in the front. Although she could feel something beneath her. "You are no periwinkle," she observed.

James laughed. "True." He sounded suddenly happy, without that subtle grimness that hadn't left his eyes even during the wedding ceremony.

She hopped from his lap, turning around with hands on hips. "Perhaps it's time you removed your dressing gown."

It was gratifying to see a hard pulse beating in his throat, and the way his eyes seemed to devour her. Perhaps she *could* live in a world in which she was thought ugly, as long as she had James waiting for her.

She came quite close and bent down to undo the knot holding his dressing gown in place. His eyes were hot and painfully eager. "So, is this a *winkle,* if it's not a *periwinkle?*" she asked mischievously, brushing the organ that burst up the moment she pulled the fabric to the side.

He gave a husky laugh. "You may call it what-ever you like, if you'll just keep . . ." His voice trailed off. She ran her fingers over his velvety hardness, coming down on her heels so she could see better.

"That's a great deal bigger than I realized last night," she said at last, her voice rather weak. She felt a painful little twinge between her legs at the very sight of it. A winkle indeed. With a capital W.

"But we did fit together," James said. His breath was uneven. "Do you think you might take your drawers off, as long as we're both undressing, Daisy?"

The timid side of her would rather that winkle didn't come near her again. But it was James asking, so she nodded and stood up. She twisted to reach the tiny metal hooks that fastened her drawers, when James made a hoarse sound, like a little gasp. Under her eyelashes, she saw his body strain forward. *He* didn't think she was ugly.

Instead of immediately unfastening her drawers, she started pulling pins from her hair, shaking it free so that it tumbled down over her breasts, all twisted strands of honey and cognac and amber. Her skin prickled at the touch of her hair, as if the strands were fingers caressing her.

"Daisy," James breathed.

"My drawers are fastened with small hooks," she said, hiding her smile. "I have to undo them carefully or I might tear the lace." She slowly, slowly slipped the first hook from its eye, allowing the lace garment to dip lower on her stomach. Another hook; another glance at James from under her lashes. He was beautiful, and intimidating. With the third hook, the silk started to slide down her hips, but she caught it.

"Let it fall," James ordered hoarsely. He was vibrating with impatience.

She grinned at him, feeling a flash of power. "Say *please.*"

Instead he reached out, lightning quick, and her smalls fell past the little twist of amber curls between her legs, down to her ankles.

"You don't need to wear that sort of thing," he said, his eyes feasting on her.

"I wear them because they are outrageous," she told him. "Mama never allows me to copy French modes except in matters of undergarments. Though now it's all different, of course. I no longer need obey her restrictions. I can wear whatever I choose."

"I prefer to think of you with nothing under your gown at all. No corset, no drawers . . . just you, so I can touch you under your gown any time I please. Please don't wear those things again."

Theo's eyes widened. "You wouldn't!" It came out a squeak.

"Why don't you come sit on my lap again?" James shrugged off his dressing gown and then sat back, appearing not the least shy about the fact he was utterly naked and his male organ was in such a state.

In fact, his eyes made Theo feel warm and confident, as if she weren't standing naked in a ray of sulky evening sunshine.

"Why don't you come and get me?" she asked. "You can practice whatever it is you intend to do if you ever talk me into leaving off my drawers. Which you won't." Without bothering to look at him, she scampered to the other side of the bedchamber.

James didn't run; he merely rose and padded deliberately toward her, his face as hungry as that of any self-respecting tiger. But what caught Theo's attention was his body. It had shadows and definition, like a marble statue, but the similarities ended there; she knew it was hot and alive. And his male part . . . even looking at it made her feel giddily alive, flaring with heat and desire.

A nervous giggle erupted from her mouth as he drew closer. "This is so different from last night!"

"Why?" James asked. "Now just stay still, Daisy. Stay still."

She danced sideways at the last moment and ran around the end of the bed. "Because we're *looking* at each other."

"I always look at you," he said, his voice hoarse and low. "I've looked at you ever since you grew those breasts. I just never let myself acknowledge what I was feeling while I looked. But it was hell the year you turned sixteen and suddenly started wearing lower bodices in the evening."

Theo tiptoed backward. "You must be joking!"

His mouth tilted into a wolfish grin. "I had a cock-stand under my napkin for months. *Months.*"

"I had no idea," Theo said, wonderment stopping her for a second. Which was just long enough for him to snatch her into his arms.

It felt as if they were touching for the first time. Last night, when they had consummated their marriage, it had been in the dark, and they had said almost nothing to one another. Theo had been too shy, fascinated and frightened, all at the same time, and couldn't think of a remark that didn't sound witless.

His chest brushed her breasts and a shiver went down her body. She put her arms around his neck. "Were you really lusting for *me?*" Theo marveled. "Right there in front of everyone. Really?"

"How could I not?" His hands slid to her slim hips and pulled her tight against him. "God, Theo, you were sitting there at every meal, and your breasts would peek out from the top of your gown, just begging to be touched. There was that time you spilled a glass of water down your bodice . . . do you remember?"

She shook her head. Her breath was ragged, and she couldn't think clearly. Every time he nudged her or touched her, a swell of pleasure overtook her body.

"Your nipples turned into little acorns standing out against your gown," he said, wrapping a hand around one of her breasts so they both looked down at his bronzed hand holding her. "All I could think was that they wanted *this*."

He pulled her backward onto the bed; she fell on top of him and he rolled. A second later his mouth was on her breast. Spiraling waves of pleasure swept through Theo's legs.

Her head fell back and she arched against him, feeling her breast as if she saw it with his eyes, tasted it with his tongue, felt it with his fingers. She knew with absolute certainty that in his eyes and under his hands her breast was the perfect size, the perfect shape. A groan broke from his lips and he moved to her other breast, giving it the same worship, a devotion that bordered on frenzy.

"Oh," Theo heard herself crying over and over. "Oh, James, oh, James . . ."

Her cries were inarticulate but sweet. James heard them like manna, like forgiveness. She did love him. She would forgive him. She was finding pleasure. For the first time since their betrothal, his heart was lightened by true joy.

"What do you want, Daisy?" he asked. "Tell me what you want."

"I don't know," she said, sobbing it. "But, James . . ."

"Yes?" He rolled his hips forward into the cradle of her legs. His breath caught in his throat and he did it again, slow and teasing, and all the time his fingers played first with one breast, then the other.

She was trembling, those intelligent eyes of hers dazed with longing, her elegant limbs askew. He would bet the fortune he didn't have that all those milk-and-water misses she so envied would never look as delicious as she did right now. They couldn't.

"You're so beautiful," he said, truth echoing in every hoarse word. "Just look at you, Daisy. All satin skin and long limbs, and those gorgeous breasts like the apples Eve offered Adam."

Her eyes widened. "Eve didn't offer Adam her *breasts,* silly."

James rose up, straddling her with a knee on either side of her hips. "Maybe she did. Maybe these are the apples of paradise. Breasts like yours, the perfect size, delicious, designed to drive a man mad."

Her eyes were alight with laughter now, laughter and joy and desire all mixed together.

"I would like to see you with this expression every morning," he said, leaning down to put a kiss on her lips. "Every night, and every afternoon."

"I watched you these last few years, too," she said, her hands caressing his shoulders. "You started growing up, and every time you came home for holidays you were taller, and taller, and you were hungry all the time."

She had the sweetest little tuft of hair there. He would love to touch it. But Bella hadn't allowed anything like that. "No dirty hands near my treasure," she'd say, slapping him, though she had let him play with her breasts as much as he liked.

He hadn't cared very much. It was different with Daisy, though. He wanted to watch her, to feel her desire, as much as he wanted to feel it himself.

"And now you're beginning to broaden here," she was saying, caressing his chest.

James looked down at himself. He had no illusions about his body. "I have muscles in my arms, but not in my chest yet, at least, not much. You should see the men who box regularly at Gentleman Jackson's Saloon."

"But I like you this way. Some men look like bulls. Their chests and thighs are so thick that a woman would be terrified of being suffocated. I've seen them working in the fields. But you . . ." She ran her fingers down his arms. "You're muscular without being grotesque. Beautiful," she whispered.

And then she curled up toward him, just enough so that she could dust his arms with kisses. While he was still dazed by the sweetness of it, her mouth danced to his nipple, paused, licked.

A kind of hoarse groan erupted from his chest, and she looked at him with a flash of mischief and desire. She reached up and gave that nipple another lick, and then a little bite.

Lust simmered through James's limbs and he fell onto her, about as gracefully as a fallen tree.

121

She squealed, but her body was soft and giving under his. "Are you—are you ready, Daisy?" he said in a near stammer.

A tiny frown crinkled her brow. "Can you kiss me again?"

"God, yes." His cock throbbed against her thigh, but he bent his head. Daisy's kisses were like no one else's. Not that he'd kissed many women, because he hadn't. When he kissed Bella, he was always thinking about burying himself inside her, finding her silky warmth, diving inside, and plunging away. As fast and as furious as he could. "Faster!" she would say.

It was different, kissing Daisy. She was sweet and intoxicating at the same time. When he kissed her, the blood seemed to drain from his head and he forgot about what he was doing . . . about getting there, about moving fast.

With Daisy, it felt as if minutes turned into drops of honey, and he could spend an hour playing with her tongue, nibbling and licking, swallowing the throaty little sounds she made, his fingers wound through hers.

After a while, their fingers slipped apart and hers played a symphony down his shoulders, his back. He managed to position himself so that he was almost where he longed to be. Every time he pushed forward, she gasped. She felt warm and soft.

Finally he simply had to ask her. "I would love

to touch you there, Daisy," he whispered, and then waited, holding his breath, to see if she was as revolted by that idea as Bella had been. "My hands are clean." His fingers hovered on her stomach.

"Why not?" she whispered back. Her eyes were alive with desire—and laughter. "I do it!"

A sound rose in his chest that was something like a sob as lust and gratitude flooded him at once. And then he *was* touching her there, and she was just as silky and wet and plump as he had ever imagined. Even better, his touch made her arch against him in a rhythm his body recognized.

"Do you like this?" he asked, his body aflame, more concentrated than he'd ever been in his life.

She twisted up again, a sob in her throat. Her hands clenched his arms.

He tried something else, and it must have been the right thing, because suddenly she felt wetter around his fingers, swollen and even more enticing. He'd like to kiss her there, if she'd let him. Obviously, she liked his touch. Her eyes were squeezed shut, intoxicating whimpers breaking from her lips. Maybe he could convince her that his tongue would be even better.

He rubbed harder and her eyes popped open. She grabbed his hand and pushed it further down. "Too much," she said, her breath coming in a pant. "That almost hurts."

"Here?" he breathed. He let his thumb delve lazily, slowly, into her luscious tightness. She was so small it seemed impossible that his tool had been inside her the night before.

A cry broke from her throat. He breached her passage, just barely, again and again, until she arched against him wildly, trembling, crying, her hands gripping his arms so tightly he would have bruises. It was the most fascinating moment of his life: he felt the moment she spasmed around his thumb. It was maddeningly erotic—and he knew instantly that Bella had never felt anything of the sort, at least not with him.

It dawned on him that if Daisy did that when he was inside, it wouldn't be about how fast he could ride himself to completion, it would be about her pleasure. He would be able to feel all those ripples inside her.

But that was a dim accompaniment to the dizzying thought that now, now he . . . He braced himself over her again and rather awkwardly rubbed himself up and down. She was slick and hot, and the very feel of her made him pant. But he had to keep control. He desperately wanted to feel *that* for himself, inside.

Her eyes opened again. "That feels good," she said, the echo of pleasure like a drug in her voice.

Watching her eyes as he slid down and in . . . it was fifty times more exciting than it had been the previous night. Then, he'd been wracked with guilt, too guilty to enjoy himself, too guilty to be there.

Now his heart was pounding so loudly that he couldn't hear, and his entire existence was concentrated between his legs, on the riptide of lust flooding him. Daisy was tight and incredibly small, but he slid home as if she *were* home.

He'd never felt anything so good. He wasn't all the way, or perhaps he was. He didn't know. Every movement of her hips was a voluptuous invitation. "I think I should start moving," he whispered. "I mean, I don't think I can stop myself."

Giggles burst from her lips. "I wouldn't know, James. We have to rely on your superior knowledge."

"I'm starting to think that I don't have much," he admitted, bending his head so that he could brush her mouth with his over and over.

"Well, but I don't know anything," Daisy told him, "though there is one thing I can tell you . . ."

"What?" he whispered.

"I want *this,*" she said, arching against him so that he slid the last inch into her cherry-dark sweetness. "More of *this,* James. You feel so good. You fill me up, and it doesn't hurt the way it did last night."

Her words snapped the reins that had held him back. He thrust forward, and then again, and again, long, ferocious drives that made her cry out. James couldn't think at all, his mind awash with the need to go harder and faster. He had his hands braced on either side of her, his head hanging so that her breath was against his, so he didn't miss one sobbing cry.

With Bella, he had never tried to control himself. He had thrust furiously, because that's what they both wanted. But with Daisy, he wanted her to break like that, to shake all over. He wanted to know what it would feel like to be inside her at that moment, more than he'd ever wanted anything in his life.

It didn't happen, and it didn't happen . . . she twisted beneath him, sobbing in an effort to get there. James could feel his body tightening, knew he couldn't wait much longer.

He braced himself a bit awkwardly on his left arm and slid his hand between their bodies, touching her in the place she liked.

"No!" she cried, sharp and fierce. "That hurts!" She grabbed his arm. "Do it like this. Push here. Oh, like that!"

Joy rushed over his body like some sort of windstorm, faster than lust, faster than desire. It gave him back a measure of control, and he thrust slowly, watching her face, her tightly shut eyes, pressed and rolled his thumb, just a little. She flinched, but then she moaned. She was shuddering all over; surely she was close.

"I'm going to kiss you there," he said, the words

coming with a gasp as he thrust into her again. "I'm going to lick all that peach juice. I want it, Daisy. And I'm going to . . ."

But at that moment her grip on his arms tightened even more and her cheeks turned a beautiful shade of pink. She threw back her head and cried aloud.

It was as astonishing as he could have imagined. She began to throb around him and he froze, astonished by the way *her* pleasure spread to him and then moved in waves of fire through his body, until his brain shut down completely and his craving body took over.

She began gasping again. He could feel her breath against his neck, but he couldn't even pay attention, because all of a sudden she started tightening again, throbbing down there, and he was gone in a white blaze of fire.

He wasn't James anymore, nor an earl, nor a future duke. And she wasn't Daisy, nor Theo, nor a future duchess of any kind.

They were two bodies knit together as tightly as puzzle pieces.

Till death do us part, James thought gratefully. *Till death do us part.*

Eleven

Dawn came, and with it a conviction on Theo's part: she would never walk again. In fact, a brief experiment convinced her it might be best not to move her legs at all.

After the second time they had made love, she had been so tender and swollen that James had poured cool water into the basin on her dressing table and gently sponged her, which felt so good that she started to giggle.

At some point they had supper, but then James made good on his promise to kiss her down there, and before she knew it, she was begging him and begging him, pulling at him with all her strength.

When he gave in, her whole body sang.

So the sun was up and still they were lying about, unable to get over the wonderful strangeness of having another body in the bed. A plaything. A playmate.

"I love your knees," James said, planting a kiss on one round kneecap. "They're so elegantly spare."

"Don't you dare touch me above the knee," Theo ordered. "I'm crippled."

"Surely not."

"Yes, I am. You owe me something."

"Anything." He lay on his stomach, running his fingers delicately over her ankles. "These are the most exquisite ankles I've ever seen. Like those racehorses who look too delicate to jump a stile, let alone gallop."

"I would like you to sing to me," Theo said, watching as pink light came in the window and played on his skin. It was whisky colored to the waist, and then turned stark white where it curved into a muscular buttock.

James groaned and dropped his head into the covers. "You know I hate singing."

His voice was muffled, but she made out his words. His mother had loved to listen to him sing, but after her death he stopped singing entirely, except while at church.

Theo felt like testing her power, stretching her wings. "Will you do it, for me?"

He rolled over. "Wouldn't you like something else, something that only I can give you? Anyone can sing." His blue eyes had a lustful gleam that she was learning to recognize.

"Absolutely not."

"I hardly know anything but hymns anymore."

She tugged at him. "Come, sit with me." She was leaning against the bedstead. "Sing me that song your mother loved so much, the old one from Queen Elizabeth's time." She held her breath. Would he do it? It wasn't a fair trial, not when they'd been married scarcely more than one day.

"'Song to Celia,'" James said, his face

129

expressionless. But then he looked at her and smiled, and came around to the head of the bed and crowded her in such a way that she found herself leaning against him instead of the bedstead.

And he wrapped his arms around her, took a deep breath, and sang, "Drink to me only with thine eyes, and I will pledge with mine."

Theo's heart almost stopped at the liquid beauty that filled the room. His voice was an extension of him, a perfect voice emanating from a perfect body.

He paused. "Sing with me."

She was no great shakes at music, but, like any gentlewoman, she was trained. Their voices entwined and his made hers all the better: "Or leave a kiss but in the cup, and I'll not look for wine."

As they sang, the light strengthened, sunbeams gaining amber edges, creeping up the coverlet.

When the song ended, Theo was so happy that she couldn't say a word. James dropped a kiss on her ear. "If you ever tell anyone that I sang to you, I'll tell your mother you went to the Devonshire ball without your chemise."

Not for the first time, Theo thought that his mother had done her son a disservice by ordering him into the drawing room to sing every night. After all those performances, he could not enjoy his own gift. "I promise," she said, leaning her head back so that she could catch his kiss. "Will you sing to me every morning?"

His smile was in his eyes, not on his mouth. "Only after nights like this one," he whispered.

He returned to his room then, leaving emptiness in her bed. Maybe, she thought fuzzily, I will be able to persuade him to sleep with me one night. Whatever they had done together—and she blushed just to recall some of it—there had been no sleeping. At least, not until now he'd gone to his own bed; euphoria notwithstanding, Theo wanted nothing more than to sleep for hours.

At some point Amélie peeped in the door. "Hot water, my lady?" she whispered.

Theo nodded. "What time is it?" she asked, coming up on one elbow. Even that made her wince.

"Eleven in the morning," the lady's maid said. "His lordship said not to wake you for breakfast."

"Thank you," Theo said, absently watching the sun on the pale carpet. That lovely variegated cloth being woven in India looked like that. Perhaps the Ryburn Weavers could make a silk that would shift from buttercup to cream. Though she thought dimly that silk was made from worms that lived on pods? Something like that. And she'd never heard of a silk pod tree in England.

A short time later Amélie announced that her bath was ready. If no one had been looking, Theo would have hobbled on her way to the bath, but she didn't want Amélie to guess how she was feeling, so she straightened her back and pretended everything was normal.

But after a half hour soak in hot water, she felt considerably better, and she sat at the window to dry her hair, ignoring Amélie's alarmed protestations regarding chills. She had always loved the gardens behind this house, but that emotion felt more profound now that she knew they belonged to James, rather than to his father.

To the two of them, James had said, over and over. The gardens were hers as well.

She would change that formal garden, she decided, combing through her wet hair. It was large enough for a little maze, perhaps, with an airy folly in the center.

With some sort of bed or sofa in it, she thought, her cheeks warming. On a warm summer night she and James could walk the maze. That thought led directly to the rather scandalous idea that someday she'd like to kiss him *there,* the way he had her.

"His Grace sent a message to say that he is returning sooner than he planned," Amélie said, laying out a morning gown.

"I suppose I'll see the duke at luncheon," Theo said unenthusiastically. "Not that one," she added, seeing what Amélie put out. "I wish the garments I ordered yesterday were already finished."

"At least three weeks, Madame said," Amélie reminded her.

Theo sighed. "I suppose the yellow one will have to do, though I don't like the contrast with my hair."

Amélie nodded. "A shade darker would be better."

That was one of the many things Theo loved about her maid: Amélie was as enthusiastic about fabric and color as she was.

But her mind drifted back to James. She never would have thought that she could feel so alive. That is, she'd known she was alive, of course, but last night, when their eyes met, she was more alive than she'd ever been.

Who cared if she was the "ugly duchess," as long as James looked at her as if she were beautiful beyond words?

She found herself humming that old song as Amélie buttoned her morning gown. And she couldn't stop smiling at the mirror as her maid wound all her heavy hair in an elaborate arrangement. Before her betrothal, she had thought that she'd crop all her hair off in one of those daring new cuts, but not now. Not now that she knew how much James loved it. In the middle of the night he had lit candles around the bed, and then played with her hair. No. She would never cut her hair.

She looked up and met her maid's eyes in the mirror.

"I am just so glad to see you happy, my lady," Amélie said, her French accent lending charm to her sincerity. "We all are. Those *bâtards* who named you so . . . they should be beaten. But his lordship made it all better. As a husband should."

Amélie's smile was purely wicked collusion.

"He did," Theo said, smiling in return. "He did. The nickname still stings, I have to admit. But being married means that only one person's opinion matters, doesn't it?"

"I have never been married," Amélie said. "But I do think so. Most men are *imbéciles*, but his lordship, he has always known you were beautiful. He watched you during meals, that is what Mr. Cramble said. And he could not take his eyes off your bosom."

"That's what *he* told me! I cannot believe I never noticed it when Cramble did."

"You are young in the ways of men and women," her maid said wisely.

Theo threw her a mock glare. "And are you pretending that you're old, Amélie? Because we both know you turned eighteen a week after I turned seventeen."

"*Je suis française,*" Amélie said with smug exactitude. "Here is the scarf you wanted, my lady."

"Watch this!" Theo picked up the pair of miniature scissors that Amélie used to trim her fingernails and briskly cut the scarf in two.

Amélie gave a shriek. "Indian silk!"

Theo shook out the half square of heavy silk. "It will make all the difference to this insipid gown." With one sharp wrench she pulled out the lace fichu tucked into her bodice and replaced it with the scarf. It flashed raspberry red against the almond-colored muslin of her gown.

She turned to the mirror again. "I like it," Amélie said. She reached out and deftly rearranged the silk. "I will pin it here and here, my lady."

"It draws attention to my bosom," Theo said, wondering if James would notice.

"That should hold," Amélie said, stepping back a moment later. "I can sew it in later."

"I don't think I'll leave the house today," Theo said. It was one thing to tell herself that James's opinion was all that mattered. It was another to walk down Bond Street with all those etchings staring her in the face.

"Let the excitement fade," Amélie said, nodding. "By next week, there will be some other poor soul under attack."

"Perhaps I'll see if my husband would like to go to Staffordshire, to Ryburn House." Suddenly she was quite sure that James would go wherever she went. She could feel a pink flush rising in her cheeks, but she kept her voice steady. "In fact, if you could pack my clothing, Amélie, I believe we will pay a visit to the country, perhaps for as long as a month."

"You are leaving London for the rest of the season?"

"Do you think I am being a coward?"

"Never!" Amélie said. "But there might be even more talk if you retire to the country, my lady. Because they will think you are afraid, you see."

"We can return for the Elston ball," Theo decided, thinking aloud. "By then my new wardrobe will have been delivered; Cramble can send it to the country and we'll have the final fittings there."

She stood up and took a last look at the mirror. The dress was still altogether too virginal, but the jarring touch of raspberry helped turn it to something with a claim to style.

Her heart beat a little rhythm at the idea of seeing James again. Though by now he was likely out of the house, on a horse, or boxing at Gentleman Jackson's. He had a ferocious amount of energy and couldn't be kept indoors or he started to look tormented, like a caged tiger.

She'd have to keep that in mind, she thought idly, her fingers trailing down the polished banister as she descended the stairs. Her husband needed regular exercise. Rather like having a dog.

Though James was far from a *pet*. There was something wild and undomesticated about him, something that was unlike any other aristocrat she'd met. The most she could hope for was to lure him to her.

It wasn't quite time for luncheon. If James was home, he was probably in the study. A thrill of feminine power went through her. Perhaps he had decided to stay home, at least until he saw her. Perhaps they could go riding in Hyde Park. Now that they were married, she really should become a better rider.

But not until she could wear a charming riding habit of her own design, with braided trim, epaulets, and military flare.

Twelve

Her husband strode through the library doorway the moment Theo reached the bottom of the stairs. His face was dark with rage—but at the sight of her, it cleared, though his eyes remained troubled.

"Hello," she said, feeling acutely self-conscious.

He said nothing, just grabbed her hands and walked backwards into the library. He smelled faintly of leather and a high wind.

"You've been out for a ride," she said a short time later, when they stopped kissing for a moment.

"God, I'm mad for you," he whispered in her ear, ignoring her comment altogether. "But I'm surprised you're able to walk. We shouldn't have done it, that last time."

"I wanted you," she said against his lips. "I want you now."

"You smell so sweet, like a daisy."

"You simply *must* stop calling me that! I insist on being addressed as Theo."

He had backed her against the wall and a hand was now wrapped around her breast. "I can't," he said, rather thickly.

"Why not?"

"Because you may be Theo when we're at breakfast, or at a play or something, but when I'm holding you like this, you're my Daisy." He took her mouth again and Theo melted against him, thoughts fading before the onslaught of his mouth and his hands and the arrogant strength of his body against hers.

"Can't do this," James said hoarsely. "You're too sore. We're only kissing." He guided her over to the sofa on the far side of the room and began plucking her hairpins, destroying all of Amélie's work in seconds. He was unweaving a braid that had taken Amélie a good ten minutes to concoct. "Couldn't you just leave your hair down when you're at home?"

Theo giggled. "Can you imagine Cramble's face if I begin wandering about the house with my hair around my shoulders?"

James's face loomed over hers, and he kissed her again, hard and dominant. "What if, as your husband," he growled, "I ordered you to?"

Theo felt a shiver go all the way to her toes. When James got that look, that possessive, tigerlike look, she felt the most embarrassing desire to simply melt into him and do whatever he demanded.

"I'm sorry," she said, tracing the line of his full bottom lip with her fingers, "but no one can ever dictate how I look or dress again. I made that promise to myself five years ago, when Mama began trying to compensate for my face by embellishing my gowns with frills and ruffles."

James frowned.

"She can't bring herself to admit it, but she wanted to make sure that everyone knew I was a girl," Theo explained.

He had discovered the precariously attached scrap of raspberry silk and pulled it out without further ado. Without a fichu, her bodice showed a great deal of cleavage. "She thought you didn't look enough like a girl," he said, sounding stunned. He bent his head and licked a wet, warm path over the curve of her breast.

Then he reared up again. "What if, as your husband, I ordered you to leave off your drawers?"

She laughed at him, loving the way he was testing the limits of his power. "That would depend on how I felt about you at that moment."

"And how do you feel about me at this moment?" he demanded.

She arched up, just enough so that she could run her tongue along that sweet lower lip of his.

"What would *you* do if I ordered you to do something?"

His lips parted, and he took a deep breath. "Whatever you want," he said, his voice fervent. "I'll do whatever you want."

"Then I'd like you to sit quite still," she said, twisting about and tumbling off the sofa.

James sat obediently. His eyes were black with excitement. "I am yours to command, my lady."

"Pull down your breeches," she said, her blood racing.

Without blinking, James stood up and did exactly as she demanded.

Theo stayed on her knees and pointed back to the sofa. He sat down. His organ seemed, if possible, even bigger than it had the night before. At the very sight of it, a little warning twinge came from Theo's private place.

"All the time you were kissing me last night," she said, reaching out to caress him, "all I could think about was what it would be like to kiss *you.*"

"Oh Lord," James whispered. "I won't survive it. I won't."

"*I* did," Theo said, throwing him a saucy smile. She bent over and tasted him.

James let out a hoarse sound and Theo dipped her head a little lower, exploring the velvety feeling of him.

It must have been his groan that prevented her

hearing the sound of the door opening. Or perhaps it was the dizzying sense of power Theo felt.

But a second later the sound filtered into her head. She leapt to her feet, met the eyes of her father-in-law, and fled in the opposite direction, straight through the closest door, which led into the morning room. She slammed the door and leaned back against it, her heart pounding as if she'd run from an assailant.

She felt sick. The duke had seen . . . He'd seen everything. He'd seen her there, bending over James's lap.

"Oh God." Her knees were too weak to support her; she slid down until she was sitting on the floor. Through the door, she heard the rumble of James's voice as he spoke, but the words were indecipherable. The sound reminded her, with sickening vividness, of how he had been sitting before her, breeches around his ankles, and she buried her face in her hands.

Did it *have* to be the duke? Hadn't she suffered enough humiliation in the last few days? Would it have been worse, though, if a footman had interrupted them? She could have dismissed a footman. No, she would never turn out a person for being unlucky enough to see her behave like a doxy.

They'd have to retire to the country for the next month. Or year.

The muffled sound changed pitch; her father-in-law was speaking.

Shifting to the side, she stretched up and opened the door slightly. If he was calling her a brazen slut, she might as well know the worst.

But he was laughing.

Laughing!

Her heart thudded a panic-stricken rhythm in her throat. Was laughter better than scorn? Or worse? It felt better. Maybe this sort of thing happened often to newlyweds. After all, she and James could have been caught actually making love. And if she hadn't been so sore, they probably would have been. Theo turned her ear to the crack of the open door.

"I returned to London because I heard about the ugly duchess business," the duke was saying. "Thought you'd want me to threaten a few reporters, maybe even shut down one of those scandal rags. But it looks as if you've been too busy to worry. Who cares if she's ugly? Obviously it makes her more grateful, huh? I could scarcely believe my eyes when I saw she was servicing you as eagerly as any tavern wench might for tuppence."

Theo's head dropped forward onto her knees. What did she expect from the duke? Her mother had declared him a coarse fool years ago, and she was obviously right.

"In fact, it's *because* she's ugly," the duke

142

continued. "You could never get a proper lady on her knees like that—"

"Silence!" James snapped.

Thank God he was saying something, Theo thought numbly.

"I don't care for your tone," his father responded, instantly switching to his characteristic angry bluster.

"You are not allowed to *ever* say anything about my wife," James replied. His voice, in contrast with his father's, was icy cold, controlled, and yet deeply dangerous.

Theo took a shuddering breath. At least James was defending her.

The duke seemed not to notice the threat in his son's voice. "I'll say anything I want!" he bellowed. "I picked the girl out for you, didn't I?"

"You did not!"

"I did! You didn't want to marry her, but I expect you're glad now. I told you, didn't I? I told you they were all alike in the dark."

"I'm going to kill you," James stated. Years of experience with James's temper told Theo that his self-control was reaching its limit. He hated it when that happened, when his shouting resembled that of his father.

But as the duke's words—*I picked the girl out for you, didn't I?*—came into her consciousness, she stopped thinking about James. *What?*

"I may not have had your marriage in mind at

143

the time," the duke was saying. "I may not have thought of it in precisely that way—"

"While you were embezzling her inheritance!" James roared. With this, Theo realized two things simultaneously: the first was that James's self-control had finally snapped . . . and the second was the significance of what he had just said. About embezzlement. It couldn't be true. *Could* it be true?

"I only borrowed from it," the duke said, sounding pained. "You needn't cast such an ugly light on it. After all, look what I've done for you. Got you a wife so grateful that she'll do you in the broad daylight, when Cramble might have walked in any moment. I apologized for her looks when I forced you to propose, but I take all that back now. I never heard of a lady doing such a thing. Never. You'll save a fortune on mistresses. Just blow out the candles first."

Theo's breath was coming in little sobs. Her entire world was toppling, falling about her ears. The duke had *forced* James to marry her. He had apologized to James for how ugly she was. She had done something that no lady would do, though she hadn't known it. Still, she did know that intimacies belong only in the bedchamber. Even the servants knew that.

"Do not say a word about my wife," James shouted. "Damn you!" Rage boiled in his voice now, but Theo didn't care. He wasn't denying it.

144

He wasn't denying any of it.

The duke—her late father's closest friend—had embezzled her dowry. Mr. Reede, the estate manager, had to have known that when they were talking the day before. *James* knew. James knew the entire time. He had sat there and talked about how they could pay the duke's debts from her inheritance, and the entire time he knew that his father had already stolen whatever money he wished from it.

Her mind spun, putting it all together. She had never seen James drunk. But when he was foxed at the Prince of Wales's musicale . . . he must have had to drink deeply so that he would have the courage to propose to someone like her.

In the weeks and years to come, when she looked back she identified that as the precise moment when her heart broke in two. The moment that separated Daisy from Theo, the time Before, from the time After.

In the time Before, she had faith. She had love.

In the time After . . . she had the truth.

Thirteen

In the library, James looked up and saw the door to the morning room ajar. He flinched, looked closer, saw a flash of yellow near the floor. Daisy had heard. She'd heard everything.

James jerked his eyes away from the door and turned back to his father.

His stupid, contemptible father.

"I don't want to see you again." He felt his throat closing. "She heard you. She heard you. You ass."

"Well, I said nothing that isn't true," the duke said, instantly defensive, swiveling to look at the door.

"She will never forgive me," James said, knowing it in his bones.

"Given what I saw—"

James bared his teeth, and his father shut his mouth. "We had a chance, you know. Even after the way it happened."

"I've no doubt that she'll be tetchy," Ashbrook said. He lowered his voice and added conspiratorially, "Diamonds. It always worked with your mother. Helped us rub along together for years."

James had stopped listening. "I shall spend my life trying to—to make up for it." For the first time in years, he wanted his mother. He hadn't felt a wash of fear like this since she lay dying.

"You'd better leave," he said now. "Find somewhere else to live. I think that we're probably done with the pretense that there's any true feeling between us."

"You are my only son," the duke said. "My *son.* Of course there's feeling between us."

"The kinship means nothing," James said, a

terrible feeling of fury and misery swelling in his heart. "I am nothing to you, and Daisy is nothing to you. We are just people you walk by in the hallway, people you use when you need us and then throw away."

His father's eyes narrowed. "You're hardly the victim here!" he said, voice rising. "You're the one who threw yourself at the girl. No reason for *you* to whine."

"I betrayed her—my wife—in order to save you."

"You didn't do it for that," the duke said. "You did it to save your estate and shore up the title. You could have told me to go to blazes, but you didn't. I thought you'd go all moral and tell me to go to the devil. But you turned out not to be the sticker you pretend to be. We're not so different."

James's fists were clenched. He couldn't strike his father.

"In fact," Ashbrook went on, "the apple doesn't fall far from the tree, and don't you forget it. Your mother didn't fool herself that I was a perfect man, but we were married, and that was the end of it." His lip curled. "There's one way that we are different, though: I'm no whiner. I may have been surprised when you went through with it, but I'm not surprised you're crying about the results. Be a man, for God's sake. You're an embarrassment. You've always been an embarrassment, with all that singing. I blame it on your mother."

"You don't love me in the least," James said, breaching the unspoken rule that English gentlemen never discussed such matters. "Do you?"

"Of all the asinine questions, that has to be the most," the duke said, color exploding into his cheeks. "You're my heir, and that's the end of it."

"People who love each other don't do this sort of thing," James said dully. He walked over to the library door, opened it, and stood beside it. "Go."

"You'll have to talk to her," the duke said, not moving. "Take charge of the situation. You're the man here. Assert yourself. Don't let her go into hysterics; it might set a pattern."

"Go," James repeated, not trusting himself to say anything else.

The duke huffed, but he walked toward the door. He stopped with his hand on the knob, but didn't turn around. "I love you," he said, quietly for him. "I—I love you." And then he left.

Staring at the closed door, James was struck by another blinding wave of longing for his mother— for the days when his mother, or at least his nanny, could make anything better. He had to go into the morning room. He had to talk to Daisy, tell her how much he—how much what? She would never believe he loved her.

He'd just said it to his father: People who loved each other didn't do cruel things to each other.

The leaden feeling in his chest spread through

his body. Maybe he was incapable of loving anyone. He was like his father. He should just leave. She'd be better off without him.

He made his way to the morning room door.

For a long time Theo didn't move, her muscles frozen, her eyes shut. The bitterness in her stomach threatened to rise into her throat.

Fighting for control, she didn't even notice at first when a pair of boots moved directly into her line of vision.

Standing up and meeting her husband's eyes took every bit of backbone Theodora Ryburn had. But stand she did, and she met his eyes, too. And she saw exactly what she expected: shame. That answered her last, lingering question. He had never wanted to marry her.

So she steeled herself. "I hope you enjoyed that," she said finally. "As I'm sure you have guessed, it's the very last time your wife will service you."

"Daisy."

"Must I spell it out?"

"Don't leave me," he said, choking out the words.

Theo had retreated behind a thick ice wall, where she felt utterly calm. And her brain was working with remarkable adroitness.

"Don't be a fool," she said. "I'm not leaving you; I'm throwing you out. I'll mend the estate with whatever is left of my embezzled dowry. I think we can both agree, after your behavior at yesterday's meeting, that you would be utterly unhelpful and won't be missed."

He swallowed, a faint sign of mortification that she welcomed.

"That being the case, there's nothing to keep you here," she observed. "You and your father are obviously not on the best of terms. He's a vulgar, despicable criminal, and you are a weak-kneed fool—who deliberately ruined my life in order to cover up your father's crimes."

His eyes were burning, but still he was silent.

"You will leave this house, and then you will leave England altogether. You may have that boat you visited yesterday—take it somewhere. I don't ever want to see your face again."

James shifted from foot to foot, for all the world like a guilty child.

"The damnable part is that the marriage was consummated," she continued. "There's no getting out of it."

"I don't want to get out of it." James's words came out in a strangled growl.

"I expect you don't. After all, there I was, kneeling at your feet, begging for favors you might toss my way. As your father so kindly pointed out, any man would be in seventh heaven; I gather such eagerness is generally paid for. I suppose you were reiterating the sort of demands you give a doxy when ordering me to not wear drawers? And to wear my hair down?"

"No!"

"Don't bellow at me," Theo responded. "I'm not a terrified scullery maid facing your father. If you throw a china shepherdess at me, I'll pick up the bloody dining room table and throw it at your head."

"I have never thrown anything," James stated.

"You're just coming into your own. I'm sure when you're as old as your father you'll have equal bragging rights to being a bastard. Or . . . wait. I think you've already earned them."

"I'm sorry," he said, his voice breaking. "I'm just so sorry, Daisy."

His face was contorted, as if he was trying not to cry, but she didn't feel a bit of pity. Safe behind her icy wall, she felt nothing.

"You're beautiful, and I'm not. But you know something, James? I'd rather be me a hundred times over. Because when I fell in love with you, I did it honestly. I was a fool; I realize that now. But I loved you last night. I truly loved you. I hope you enjoyed it, because I think I'm probably the last person stupid enough, and fooled enough by your beautiful face, to think that there's anything worthwhile inside you."

His jaw tightened, but he said nothing.

She had one more thing to say. "When someone falls in love with me—and he will, because life is

151

long, and this marriage is *over*—he'll love me for who I am, not for my face. He'll be able to see inside me, and he'll want me for more than my dowry, or the fact that I could be ordered about and turned into a prostitute without even understanding my own humiliation."

"I didn't do that!"

She managed to keep her voice steady. "You are disgusting. Utterly disgusting. But the saddest part of this is that I did all that with you because I thought I was in love with you, and that you loved me as well. I didn't do it for money, which is why you did it. So I think your father had it wrong: it seems that I just had two very expensive nights with a cicisbeo."

"Don't do this," he said, his voice little more than a rough whisper. "Please, Daisy, don't. Don't do this."

"Do what? Tell you the truth?"

"Break us apart."

She waited, but he found no more words.

"There is no us," she said, feeling suddenly shattered. "I'll expect you to leave the house within the day." To her horror, she realized that the sight of him still warmed some errant part of her heart, and the very realization drove her on.

"I would never have done this to you." For the first time, her voice almost cracked. "I loved you, James. I really loved you. The odd thing is that I didn't even realize it until we were married. But even if I hadn't loved you that way, I wouldn't have betrayed you, because you were my closest friend. My *brother.* You could have just asked me, you know."

His face had turned deathly white. "Asked you what?"

"Asked me for my money," she said, head high, eyes dry. "People who love . . . they share. They give. I would have given you that money. You needn't have walked over me to get to it."

She turned and left, closing the door precisely behind her.

She climbed the stairs to the second floor feeling as if she were a hundred years old, as empty and wizened as a beldame. As she walked down the corridor, the duke emerged from his chamber.

She met his eyes without even a tinge of shame. *She* was not the one to be ashamed.

His eyes fell.

"I own this house," she told the top of his head. "I want you out of it. As I learned yesterday, I seem to have promised you a generous allowance. You can rent your own damned house with it."

His head jerked up and he bellowed, "You can't do that!"

"If you are not out of here by tomorrow, I will take that lying estate manager, Reede, and deliver him and his records directly to my solicitors, not to mention to Bow Street. Say what you like. Tell your friends that you can't bear to see my ugly face in the morning. But move out."

"Tell her she can't do that!" her father-in-law shouted.

She glanced down and saw James standing at the bottom of the stairs, his hand clenched on the banister. "He's leaving, too," she told the duke. "I'm closing this house to save the expense of running it. I'll be living in Staffordshire for the foreseeable future, but if either of you wishes to communicate with me, you can do it through my solicitor."

"I will not communicate with my wife through a solicitor," James said from below.

"I agree. I would prefer that you not communicate at all."

"You're a virago," the duke snarled, his voice shaking with rage.

"There's nothing to throw in this hallway," she said, looking at him with distaste.

"You cannot make me leave my own house, the house my grandfather built."

"No, I can't. But I can air the evidence of your embezzlement of my dowry, left in your care by your best friend. Interesting, that." She glanced back down at James. "Best friends seem to be no more than fodder for betrayal in this family."

The scorn in her words seemed finally to penetrate the duke. He wheeled and stalked back to his chamber without another word.

Theo did not look down the stairs to see if James was still there. She knew he was staring up at her; she could feel his eyes on her back.

But she walked on, leaving Daisy behind. Leaving her marriage behind.

Leaving her heart behind.

Part Two
After

Fourteen

Nine months later
Aboard the Percival
Somewhere in the Maldives

"We can't outrun it, my lord. We're too heavy."
The quartermaster, a stout man named Squib, had
to shout at James to be heard. Wind stripped the
fear from his voice, but not from his face.

"Hold the wheel." James turned around,
scanning the horizon. The approaching ship was
barely visible, but she was skimming the waves as
if she had taken wing. "You're sure she's a pirate
vessel?"

"Lookout confirmed it," Squib said, blotting his
forehead. "I've managed to avoid pirates all these
years, dammit, and I have new grandbabies at
home. I should have just stayed in London."

"Is she flying a black flag?"

Squib nodded. "We're done for. It's the *Flying
Poppy.*" He gave an involuntary moan. "Got a red
flower on black; easy to spot."

James had been standing at the rail, rigid,
staring at the ship as if his hard stare could make
it disappear. The moment he heard the name,
relief made his shoulders slump. He knew about
this ship, and if he was right, they had a chance. A
slender chance, but it was better than nothing.

"Could be worse," he said, hoping he was right.

"The *Poppy* has taken five ships this season alone, from what I heard at the last port. The only thing can be said is that they don't generally kill the crew, but they sink the vessels. We're done for, my lord."

James grunted. "Are the cannon ready to fire?"

"Yes."

"We're not done for until the last moment. Steer ahead. Doesn't really matter where you go."

James leapt down from the forecastle and ran below decks. His crew was busy with the cannons, slamming the huge sticks that tamped the powder into place. They didn't pause until he addressed them.

"Men!"

They all looked up. An hour earlier, they had had the sun-bronzed lethargy of men on a long voyage, tired of salt beef, tired of flying fish, their eyes and noses full of salt. But now, to a man, they were terrified.

"Our goal is to stay alive," James told them.

There was a moment of surprised silence.

"We'll give the cannon a try. We might get lucky and hit her broadside. But those pirates want what's in our hold. And I don't want all of you killed fighting hand-to-hand with men who have spent their lives doing it. If we don't sink the ship on the first go, I want you all on the deck. Face down."

At that, there was a babble of angry voices.

"I've never turned down a fight in me life," Clamper shouted. He hailed from Cheapside, and had a rugged face and a handy way with a dagger.

"You will now," James said. "You pull that blade of yours, Clamper, and I'll consider you mutinous."

Silence again. He and the crew had been together nine months. There had been difficult moments as he learned the ways of the sea and sailing a trading vessel, but Squib had stood at his shoulder the entire time. And he'd be *damned* if he'd let his crew be massacred. "I intend to challenge the captain," he said. "To invoke sea law."

"Pirates don't have no sea law," someone shouted.

"The captain of the *Flying Poppy* does," James said. He'd made it his business to find out whatever he could about the pirates known to operate between India and the British Isles. "His name is Sir Griffin Barry; he's a baronet and a distant relative. We met when we were both boys. He'll remember me."

"So you can talk to him in yez language," Clamper said, a flicker of hope dawning in his eyes.

"I can try," James said. Barry was an unregenerate criminal, of course. But he had gone to Eton. And they were third cousins. In short, there were other degenerates in his family besides his father and himself. "Don't fire those cannon until I give the word."

But in the end, the word never came. The crew of the *Flying Poppy* was far too canny to expose her side to a vessel they were bent on plundering, and the *Percival* was too heavy in the water, thanks to its full load of spice, to move nimbly. The *Poppy* danced around her until the pirates pulled up alongside and boarded without incident.

Men flowed over the railing in a rush. Upon seeing the *Percival*'s crew lying face down on their own deck, they spread out along the railing without a word, backs to the sea, pistols in one hand, knives in the other. Apparently the *Percival* was not the first ship whose captain had surrendered at the sight of that bloodred poppy sewn onto a field of black.

The captain was the last to board, landing on the deck with a knife between his teeth and a pistol in his right hand. He certainly didn't look like a scion of gentle English stock; he was dressed like a dockworker. A small poppy, matching the one on his flag, was tattooed below his right eye.

"Sir Griffin Barry," James said, inclining his chin precisely the degree required by an earl greeting a baronet. He stood in the midst of his prostrate men, all of them surrounded by a loose ring of pirates. He was dressed, weirdly but calculatedly, in court attire: a coat embroidered in gold thread with buttons made of gold twist. He even wore a wig—rather hastily plopped on top of his head, to be sure, but it was there.

Barry took a lightning look at this vision, then leaned back against the railing and burst into laughter. It was not a benevolent laughter, by any means, but at least he was laughing.

James felt a pulse of courage at not being shot on sight. "Under sea law, I could challenge you to a duel," he remarked, his tone as casually fearless as he could muster.

The baronet's eyes narrowed, and his hand tightened on his pistol. "You could."

"Or we could simply retire to my cabin and have a drink. After all, we haven't seen each other in—what?—five years?"

His entire crew could be dead in a matter of three minutes, by his estimate. But James was gambling on the ancient system of British courtesy, drilled into the head of every aristocratic boy from the time they could toddle. He added, deliberately, "I believe our late Aunt Agatha would prefer the latter."

"Bloody hell," Barry said, his eyes widening with dawning recognition. "Thought you were any fool aristocrat. But you're the Dam'Fool Duke's son."

James bowed, flourishing the pristine lace at his wrists. "Islay. James Ryburn at your service.

Something of a pleasure to meet you again, Sir Griffin Barth—"

Barry cut off the utterance of his second name with an obscenity. James felt a prick of satisfaction, along with another wave of courage. Who knew one could intimidate a pirate captain with private information such as the fact his middle name was *Bartholomew?*

"What in bloody hell are you doing out here, other than waiting to be marauded by me?" Barry growled. But the balance of power had shifted. James's status as heir to a dukedom had leveled the playing field, for all Barry was both a pirate and a baronet.

"Making my fortune after my father lost one and embezzled another. Surely you, Coz, could be the one to teach me to do that? The *Poppy Two*, perhaps?" Holding his cousin's eyes, he threw off the embroidered coat, revealing the coarse shirt underneath. With another quick gesture, his wig spun through the air and overboard.

"I've been captain of this vessel for nine months. I've learned the wind and the water and the stars. I have a hold full of spice, but I'd like to do something new. You might say, Coz, that the criminal instinct runs in our family."

Whatever Barry had expected to hear, it wasn't that. James held his breath. He didn't let his eyes drift downward toward his men, lest it be taken as a sign of concern and therefore of weakness.

"I'll have that brandy," Barry said, finally.

"My men are unarmed," James remarked, as if he were commenting on the weather.

Barry jerked his head toward one of his men. "Round them up and put them over there by the rail while I talk to his lordship here." He looked back at James, the cold ruthlessness of a pirate captain in his eyes. "If I don't come above deck in an hour, kill them all, Sly. Kill them all."

An hour passed, and Barry did not reappear. Sly, however, knew better than to carry out his captain's orders before taking a peek downstairs. By the time he took a look, James and Griffin were well into their second bottle of cognac.

Night fell with the *Percival* towing the *Flying Poppy*, their respective crews conducting their business in an orderly fashion (albeit with a few pirates looking over Squib's shoulder).

James and his cousin, whom he had reverted to addressing by his given name, continued drinking.

"Can't drink like this normally," Griffin muttered at some point. "Captain can't fraternize with his men."

"I'll remember that," James said, slurring his words a bit. "Do you remember what we did when we first met?"

"Climbed up on the roof," Griffin said after a brief pause to recollect, "slung a rope from one of the chimneys, climbed down far enough to bang on the nursery windows and try to scare your nanny to death."

"That was the plan," James agreed, taking another slug of cognac. They drank straight from the bottles. "Didn't work out that way."

"My sister ran around shrieking, but yours didn't. She opened the window, remember? I thought she was pulling us in, but instead she threw a basin of water at us, laughing as if she was cracked. She could have killed us."

"Not my sister," James said rather owlishly. "I married her. She's my wife." Before he knew it, he found himself talking, for the first time, about what had happened nine months before. It spilled from his mouth. Not all of it—not what he and Daisy had been doing in the library—but enough.

"Damnation," Griffin exclaimed. "She heard it, all of it?"

The ship caught the side of a wave and James nearly fell from his chair, but he managed to catch himself. "Drunk as a stoat," he muttered to himself. "She heard every word. Told me never to come back. I took over the *Percival* the next morning."

"I've got a wife somewhere, too," Griffin said, not sounding in the least regretful at having misplaced her. "Better off without."

With rather elaborate care, they clinked their bottles. "Here's to the *Poppy*," James said.

"And the *Poppy Two*," Griffin added. "See this?"

He tapped the wrong cheek, but James understood what he meant and felt a surge of apprehension. No tattooed man could ever return to English society. Tattooed men did not bow before the queen, nor dance the minuet at Almack's, nor kiss their wives goodnight.

There were times, in the dark of the night, when he yearned for Daisy so much that he could hardly breathe. Times when he thought he *must* return to her, beg her to take him back, sleep at her doorstep if need be. They had been friends his entire life, after all, and lovers . . .

He still woke up shaking and aroused from dreams of her.

But if he were tattooed, those dreams would be over. There could be no prospect of going back. And that's what she wanted.

She had told him to never come back, that she never wanted to see his face again. Daisy never said anything she didn't mean. She was straight as an arrow. Not like him.

"Right," he said, standing up with hardly a wobble. "Have to board your ship, I suppose. Gotta get my tattoo so I can be a real pirate."

"You can come over there, but no poppy," Griffin said. "You have to earn your tattoo. You can't just get one for the asking."

James nodded. "Damn, my head is starting to ache."

"Three bottles of cognac," Griffin said, standing

as well. He lurched against the wall. "I don't hold my liquor so well anymore. Did I tell you never to drink with the crew?"

James nodded, which made his head throb. "I'll learn it all," he said.

Back on the deck, the sea air woke them up.

"How are we going to get to your ship?" James said. The *Poppy* had drawn close to the *Percival* earlier, close enough that the pirates had easily leapt from their deck, caught the *Percival*'s railing, and swung over. But now the two ships were tethered with a good distance between them, sails furled.

With a wild shout, Griffin kicked off his boots and launched himself straight over the railing and down into the blue water.

"Mad," James muttered. English lords didn't do more than dip in the ocean, though, of course, he could swim.

But over he went, dropping into water as warm as a bath, stroking after his cousin, who swam not like a fish but like a shark.

Then up a rope ladder, hand over hand nearly as fast as Griffin. James's head had cleared, and he was almost sober as he pulled himself over the railing.

For all the brandy and the bonhomie, Griffin was a pirate lord.

His pirates were clustered around him now. They turned as James drew himself upright, dripping.

Griffin's face was different in the midst of his men: it was sinister and grim, without a trace of his fine breeding to be seen. "This is my cousin," he stated. The pirates nodded, though a few narrowed their eyes. "He'll be captaining the *Poppy Two*. You can call him The Earl."

They went below to Griffin's cabin, where Griffin threw James some dry clothes: rough clothes, fit for a fight at sea. Without ceremony, he took a pair of scissors and chopped off James's hair above his ears. "The last thing you want is some cutthroat to jerk you backward by your pretty locks," he explained.

James looked at himself in the glass and approved. Not a trace of an English earl looked back at him. He looked like a man who cared for no one, not for his wife or his family or his heritage.

That wasn't quite true, but he could make it true.

Now he was a pirate.

One year later

Using their perfected (and extremely successful) pincer action, the *Flying Poppy* and the *Poppy Two* had just divested yet another pirate ship, the *Dreadnaught*, of her ill-gotten gains. Pallets of teakwood and barrels of China tea were now nestled in the hold of the *Flying Poppy* together with the *Dreadnaught*'s crew, their ship having followed the body of their captain, Flibbery Jack, into the depths of the Indian Ocean.

Griffin and James were sprawled in Griffin's cabin, celebrating their latest conquest with a glass or two of cognac. After that first night together, they had not overindulged again; it wasn't in their natures.

"We're surprisingly alike," James said, following that thought to its logical conclusion.

"Damn good sailors," Griffin replied. "Just when I think that the *P-Two* can't possibly sidle up where I'd like her to, you manage it."

"Pity about those men."

"The dead ones?"

"Yes."

"Didn't lose any of our own. And the crew of the *Dreadnaught* were feared through the East Indies," Griffin pointed out. "We've done the world a favor. Another favor, given that we scuttled the *Black Spider* last month. And may I point out that the *Dreadnaught* gained her reputation by capturing a passenger ship bound for Bombay and walking every single man, woman, and child down the plank?"

"I know it," James said. All his research on pirates and their routes had served them well in the last few months. The *Poppy*s were now as feared by pirates as pirates were feared by trading vessels.

"We're bloody Robin Hoods, we are."

170

"With the tiny exception that we don't give to the poor," James said dryly.

"We returned that golden statue to the King of Sicily. We could have sold it." Griffin was not one for the magnanimous gesture.

"Ferdinand's letter giving us the right to fly his flag as privateers is worth more than Saint Agatha, even if the statue wasn't hollow—which it was, may I point out."

Griffin just shrugged. He didn't like giving anything away for free, but even he had to admit that privateers lived an easier life than pirates, though the distinction was certainly a foggy one.

"What are you going to do with all that fabric you put in your cabin, by the way?" he asked. "Are you planning to lure a woman on board? The men won't hold with it. The first storm that hit, you'd look around for your popsy and find they'd tossed her overboard to appease the sea devils, or Poseidon, or what have you."

"I thought I'd send the fabric to my wife. She always talked about cloth more than she did dresses themselves, and the silks are lovely. The *Dreadnaught* must have caught a silk trader."

"Why on earth would you do such a thing?" Griffin asked, clearly astonished. "She booted you out the door, and quite rightly, from what you said. Why remind her of your miserable existence?"

"Good question," James said, throwing back his

cognac. "Forget the fabric; we must do something with the gold."

"Bank it," Griffin said promptly. "When I think of the way I used to simply stash it in a cave before you came along, it makes me twitch all over. Shall we stow it in Genoa or open a new account somewhere else?"

"I'm worried about our account in that Paris bank, given Napoleon's sticky fingers," James said. "I think we'd better head there and close that account. We'll put the lot in Genoa."

Griffin put his empty glass to the side and stood. "Look, James, I have some bad news. The bos'un on the *Dreadnaught* was taken on in Bristol two months ago, and he had this."

He walked to the sideboard, picked up a newspaper lying there, and handed it to James. A black-bordered notice announced that the Duke of Ashbrook had died suddenly.

James stared down at the paper. His father was dead, and had been for two months. Just like that, his world changed. Then, after a few seconds, he rose, quite calmly, and said, "I'll go back to the *Poppy Two* and tell the men that we're en route for Marseille. We'd better swap out the sails and turn into privateers."

Griffin gave him a swift punch in the arm. "Don't think I'm going to 'Your Grace' you. Do you suppose the men will catch on if we announce your name is changing to Duke? Earl doesn't really seem fitting for one of your grand stature."

James didn't bother to answer. He climbed the stairs wearily. They had a crew member whose only job was to row back and forth between the *Poppy*s, and a moment later he was once again crossing the short distance. Dusk had fallen, and the ocean seemed drained of color and detail, as if the rowboat plowed through a gray mist.

Back in his own cabin, he felt so exhausted that he dropped on the bunk without undressing. It had been a long, grueling day: from the moment a pirate ship was spied, he and the other men often didn't sleep for forty-eight hours, a period of tense watchfulness that generally culminated in a bloody battle. Pirates always fought hard, and beating them was a ruthless, hand-to-hand business. Today's taking of the *Dreadnaught* had followed the pattern.

Despite his physical exhaustion, his mind felt frozen, unable to think of anything but his father's death. His man appeared with a basin of hot water before quietly departing. James heaved himself from the bunk and stripped off his clothing, memories ricocheting around his brain.

He had spent a good deal of his life loathing his father, but he had never thought of him not being there. Never. The duke wasn't terribly old, but then James remembered the purple color in his cheeks during his attacks of rage. His heart had burst, no doubt.

And yet . . . and yet for all his father had done, James had never truly questioned whether he loved him, James, his son and heir, his only child. The duke was a fool, a gamester, a reckless man who trampled the feelings of those around him. And yet he *did* love James. The fact that he had died without knowing that his son was alive or dead: that felt like a knife under James's ribs.

The memories flooded in, and not those to do with stealing Daisy's dowry or anything like that. No, they were the way his father used to burst into the nursery and swing him onto his shoulder; the way he'd let him hide under his desk so that his tutor couldn't find him; the way he'd show up at Eton completely unannounced and use his title to bully his way into the classroom and then take James and all his friends out boating on the river Thames.

Grief was locked together with guilt. The two emotions sat at the base of his chest like a stone, telling him that his father died broken-hearted.

He knew it.

He should have . . . He should have . . . What? It hardly mattered now. He had done nothing. And the duke was *gone*. As lost to James now as his mother was.

Daisy would have managed it all, the funeral, and the rest of it. Daisy would have made sure her father-in-law, no matter how despised, had a proper monument.

His sponge bath finished, he stared at the pile of fabric in the corner as he dried himself. He was desperate to think about anything other than his father's death.

The fabrics glimmered like the souks of North Africa and the bazaars of India from which they'd come. His gaze fixed on one cloth that captured the pale blue of a hot summer day in England, when the sky seems so high and far away that it might as well be heaven.

Even as he stared, willing his mind blank, he could almost hear his father screaming at him, telling him to stop being a horse's arse and come back, face his responsibilities, take over the dukedom.

Yet now that voice was forever silenced. James's memories of his father felt useless and far away, as if England were no more than a kingdom under the sea, a land of fishes where he would fit in as well as a trout behind the pulpit of St. Paul's.

The hell with it.

He had stopped dreaming of Daisy, but that didn't mean he'd stopped thinking of her altogether. He still did, though mostly alone in his bunk, when recovering from a knife wound.

If he were given the chance to do it over, he wouldn't have fled England. He would have carried his wife upstairs and thrown her on the bed, and made her understand how he felt about her. But it was too late for that: those dreams were as dead as his father.

There was nothing in England for him. He had to be gone seven years before they could declare him dead. Well, in a mere month or two, he would have been at sea for two years. Pinkler-Ryburn was a decent fellow; he'd assume the title in five years if James failed to return. Then Daisy could marry again. Severing all ties to England would extinguish, for once and all, this odd and shameful longing to return home to her.

He could hear Daisy's voice as clear as a bell in his ear when she had told him their marriage was over. And when she had said that another man would fall in love with her, a better man than he.

That was easy enough to imagine. James had never loathed anyone as much in his life as he loathed himself.

He shouted, and his man popped in the door. "Throw that lot overboard," he ordered, nodding at the cloth. The man gathered the cloth into his arms and scurried from the cabin.

An hour later, James had a shaved head and a small poppy tattooed beneath his right eye. He appropriated a name from Flibbery Jack, the pirate captain who would no longer be needing it, and gave it to himself.

Long live Jack Hawk.

Because James Ryburn, Earl of Islay and Duke of Ashbrook, was dead.

Fifteen

June 1811
Ryburn House, Staffordshire
Duchy of Ashbrook

Theo ran a hand through her short hair, loving the fact that her head felt light and free. She'd cropped her hair the day after her marriage fell apart, and she had never regretted it. "What did you say, Mama? I'm afraid I wasn't listening."

"May I offer you a piece of apple cake?"

"No, thank you."

"You must *eat,*" Mrs. Saxby said rather sharply, handing Theo a piece of cake nonetheless. "You do nothing but work, darling. Work, work, work."

"There's a great deal of work to be done," Theo said reasonably. "And you must admit that it's all going quite well, Mama. We are producing our very first ceramics sometime this month. And the Ryburn Weavers has fourteen new orders. Fourteen!" She couldn't help a triumphant grin at the very thought.

"That's all very well," Mrs. Saxby said, "but you look almost gaunt. It's not becoming."

Theo let that pass. After a few months that she still hated to think about, she had settled into acceptance of her "ugly" status. When James had fled London, the *ton* assumed, quite naturally, that he couldn't contemplate more than two days of marriage to an ugly duchess-to-be. No one talked of anything else for a good month, evidenced by what gossip filtered its way into the newspapers. Theo had not been there to experience the firestorm in person; she had left the city the same day James did, retreating to Staffordshire, where her mother had joined her after returning from Scotland.

By the time people discovered that James had taken the *Percival* and set off for foreign parts, she was safely ensconced in the country and, though occasional sorties to London were unavoidable, she hadn't ventured back into polite society—the very word made her lip curl—since.

"Mr. Pinkler-Ryburn's wedding is approaching," her mother insisted. "We must both look our best."

"As I said when the invitation first arrived, I see no reason why I should attend the wedding of my husband's putative heir to the cretinous Claribel. Besides," she added more reasonably, "it would take nearly a week, since the nuptials are being held in Kent. I couldn't possibly spare the time; August is a very busy month."

Mrs. Saxby's teacup joined its saucer with a bit more force than necessary. "Darling, I hoped not to have to say this to you, but you are growing rigid." Her hair had turned a little gray, and she'd lost some of the bounce in her step after her son-in-law's dramatic departure, but she had never weakened in her adherence to courtesy. "You must attend as a representative of the duchy. *And* because Mr. Pinkler-Ryburn is a very good man."

"His worth has nothing to do with it," Theo said. "I simply cannot hare off to a wedding when I need to be here." She could be quite as stubborn as her mother.

"You have taken a very *pinched* view of life," Mrs. Saxby continued. "You may have had an unhappy experience of marriage, but is that a reason to turn into a sharp-tongued, unhappy woman?"

"I'm not unhappy," Theo said, adding honestly, "most of the time. Besides, happiness is not something one can control."

"I disagree. Life dealt you a few blows. But what happened to the daughter I used to know? Where is your list of style rules? You always said that as soon as I stopped dictating your apparel, you were going to throw your pearls to the swine, and so on. I didn't always agree, but I was very interested to see what you would make of yourself."

Theo glanced down at her gown defensively. "There's nothing wrong with my gown. We're in mourning for the duke, after all."

"It was made in the village. The only thing that can be said in its favor is that the seams are reasonably straight."

"I am not interested in adorning myself; that was

a girlish dream that I put aside. Besides, I spend almost all my time in the study. Why would I need a gown created by a modiste, especially one in mourning colors, when I have no one to display it for?"

"A lady does not dress for an audience."

"I beg to differ. As a debutante she dresses in order to find a husband, God help her—"

"That's just the sort of comment I mean," her mother put in.

Theo sighed. "I suppose I could order a gown or two from London once we're out of mourning, if it would make you happy. But I'm certainly not traveling back for fittings, and I shall not attend Pink's wedding."

"Happiness," her mother said, returning to the subject, "is a matter of self-control. And you are not exhibiting enough of it."

For the first time during the exchange, Theo felt a prickle of real annoyance. How could anyone, least of all her mother, claim she did not exhibit self-control? In the last years, she'd stayed in the study for hours after the household went to bed, poring over books describing Italian ceramics and Elizabethan furnishings.

She had traveled around the entire estate once a week in a pony cart, to ensure that the sheep herds and the conditions of the cottagers were improving. Her trips to London were taken up not with theater and the shops, but with visits to

Cheapside and a building full of clanking looms. "I think I show self-control," she said, making an effort to prove it by not allowing her annoyance to show.

"Oh, you work," Mrs. Saxby said dismissively.

"The estate is now profitable, even after all the allowance we had to pay the embezzling duke," Theo snapped. And then, hearing the hectoring edge in her own voice, she felt a wave of remorse. "Please forgive me. I certainly didn't mean to turn into a virago. And it wasn't a kind statement as regards His Grace, given that he's dead."

Her mother reached over and patted her hand. "I know you didn't, darling."

But she did not deny that Theo had become something of a harpy. Drat. "Buying fine feathers in London won't make me someone other than who I am," Theo pointed out.

"You are beautiful," her mother said now, once again demonstrating her ready ability to overlook the obvious. "The more beautiful for not looking like everyone else."

Theo sighed. "Any feathers and furbelows I add to my person will merely diminish my dignity. My self-respect. If I play the game of making myself look pretty, I will not succeed, and I will just look foolish and vain."

Her mother put down her teacup again. "Theodora, I did not bring you up to be such a weak-livered, cowardly person. You are not the first woman to receive a blow to your self-regard, and you will not be the last. But that does not excuse you, nor make it acceptable to wallow in self-pity. By avoiding the *ton*, you make yourself a continuing subject of conversation and speculation. Even more importantly, by dwelling on the less fortunate side of your marriage, you make yourself disagreeable."

"I do not dwell on my marriage! And in truth, Mama, what would you deem the 'fortunate' side of my marriage?"

Her mother met her eyes. "Theodora, it is my distinct impression that you enjoy the way everyone on this estate listens to your every word. And that's not to mention the effort you've put into the weaving concern and the ceramics factory."

This was indisputably true.

"You would never have had this opportunity had you married Lord Geoffrey Trevelyan. I saw him at the opera a fortnight ago, by the way. It was a production of *Così fan tutte*, sung in Italian."

"A nice way to make your point," Theo said, grinning. "You're right. I would rather not be made to endure hours of opera."

"Still, you refuse to allow yourself to be happy. You are bent on seeing yourself as an injured party, whereas in fact you have triumphed over adversity. You threw your husband out the door, and in what I can only imagine was a paroxysm of guilt, James obeyed you."

"He wanted to go," Theo countered, having realized it at some point, and more or less made her peace with it. "He married to protect his father's honor, but that doesn't mean that he wished to stay married, at least not to me."

Her mother looked at her, and then back down at the teapot. "May I offer you a fresh cup, my dear?"

"No, thank you. I just did it again, didn't I?" Theo asked, with a sort of wry chagrin curling in her stomach.

"Life is a good deal more complicated than you admit. I would certainly, for example, contest your characterization of James's motives, but it seems irrelevant at this moment. After all, the poor man may be dead."

Theo flinched. "Of course he's not dead! He's staying away in a sulk. I did not say that he needed to stay out of England forever. I merely said that I did not wish to see him again."

"In my opinion, James's deepest attachment in England was to you. When you dismissed him, he likely severed all attachments in order to protect his heart. His father reminded him of nothing more than his ill-mannered behavior to you, and now the poor duke is dead. There is nothing to bring James back to England."

"'Ill-mannered!'" Theo said, stung. "I would call it rather more than that."

Her mother ignored that comment. "No matter how irresponsibly the late duke handled his money—and your inheritance—he opened his house to us on your father's death without a second thought. Ashbrook was never happy again after James disappeared, and you do bear some responsibility for that, Theo. He loved his son dearly."

"You keep speaking as if James is dead," Theo said, surprising herself with the vehemence in her tone. "James is *not* dead."

"One must hope not." Her mother rose gracefully from her chair. "I must finish going through the linens with Mrs. Wibble. I will join you at luncheon, dearest."

It was a dramatic exit, Theo had to admit.

James was not dead. She would know if he were dead.

She did not bother to ask herself why she was so certain of that fact. Instead, she jumped to her feet. She had just remembered that she promised to send a new set of sketches to the factory that very afternoon.

Aboard the Poppy Two

A few weeks after Jack Hawk came into being (and James Ryburn, Earl of Islay, was declared dead by one who should know—that is to say, himself), the *Flying Poppy* and her shadow, the

184

Poppy Two, docked at an island in the West Indies on their way to France, and James—now known as Jack—succumbed to the amatory blandishments of a plump and jolly widow named Priya.

She taught him a thing or two, even though he felt terrible after the night with her. But his marriage was over—practically, if not formally. Could he truly remain celibate for the rest of his life? Of course not.

Unfaithful . . . unfaithful. He didn't like the word. It knocked around in his head for a month or two until he managed to cram it into a dark corner of his mind and shut it up. His wife had ended their marriage. Therefore, he was free to act as he would if he were not married. It wasn't adultery. It wasn't.

He was acting in the only way a grown man could whose marriage had ended. He was staying away so that, after the requisite seven years, she could have him declared dead. He was living his life instead of simply reacting to it. His heart gave another painful thump at the memory of his father.

James learned even more from a Parisian mademoiselle, and the next year, from a girl named Anela, who lived on a Pacific island and thought the rising sun should be worshipped from a horizontal position.

Jack proved to have a knack for prayer.

For his part, Griffin was never happier than when he had a lass on each arm and French letters stowed all over his person. Since neither of them was greedy—in bed or out—the very sight of the *Flying Poppy* and the *Poppy Two* rounding into a cove soon enough became reason for rejoicing in certain parts of the world.

"Jack Hawk" became a name that pirates loved to curse. Every day was hard work, all of it physical—clambering up the rigging, engaging in hand-to-hand combat, swimming between the *Poppy*s, praying with Anela. Jack's skin darkened and his chest broadened, until his own mother wouldn't have recognized him. He even grew a few inches taller; he developed the powerful shoulders and thighs of a man who rules the waves.

But at the same time, his blue eyes and high cheekbones signaled aristocrat, though the small inked poppy under his right eye signaled something quite different to pirates: *death*.

Sixteen

August 1812

Mrs. Saxby and Theo had just finished breakfast one morning when the subject of James arose once again.

"Someday you'll take him back," her mother said.

"I will not," Theo said, nettled. "I don't even think of him any longer."

"Have you resolved never to have a child of your own?" Mrs. Saxby asked. It was typical of her parting shots. But this time she paused and leaned her head against the doorframe for a moment. "Oh dear, I have such a headache."

Theo leapt to her feet and went to her mother's side. "Would you like me to have a tisane made up? Let me help you to your bedchamber. A few hours in the dark with a cool cloth on your head and you'll feel much better."

But Mrs. Saxby straightened her back and said firmly, "I can certainly climb the stairs by myself, dearest. I'll have a nap and be right as rain." But she did not leave immediately; she put a hand on Theo's cheek and said, "Having you has been my greatest joy in life. I merely wish the same for you: a child of your own with the husband you love, though you may deny it as often as you wish."

Theo wrapped her arms around her mother. "This will make you happy, Mama. I've resolved to have a wardrobe made in London all the better to pay a call on the newly wedded Mr. Pinkler-Ryburn, not to mention the delightful Claribel."

Her mother laughed at that. "And I can't wait to see your new gowns. I do love you, darling." And with that, she turned and retired to her chambers.

Mrs. Imogen Saxby never woke from that nap. Theo moved through her mother's funeral and the attending visitations as if she were in a dense fog.

Weeks passed before Theo accepted the truth of it: her mother was truly gone. The house echoed. She sat alone at meals and wept.

Unfortunately, business does not stop merely because there is a death in the family. It was inconvenient to cry in meetings with the estate manager. It was inconvenient to cry in church, at breakfast, and on the way to London.

It was also undignified, but she did not care; the emptiness in her heart was so consuming that what people thought of her was of no importance.

Yet Theo carried on, somehow, knowing that a great many people were depending upon her and she could not let them down. *Would* not let them down.

At last the mourning year was at an end. She had thought often of the conversations she had with her mother about her marriage, and she gradually reconciled herself to the idea that she and James couldn't go on like this, without resolution of any kind. Four years had now passed since he'd left, with no word from him, or indeed *of* him. She made up her mind to find him. After all, it had been her mother's express wish not only that Theo return to society but that she return to James as well.

Without further ado, Theo instructed her solicitors to engage as many Bow Street Runners as necessary and send them out into the world searching for news of her husband. The success of the estate's businesses meant that the cost of their search—and it might take them a year or more to return with news—was of no object.

And then she did her best to put James out of her mind. There was nothing she could do about him for the time being.

Theo had employed her taste in the last years in shaping Ashbrook Ceramics into a thriving business that made the finest ceramics for a very select few who shared her interest in ancient Greek pottery. And she had poured her love of color into Ryburn Weavers, guiding its focus on reproductions of French and Italian textiles from the previous two centuries.

But now the weavers and the ceramics factory were on a steady keel. They no longer needed Theo's daily involvement. What they could most use, in fact, was a highly visible patron: a person whose taste and discernment were uncontested throughout the *ton*, someone who would spur desire for Ashbrook wares.

It was a brilliant idea in every respect but one: Theo was still in self-imposed exile from the very people she most needed to impress.

She had learned to trust herself and her taste, even if she hadn't bothered to apply her dictates to her own attire. Style, after all, is a harmonious arrangement of parts that, in Theo's opinion, was better than physical beauty. What's more, it was often mistaken for it.

She didn't think it would be terribly difficult to transform herself into the imagined ideal client. She even unearthed her list of style rules, written carefully all those years ago in round schoolgirl hand and particularized with a passion that made her smile. Rereading them, she was delighted to find that not one caused her to wince with embarrassment. That settled it. She would become her own best patron.

After some thought, she decided to visit Paris for a few months before she conquered London. The papers were full of the welcome news that the Treaty of Fontainebleau (and Napoleon's abdication) meant that France would once again be welcoming English visitors. No nationality more than the French understood that while beauty is a matter of birth, art—the art of dressing oneself—is available to all who care to learn.

In May 1814, the Countess of Islay (for James had yet to take up the title of duke) closed up her country estate and moved to a magnificent town house on the Seine, opposite the Palace of the Tuileries. She intended to apply herself to the study of elegance with all the passion she had devoted to ceramics and to weaving.

And she had every expectation of success.

Seventeen

Paris, 1814-1815

Within a month of entering Parisian society, the Countess of Islay was considered an "interesting" Englishwoman; by the end of a very few months, she was an honorary Frenchwoman. No one referred to her by such bland words as *ugly* or even *beautiful:* she was *ravissant* and—above all—*élégant.*

It was widely known that the duchesse d'Angoulême, the niece of King Louis XVIII himself, consulted Lady Islay when it came to tricky questions regarding fans and other accoutrement. After all, a lady's bonnet, gloves, slippers, and reticule were the most important elements of a truly elegant appearance. Parisians gasped when Theo paired brown with black— and then found themselves even more shocked when she wore a black corded silk evening gown sewn with amethysts, and later, a purple riding habit with sour-green gloves.

They gasped . . . and rushed to imitate.

What the French loved most were Theo's epigrammatic rules. They were collected like precious jewels, and even the poorest shopgirls ripped the lace from their Sunday frocks when she was reported to have remarked, *"Wear lace to be baptized. Period."*

It caused a sensation when she was reported to have declared that *discretion is a synonym for intelligence.* By the time everyone deduced that she had been commenting not on fashion, but on the Marquis de Maubec's decidedly indiscreet adoration for his father's third wife, a number of Parisians had leapt to the conclusion that a "discreet" woman would not wear lashings of jewels. In fact, the countess *had* remarked, of a particularly ostentatious lady, that "she was wearing so many carats she looked like a vegetable garden."

Attention to her words was at such a fever pitch that Theo was visited by a delegation of three diamond sellers who begged her aid. That very evening Lady Islay appeared at a ball wearing a necklace that featured no fewer than eight strands of diamonds, caught together by an extraordinary pear-shaped diamond pendant, and casually remarked that she thought a woman should rival the Milky Way at night: *We give babies milk, but ladies? Diamonds.*

By the time Theo turned twenty-three, her husband had been missing for close to six years, and none of the Bow Street Runners—though some had not returned to London—had yet reported news of him. She always told people, whenever they asked, that her husband had been misplaced, rather as one might misplace an abhorrent silver candelabra given by a great-aunt.

But inside, she didn't feel so nonchalant. Silence wasn't like James. Or was it? He had the most ferocious temper of anyone she'd ever known, except perhaps his dead father. Anger at her—or at himself—could drive him to live in a foreign country without giving a thought for his old life. But would he really brood for this long? Wouldn't he want to come home and have it out with her?

Unless he had another life, another wife, in some foreign place . . . perhaps he had even taken another name.

It was an unpleasant thought, but it was better than what Cecil Pinkler-Ryburn, in line to be the next duke, believed. Her husband's heir and his wife, Claribel, had appeared in Paris a few months after Theo, following a rush of fashionable people who deserted London for the Continent. Though Claribel was unfashionably maternal and preferred to stay at home with her little ones, Cecil had become one of Theo's most frequent callers, as they found (rather to Theo's surprise) that they enjoyed each other's company very much.

But Cecil firmly believed that if James were alive, he would have returned to London as soon as he learned that he was now a duke; according to Cecil's logic, because he did not return, James must be dead.

Theo tried not to think about it. She was having a wonderful time in France, rootling out antique fabrics and sending them back to her weavers;

snatching up Greek designs wherever she could and sending those back to Ashbrook Ceramics; being fêted at the French court. Yet the sad truth was that behind every success was a faint mindful awareness of what James would think.

She seemed to carry James with her as a silent audience of one. Over time she had forgotten (more or less) about the unpleasant aspects of their marriage and just remembered what a friend he had been, and how he had encouraged her during her debut as a wallflower with a hopeless adoration for Lord Geoffrey Trevelyan.

Her closest friend now was Cecil, though he bore no resemblance to James in character or figure. He had grown quite plump, particularly around the place where his waist used to be. He had learned to care more for a turbot in a good wine sauce than the height of his collar, and he was steady and devoted in his new passion.

He had also dropped the excesses of fashion that characterized him as a younger man, though he had not deserted fashion altogether: these days he frequently wore Ryburn silks. In particular, Cecil benefited from a colorful cravat—a new style in Paris—because it drew attention away from the fact a second chin had joined his first.

"Is that a new cravat?" Theo asked now, taking tea with him.

"Indeed," he said now, his smile emphasizing the rather charming laughter lines around his eyes.

"My man didn't care to pair a pink cravat with a violet coat, but I cited your example and he gave in. I must say, there's something wonderful about watching a Frenchman accede to an English-woman's dictates. I would never be able to face him down without you to back me up."

Theo poured him another cup of tea. "I do appreciate the fact that you haven't been in the least forceful about asking me to do something formal regarding the dukedom."

"Lord knows I don't want the title," Cecil said with a shrug. And he meant it. He was cheerfully indolent and viewed with horror the duties associated with the duchy. "The only thing I would find even remotely interesting about becoming a duke would be if one of my fellow peers murdered someone and we got to sit in judgment. But frankly, that happens all too rarely."

"Bloodthirsty wretch," Theo said affectionately.

"I have more than enough money of my own. It's my father-in-law who's chuffed at the prospect."

"We cannot declare James dead," Theo said, the words coming in a rush, "without making another effort to find him first. I've been thinking that I had better return to England and see what's happened to all those Bow Street Runners I sent out. After Christmas, in time for the season, perhaps. I can't stay in Paris forever."

Cecil cleared his throat. "My father-in-law also hired a runner two years ago."

"The man found nothing?"

"I saw no point in telling you unless we had been able to find James. There are statutory regulations, you know . . . the duke has to be missing for seven years."

"It will be seven years come June after this," Theo said, scowling into her teacup. "Did your man travel to India? I remember James talking of that country."

"I will ask," Cecil said, heaving himself out of his chair.

The 1814 Christmas season was lovely; the city danced, as only Paris can. But Theo found herself increasingly aware of a bleak fear in her heart. Could it be true that something frightful had happened to James?

It would be awful if she had forced him to leave England and he had died on some foreign shore. Or worse, aboard a sinking ship. She found herself waking in the night, unable to sleep as she imagined the *Percival* capsized in a storm, James's last gasp as he slid under the waves. She would push the image away, sleep—only to wake again with the realization that death would explain why James never contacted his father.

It was bewildering to discover that she cared so much for an absent, less-than-truthful spouse.

Finally, she sat up one morning and found she was weary of the guilt, the grief, the pesky longing that wouldn't go away.

"He *is* dead," she told herself, trying the words aloud in the chilly morning air. It was a painful thought, but not an overwhelming one. Six years, almost seven, is a long time, after all, and they had been married all of two days. She missed her childhood friend far more than she missed his brief incarnation as her husband.

She summoned Cecil to her house. They were both planning to return to England in February.

"We'll give it one more year," she told him. "At that point, we'll do whatever necessary to shift the title to you."

"And then you must marry again," Cecil said. "Claribel and I both wish to see you in a happy marriage."

What sort of man to marry? That was a real question.

She kept coming up with the same list of desired qualities. She would like a man with a singing voice, because she'd never forgotten the way that James sang to her in the dawn, after they'd made love all night long.

She wanted someone with blue eyes. She would like him to have a generous smile and a sense of humor and a deep kindness.

It didn't take much of an intellect to add up her list of requirements and discover they pointed toward a man who was absent and almost certainly dead. So she redoubled her efforts to convince herself of James's perfidy. Would she really want to take back a man who had married her when commanded to do so by his father?

The answer was dismal. Yes. Yes, she would.

As long as he would make love to her, and sing to her afterward.

Eighteen

April 1815

The opening ball of a given season is the most interesting for any number of reasons, some of them obvious, and some more esoteric. Not only do all the young ladies entering society for the first time make their debut appearance, but the composition of the *ton* becomes clear. Who is in mourning and staying in the country? Whose marriage has fallen into such disarray that husband and wife are living in separate establishments? Who has lost so much money at the races that he appears in a coat that is dismally old-fashioned?

It was at a first ball that Beau Brummell made his appearance, immaculate in black and white. It was at a first ball that Petunia Stafford exhibited the cropped curls that made her look like a giddy yet dazzling child; at another, Lady Bellingham appeared in dampened petticoats (and there were those who questioned to this day whether she had worn a chemise).

Theo chose to skip the opening ball of the 1815 season. It would be too obvious, and she considered it an unspoken rule that the Countess of Islay never did what was obvious.

Of course she had been invited. Once it was seen that the knocker had been replaced on the door of 45 Berkeley Square, signifying that Theo was in residence, invitations poured in the door.

There were many who barely remembered her, as she was married halfway through the season of '09 and never again glimpsed in polite London society. They longed to make a judgment about her ugliness themselves.

But there were also those who had visited the French capital, or had heard the news from there, and they confidently reminded all and sundry that ugly ducklings—and duchesses—sometimes turn into swans.

In fact, Theo elected not only to skip the opening ball, but to wait out the first three weeks of the season as well. She had decided to make her first appearance—her reentry into British society—at a ball being thrown by Cecil and Claribel.

Claribel was just as dazzlingly empty-headed as she had been a decade before. Her milk-and-water prettiness had not aged well: she was beginning to resemble a wilted rose, the kind that goes blowsy before all its petals drop. And like Cecil, she had broadened considerably around the waist.

Theo's angular slimness and strong features, on the other hand, had come into focus in her twenties. She knew that she had never looked better—but each time she allowed herself the thought, it was followed by a tinge of regret: her mother would have abhorred such a vain and self-regarding observation. It was truly astonishing that one's mother can pass away and yet one constantly hears her talking in one's ear.

When Mr. and Mrs. Pinkler-Ryburn opened their ball, the subject on everyone's lips was the Countess of Islay. The news had spread that her ladyship had accepted her relatives' invitation.

"Did we invite Lord Tinkwater?" Claribel asked her husband, watching as the butler ushered in a fantastically drunk lord, who had the wisdom to have developed a method of walking that didn't require a sense of balance.

"We did not," Cecil said. "All sorts of people have come whom we didn't invite, darling."

He squeezed Claribel's arm and turned away to greet Lord Tinkwater.

But by the time they decided to close the receiving line, there was still no sign of Lady Islay. They had barely made their way down the steps into the ballroom when a terrific noise erupted behind them.

"That'll be Theo," Cecil said, turning to look back up the stairs. "She planned her entrance perfectly, of course." And then: *"Damn!"*

Claribel was about to reprimand him for using a profanity in her presence, but her jaw dropped instead.

The woman poised at the top of the stairs, looking down at all of them with a little smile that indicated absolute self-confidence, looked like a goddess who happened to come down to earth by way of Paris. She radiated that sort of ineffable glamour that simply cannot be learned—as Claribel knew to her sorrow, having made multiple efforts.

The fabric of Lady Islay's gown certainly cost as much as Claribel's entire quarterly allowance. It was a pearly pink silk taffeta shot with threads of silver. Her breasts were scarcely covered, and from there the gown fell straight to the ground in a hauntingly beautiful sweep of cloth.

The pink brought out the color of her hair—burnt amber entwined with brandy and buttercup. If only she had left it free around her face and perhaps created some charming curls! Claribel made up her mind to tell her privately about the newest curling irons. She herself had lovely corkscrew curls bobbing next to her ears.

Even so, there was something magnificent about

the countess tonight, almost hypnotic. The *pièce de résistance* of her costume was a formal cape that gleamed under the light, soft and lustrous, almost as if it were made of fur.

"Damnation," Cecil said again, scarcely under his breath.

She glanced at him and saw to her astonishment that his eyes were gleaming with an appreciation that she recognized—and was used to reserving for herself and her own rather generous figure.

"I see no reason for profanity," she observed. Then she started forward to greet her guest.

"You look lovely, Lady Islay," she told Theo earnestly, a moment or so later. "Your gown is exquisite. Would you like Jeffers to take your cape? I'm afraid it must be rather hot, beautiful though it is."

Cecil was bending over Theo's gloved hand. "Oh no," he said, before Lady Islay could even answer. "I'm quite certain that Theo plans to wear her cape for at least part of the evening." There was a note of amusement in his voice.

"If you're quite sure that you won't grow overwarm," Claribel said uncertainly, eyeing the cape. It sprang out from Lady Islay's shoulders and then swirled to the ground, managing to look surprisingly light. The inside was lined with a gorgeous rosy silk, and the outside . . .

"What on earth is that made of?" Claribel couldn't help asking as she reached out to touch it.

"I can guess," Cecil put in, the thread of amusement in his voice even stronger.

"Oh, can you?" Theo remarked. "Then tell me this: am I being altogether too obvious?"

Claribel hadn't the faintest idea what she meant. But Cecil, clever Cecil, obviously did, because he bellowed with laughter.

"Swansdown," he said. "Gorgeous swansdown, and every man and woman in this room has taken note of your swanlike triumph."

"I could not resist," Theo said, with that smile that was all the more attractive for being so rarely seen. "How lucky you are in your husband," she said to Claribel. "It's a rare man who knows his fairy tales."

"I know, of course, I know," Claribel said, babbling a bit. There was something about Lady Islay that was rather daunting. She was so *elegant,* for one thing. And that severe hair, which should by rights look positively awful, looked sensual, though it wasn't a word Claribel cared for.

Plus, now she realized that her gown was scandalously thin. No wonder she wasn't worried about being overly warm. Why, when Lady Islay turned away to greet Lord Scarborough, Claribel clearly saw the line of her bare calf.

She suppressed a sigh. Of course she loved her three darling children, but carrying them had had a deleterious effect on her figure. She felt like an overstuffed pincushion in comparison.

"Looks marvelous, doesn't she?" her husband remarked.

"I think she's a trifle underdressed," Claribel said. Despite herself, her tone was a little hurt.

Cecil took one of her gloved hands and raised it to his lips. "You cannot possibly imagine that I find Theo as attractive as you?"

"Her figure is perfect," Claribel said wistfully. "Just perfect."

He leaned closer. "A man doesn't care about that, my sweet buttercup."

Claribel rolled her eyes.

"She's chilly," he said, more quietly. "I do adore her, but I don't envy the man she marries. Just look at her."

They both turned, to find the countess surrounded by a gaggle of men as tightly pressed together as ha'pennies in the church box.

"They're fascinated, intrigued, even adoring," Cecil said. "But I saw the same reaction in Paris many a time. If you ask me, that's why there's never been even the faintest whiff of scandal about her in the last six years. No one would want to actually *bed* her."

"Cecil! What a thing to say!"

He gave her a twinkling glance. "Now *you* are a different story. Alas, my figure is not what it once was."

"As if I cared about that!"

"Then why would you think that I do not relish

every one of your curves?" he said, and the look in his eyes confirmed his words. "But even more, Claribel, I love the fact that you come to our bed with pleasure. You are my—"

"Mr. Pinkler-Ryburn!" Claribel exclaimed. "You forget yourself." But her cheeks were hot, and her fingers trembled in his. "We are fortunate," she added, as softly as he. Then she whisked her hand away. "Enough of this foolishness. What on earth was Lady Islay saying about fairy tales?"

"All those people who called her 'the ugly duchess' are eating their words," her husband said. "The countess has turned into a swan, and she's dropped them all on their arses by making fun of it."

"I'd forgotten all that," Claribel said, wrinkling her nose. "My mother said it was all frightfully ill-bred and wouldn't let us read the papers for a week."

Cecil bent over and dropped a kiss on her nose. "I know, darling. That's why you are the sweet tartlet that you are, and Theo is the rather stern and magnificent cake that she is."

"I am not a tartlet." But she couldn't help smiling.

Nineteen

The Pinkler-Ryburn ball reminded Theo of nothing so much as a host of sparrows perched on a railing. They would descend from a tree in a huge group, chattering madly. One bird would take wing and the rest would hysterically soar up after, the whole group coming down almost immediately on a railing all of ten yards to the left. Or to the right.

The key to controlling the evening, she decided, was to be the sparrow that determined the behavior of the flock. When the ballroom became intolerably crowded, Theo drifted onto the terrace, taking with her a core group of gentlemen glued to her side by a pleasing mixture of lust and admiration. What's more, they were men who conformed to her sense of elegance.

When Mr. Van Vechten joined them, his velvet coat an aggressive shade of purple striped with peach, she was just dismissive enough that he retreated as quickly as he had come. The same went for Mr. Hoyt, who was rumored to have a fortune in gold, but unfortunately had a penchant for displaying his treasure in the form of garish buttons.

Glimpsing her little group, convulsed with laughter as Theo sparked jokes with her coterie, the ballroom emptied onto the terrace.

Feeling nearly as constricted as she had inside, Theo decided, rather mischievously, to go for a walk in the gardens. There was no question as to her companion; she tucked her arm under that of Lord Geoffrey Trevelyan.

They had both grown older. She learned that he had married that first season (though not, obviously, to Claribel), and that his wife had died some two years after. There were creases at the corners of his eyes now, and a lean cast to his cheeks. But everything else was the same: the dark, slanting eyes and the wicked little smile flickering around his lips. And her heart still gave a little thump at the sight of him.

By the time she and Geoffrey had returned to the terrace, Cecil's guests were rocketing tipsily down dark paths, pretending that they were in Vauxhall.

Theo led the way into the ballroom, now thin of company, and allowed Geoffrey to sweep her into a waltz. She was besieged when that waltz drew to a close and another followed; it seemed that everyone wanted to dance with the swan, and they didn't want a quadrille.

No, they wanted that low husky laugh at their jokes, and those slender, coltish legs thrillingly near their own.

"There's something about the look of her," Colonel MacLachlan told Cecil, longing tangible in his voice. "She's not my usual type at all, I don't mind saying. I like small and round. Plus, she mocked me, and I know she would no more consider bedding me than the Regent himself!"

But his eyes still followed Theo down the length of the ballroom. She was in the arms of a man old enough to be her father, and yet anyone could see that when she smiled at him, the man straightened, took the turn of the waltz a bit more dashingly.

"Theo is like the huntress Diana," Cecil said, rocking a little on his heels. He was thoroughly enjoying the burst of popularity his cousin-by-marriage was experiencing. "Beautiful and yet slightly deadly, ready to whip out a bow and arrow, or turn a man into a squealing swine. Sensual, and yet with just a snowy touch of the virginal about her."

"Good Lord, man, you sound like a poet," MacLachlan said, startled. "Don't let your wife hear you talking like that about the countess."

Cecil only laughed. He wasn't worried about Claribel; they understood each other, and their happiest moments were their most intimate. That sort of bond meant that she knew damn well that he wouldn't stray. Besides, he was of the private opinion that Theo would be remarkably uncomfortable to live with.

Her rules were enchanting to read about, but the same tendency to catalogue perfection could be seen throughout her life. She proclaimed, rather than suggested. She was too fierce in her opinions, too unforgiving, too witty.

Too much fuss. Too many feathers.

As befitted a swan, of course.

Even as Theo enjoyed her meteoric rise through the *ton* and the hushed attention that polite society gave to her every utterance as regards style, the constant mentions of *swans* (and never *ducklings*) was wearing.

By the fall of 1815, the papers were in the habit of asking for another of her "rules"; *La Belle Assemblée* never failed to include a detailed illustration of her every costume.

She thought that it would be quite nice if James returned to find his wife the talk of the *ton* and a force to be reckoned with.

And so it was that Theo had the ghost of one person—her mother—standing at one shoulder, and the ghost of another—James—at her other shoulder. And while she did not cast a romantic haze over the short days of her marriage, she had thought a great deal about where fault lay—and indeed, whether "fault" was a useful question in a marriage.

James, she concluded, had been pushed by his father into an action that he knew was morally objectionable. And yet, in his own way, he loved her. She was sure of that.

The limit she and Cecil had set was drawing

near, and Theo knew she must accept the fact that it would be miraculous if any news of James emerged at this point.

Just after 1815 turned to 1816, she summoned Cecil to meet with the family solicitor, Mr. Boythorn, who prosed on at length about a "death in absentia" petition to the House of Lords, detailing Theo's inability to enjoy either the duties and responsibilities of a wife, or the freedom and protections of a widow.

"We should have a memorial service for my husband," Theo said when he paused for breath. "After we declare him dead in such a cut-and-dried manner. It would be absurd, I suppose, to wear mourning for a year. But I shall wear mourning for at least a short time. James was very young when he left England, but there are many who remember him."

"When I was a boy, everyone called me Pink," Cecil put in. "James never joined in."

The solicitor cleared his throat. "A memorial service in St. Paul's Cathedral would be most appropriate. It would indeed be fitting to hold a service after Lord Islay has been formally recognized as deceased. A small plaque could also be arranged, to commemorate the life of this courageous young man. It is my belief that the *Percival* foundered almost immediately."

"Surely not," Theo said, hating to think it.

"The vessel was headed to India, by all accounts,

and never heard from again. The passage is besieged with pirates," Mr. Boythorn observed. "More than one sailor has told me that it would be a miracle if the *Percival* escaped an unfortunate fate."

Theo sighed. "Cecil, would it be acceptable to you if Mr. Boythorn began the proceedings to submit a death in absentia petition to the Lord Chancellor and the House of Lords? If we receive other news in the next month, of course, the petition would be withdrawn immediately."

"Would you prefer to wait another year, my dear?" Was there ever a more reluctant duke than Cecil?

Theo looked at him with a faint smile. "I have quite enjoyed managing the estate, particularly with regard to the weaving and ceramics concerns. But I should like to move on with my life. I know I'm practically elderly—"

"You are not!" Cecil cried with a satisfying smack of indignity in his voice.

"But I intend to throw myself on the marriage market after the petition is approved," Theo continued, "and another year would do me no good in that respect."

"As it should be," Mr. Boythorn intoned solemnly. "It is time to close this sad passage in the history of the Dukes of Ashbrook. Lord Islay was cut off in the prime of his youth, but life must go on."

And with that rattling series of platitudes, the conversation ended.

Long live the new duke.

Twenty

On board the Poppys

In 1814 the *Poppy*s sailed to India without taking a single ship on the way; they did so merely to prove that their captains would have no problem grappling with monsoon winds. But since they were there, they wandered around until Griffin decided that Sicilian noblewomen whom he had known (intimately) would fall in love with gilded birdcages; he filled the hold with them. James discovered a passion for a flavoring called curry, so he filled all the birdcages with packages of turmeric and cumin.

On the way home a pirate crew was ignorant enough to try to take them down, so they sunk that ship, dropped off the men on an inhabited island (as was their custom), and sailed on, a pile of emeralds in a corner of Griffin's cabin revealing that the *Poppy*s were not the first boats those particular ill-fated pirates had approached.

They sold the birdcages in Sicily at an outrageous profit. They sent the curry to England, where their man there (for they now had establishments to manage their assets in five countries) reported that it was slow to take on at first, but by the end of three months, it had sold at a neat seventy times the cost.

Jack had learned to control his temper. He had even come to thinking of his father with equanimity. When one kills enough men—albeit pirates who had killed hundreds themselves—embezzlement seems like the crime of a child. Perhaps more importantly, guilt became something that he refused to allow to rule his life.

And Daisy . . . he found himself irritatingly unable to forget the enchanting way her eyes had widened when he first touched her breast, not to mention all the childhood years when they played and fought together. But he told himself over and over that those were the memories of a boy named James, and Hawk prided himself on forgetting everything to do with his life in England, marriage included.

Then his luck ran out.

It was early 1816, and they had just taken down the *Groningen*, on special request from the Dutch king; the naval boat had been stolen and was being used to rob trading vessels. Everything was well in hand; the pirate captain had gone to his just reward, and only a few men from the *Groningen* were still fighting hard.

Jack was about to bellow an offer for surrender when there was a rush of movement to his right, and a pirate came up fast and hard with an open blade.

He felt the knife slice his neck, just below his chin. It didn't hurt, oddly enough, but there was a terrible sensation of flesh parting, followed by a warm rush of blood down his throat.

He reeled back, dropping his weapons and collapsing to the deck. There was a crack from a pistol, and the pirate with the knife pitched backward, landing on the deck with an audible thump.

Then Griffin fell on his knees by Jack, swearing a blue streak, screaming orders.

Jack squinted up at him, seeing his cousin against the sun as if he had a halo, a fuzzy halo. "Good run," he said, but nothing came from his lips. Of course men who had their throats cut couldn't speak. He and Griffin had come to love each other like brothers, though being men, they never expressed it. They didn't need to.

Now Griffin was bending over him, stuffing cloth under his chin. James met his eyes and discovered they were terrified. He had known the truth before he saw it in his cousin's eyes. Men with cut throats do not live.

"You will *not* die," Griffin ordered through white lips, as ferocious as only a pirate king can be. "Damn it, James, hang on. Dicksling will be here in a moment, and he'll sew you back together."

James shaped the words slowly. "Tell Daisy." No sound escaped, and the pain had flooded his body now, making black dots swim in his vision. But there was only one thing in his heart, one thing he had to say, shocking though it was to discover it.

"Daisy?" Griffin said, leaning even closer. "Your wife. Tell her what?"

But the black dots were connecting together and rushing at him as if a sandstorm suddenly rose from the sea.

And at that very moment the felled pirate made one last violent effort: the man thrust himself to a sitting position and slashed his knife at Griffin. With a howl, Griffin clapped his hands between his legs. Blood flew in the wind and splattered all over James's face.

It was over, it was all over. It was only then that James realized what he surely knew all along.

He couldn't shape the one word he desperately wanted to say.

And there was no one to hear it.

Twenty-one

April 3, 1816

The petition to declare a formal end to the life of the Earl of Islay was wending its way through the Courts of Chancery when Theo received a message from yet another of the twenty Bow Street Runners who had returned to England.

But this message was different: it claimed news.

She sat quite still with the note in her hand, staring at it.

If James was alive, the Runner, a man by the

215

name of Mr. Badger, surely would have written *I found your husband,* rather than *I bring news.* Desolation felt like a palpable thing in her stomach, like another heart beating under the first.

She summoned her new butler, Maydrop, and instructed him to request that Mr. Pinkler-Ryburn visit that very afternoon. Mr. Badger turned out to be swarthy and hirsute, a bow-legged and fierce-looking individual. One had the distinct impression that criminals would be quite sorry to find that Badger was on their trail.

"He has the whiskers of a catfish," Cecil whispered, but Theo was too nervous to smile. They were sitting together on the couch, Mr. Badger in a chair opposite them. Theo was so fidgety that she felt as if flies were dancing on her head, yet Mr. Badger methodically plodded on without getting to the point. He took forever explaining precisely where he had been assigned by his superiors, how many men he took with him, how many he hired in the islands, how long it took him to sail to his first port of call.

For the first time in years Theo had the impulse to chew on her fingernails, a habit she had broken in the schoolroom.

"The West Indies," Mr. Badger continued, "is not civilized by our standards, and I'm afraid that I employed a great deal of bribery in order to obtain the information I sought."

"*Have* you found my husband?" Theo interrupted. She could wait no longer.

"No, I have not," Mr. Badger replied.

She swallowed. "But you found news of him."

"I am of the opinion that he was not dead as of 1810," Mr. Badger said, returning to the sheet of foolscap he had balanced on his knee. "He was . . . well . . ." A look of distinct disapproval crossed his face.

"He was living with another woman," Theo said flatly.

"He was a pirate."

Cecil gasped, and Theo gave a cry—whether of horror or surprise, she couldn't say.

"That's impossible," she managed a second later.

Mr. Badger licked his finger and turned to another sheet of foolscap. "He was called the Earl by various members of the criminal establishment. I might remind you that at this point James Ryburn was possessed of the courtesy title Earl of Islay. He worked in concert with another pirate known as Griffin Barry."

"That name does sound familiar," Cecil said.

"Barry is actually a member of the peerage"— Mr. Badger gave them a lowering glance, as if they were personally responsible for this reprobate member of their class—"and it is my considered opinion that the said Sir Griffin led Lord Islay into impudent and ill-conceived, not to mention criminal, ways."

"Criminal!" Cecil gasped again. "My cousin James would never do anything criminal! I'd stake my life on it."

"I would not advise you to do that if I were you, sir," Mr. Badger stated. "There was some confusion about the actual activities of the Earl and Barry; there were those who maintained that Barry attacked only the ships of other pirates, at least, after he joined forces with the Earl. There is ample evidence for Barry's piracy before 1808, but after that date, he specialized, if one can use that term, in attacking his fellow reprobates, which makes him a 'privateer,' rather than a pirate." He paused. "To law-abiding men, there is only a slight distinction."

"Impossible!" Theo said, feeling glad for the first time that her mother was no longer alive.

"If this 'Earl' is any connection to my cousin," Cecil said, "then I am quite certain that he would indeed attack only pirate ships. His Grace is a man of honor and would no more think of harming innocent lives than he would of . . . of cheating in a game of cards!"

Theo put her hand in his and squeezed. If only James were here to listen to Cecil's fervent defense of him. "What happened to the Earl?" she asked. "Was he killed?"

"There's quite a legend built up around the man's vessel, the *Poppy Two*, but no one could tell me of its fate," Mr. Badger said, "though, of course, I left men there with instructions to find out. They are sailing from island to island making extensive inquiries at each place, while I returned here with all speed. All we had determined by the date I returned to England was that the said Griffin Barry once had a partner known as the Earl. But not very long thereafter the Earl was replaced by a fearsome character known as Jack Hawk."

"Jack!" Theo cried. "Jack is not so far from James." At the same time she wanted any shred of evidence that he might still be alive, she wasn't sure that she liked the idea. It would mean that her James was a pirate, a bloodthirsty criminal who walked innocent people down the plank. "Though I still don't believe it," she added.

"I agree there is a similarity in names," Mr. Badger said. "But the resemblance stops there. I had two people draw pictures of this Jack Hawk, as he's well known in those parts. He has a passel of women fond of him, if you'll excuse the indelicacy, Your Grace. There's not a chance that the Earl and Jack Hawk are one and the same: from descriptions of him, Hawk is a monstrously big fellow, with a shaved head and a tattoo under his right eye."

"A *tattoo?*" Cecil repeated.

"What on earth is a tattoo?" Theo asked.

"Decoration pricked into the skin with the use of pigment and a needle," Mr. Badger said. "I find it most unlikely that an Englishman, let alone a nobleman, would submit to such a barbaric procedure, which is both painful and indelible. I saw some examples while I was on the islands, and they were distinctly savage."

"I agree with you that we can discount the possibility that this pirate and Lord Islay are the same," Theo said. "In fact, I find your former supposition unlikely as well, Mr. Badger. The fact that Griffin Barry is a member of the peerage is insufficient evidence to presume that a criminal named Earl might have any connection to my husband."

"I'm afraid that we cannot offer even a partial reward for this information," Cecil agreed, chiming in. "Lord Islay was never a pirate; I find the supposition unlikely, not to mention insulting to his memory."

Theo let the reference to "memory" go by; Cecil found it increasingly difficult to speak of his cousin in the present tense. She could understand; after all, James had been gone for nearly seven years.

"I was interrupted before I could present you with a piece of evidence," Mr. Badger said, looking as satisfied as a cat with nothing left but a mousy tail. He reached into his breast pocket and withdrew a small flannel pouch, which he proceeded to open.

It held a locket.

And inside the locket . . . a curl of hair whose color ranged from bronze to brandy.

"I fail to see the significance of that object you hold," Cecil said, leaning back with a wave of his hand. "A tarnished locket with a piece of hair—" He looked sideways at Theo and broke off.

"It is my hair," Theo said, her lips moving with difficulty. "James cut it on our wedding night. Actually, the following morning." She reached out her hand. "May I have it, please?"

Mr. Badger handed it over. The locket was, as Cecil said, a tarnished and not particularly valuable one. Yet there was no mistaking her own hair. She'd spent too many years deploring its odd streaks to mistake it.

"That need not be your hair," Cecil said, peering down at her hand. "I agree that there is some similarity, but your color is much lighter than that, my dear."

"James cut it from underneath so that no one could see. The hair is darker, but you see it has all the oddness of my hair. Like a yellow zebra, James always said." To her distress, she heard her voice quaver.

"Where on earth did you find this?" Cecil said to Mr. Badger, simultaneously giving Theo's arm a little squeeze. "Not that I consider the hair necessarily to be Lady Islay's."

"Apparently, it was stolen from the man called the Earl. I had made it clear that I would pay a hundred pounds, a small fortune in those parts, for any evidence of the duke's existence. In the course of my inquiries, I extended the offer to include any details about the pirate named the Earl. This was brought to me in response."

"And yet no one knew what happened to the man?" Theo whispered. Her fingers shaking, she clicked the locket closed again. Even looking at that hair brought back the extreme joy of that day. She had never felt anything like it again.

Mr. Badger shook his head. "*The Flying Poppy* wasn't seen in those parts again for a good three to four years, which is not so extraordinary. Griffin Barry operates all over the seas, Your Grace. There's talk of him around India and then near Canada. They call him 'a flying fish' and the like."

"And when the *Poppy* returned, the Earl was gone."

"Exactly. And the devil of it is that the *Poppy* hasn't been seen in the last couple of years, and I didn't hear stories of it, either. So there's a chance that Barry has gone to the bottom of the sea, taking the truth of what happened to Lord Islay with him."

A silence ensued; Mr. Badger had at last come to the end of his narrative. It was Theo who said what had to be said. "He's gone." Her fingers closed hard around the trumpery little piece of tarnished metal. "James is dead."

Mr. Badger nodded, his gaze not unsympathetic. "I fear that is the case. Piracy is a terrible business, and I find myself amazed that his lordship survived even for a month or two, let alone as long as he did. Lord Islay would have been at a distinct disadvantage, surrounded by lawbreakers who would as soon shoot you in the back as issue a civil greeting."

"This is a rather disgraceful question, but I fear it must be asked," Cecil put in. "Is there a chance that my cousin left a child somewhere on the islands? I much dislike the idea of a Ryburn growing up under such disadvantageous circumstances."

Theo's heart skipped a beat.

But Mr. Badger was shaking his head. "'Twas Jack Hawk who has a way with the ladies. For all I know, that reprobate has scattered children all over the East Indies; he has a reputation that suggests it. But the Earl had a quite different character."

"What was it?" Theo asked, her heart feeling crumpled and helpless somewhere under her breastbone.

"He was never known to have visited a woman at all," Mr. Badger said, his eyes distinctly sympathetic now. "That fact suggests that when he embarked on this rather unusual career, Lord Islay did not discard all the qualities that distinguish an English gentleman. And, of course, he did keep the locket."

"I'm glad that the old duke didn't live to hear this," Cecil muttered. "It would have put him in the grave."

A sob rose up Theo's throat with such force that she felt her mouth distort. James was dead, killed by a pirate, his body likely thrown into the sea. And he had kept her lock of hair with him when he left England. She couldn't bear it . . . she couldn't bear it.

She rose, and Cecil's hand fell from her arm. "If you'll forgive me," she managed, feeling tears sliding down her face.

Mr. Badger came to his feet, nodding. He had the look of a man who had delivered terrible news before.

Cecil was fighting his way up from the low settee. "Go," he said, panting a little. "I'll just talk with Mr. Badger for a few more minutes. I'll call on you later, my dear."

Theo ran from the room, the locket clenched in her hand.

Twenty-two

May 30, 1816
The House of Lords
London

The Garter King-of-Arms, who was responsible for behavior and precedence in the House of Lords, was dreading the day before him. "I have to get them all in line to enter the Chamber," Sir Henry Gismond said fretfully to his wife over toast and marmalade. "Almost two hundred of them, all told, and they will wander, especially the older ones. I dread these formal occasions, I truly do."

Lady Gismond nodded. She knew that her beloved Henry hated them, even if he reveled in the chance to exhibit himself as the principal advisor to the Crown in matters of ceremony and heraldry. "It's a terribly sad occasion. Lord Islay was a lovely young man, by all accounts. I hate to think of him lost on those cruel seas."

"It's the drunkards that make the most trouble." Gismond continued his own train of thought. "You'd never guess how many of them conceal a flask under those scarlet robes, my dear. Truly shocking. I can hardly stop myself from rapping them on the knuckles on occasion."

"They won't be tippling today," her ladyship

said firmly. "How often is a peer declared dead in absentia? And Lady Islay herself will be in attendance. I'm sure everyone will respect her anguish at bidding good-bye to her young husband. They did say it was a love match, you know."

It required the help of seven heralds, but Gismond managed to shepherd the peers into line, ready for their procession into the formal Chamber of the House of Lords: dukes paired with dukes and earls with earls. "Like the bloody Noah's ark," Gismond muttered to himself, and not for the first time. "Your Grace must stay in position," he said, actually laying hands on an elderly and quite deaf peer.

Finally he was able to breathe a sigh of relief as the trumpet formally called the peers together, and he strode through the doors like a particularly magnificent mother duck leading two straight rows of quacking peers. Sunlight was flooding through the high arched windows, bouncing off the gilded chandeliers that hung from the ceiling.

Altogether, he found a rather glorious sight before him as he turned at the top of the room and waited as the crimson- and ermine-clad peers filed into benches. Lord Fippleshot seemed to have misplaced his spectacles, and His Grace the Duke of Devonshire was waggling his fingers at the crowded Spectators' Gallery, currently occupied by the peeresses. But all the same, they were in line, and no one appeared to have overindulged in brandy during luncheon.

Sadly, the room took on this crowded, excited atmosphere only when the subject at hand was a question of death—a peer accused of murder, for example, or thought to be dead, as now. Though the peeresses tended to turn up for questions of wills and illegitimacy as well. It was only the routine votes governing the kingdom for which most didn't bother to appear. But that was an unworthy thought, and he dismissed it.

There was a pause for a breath, and then a herald stalked up the aisle, the young Countess of Islay following in his wake. She wouldn't ever become a duchess now, Gismond reminded himself, feeling a little pang of sympathy. But there, Lady Gismond—who read the scandal rags with the kind of concentration some reserved for the Bible and others for the racing docket—was passionately attached to the idea of the countess's marrying again. "She needs a man of her own," Lady Gismond had said that very morning. "Never a whisper of scandal about her, but the poor woman won't have children if this drags on much longer."

All the peers rose as the countess, dressed entirely in mourning, proceeded to the front of the chamber and curtsied, first to the Spectators' Gallery, then to the assembled peers, and then to the Lord Chancellor. Formalities completed, she retired to the alcove reserved for peeresses and seated herself next to Mrs. Pinkler-Ryburn.

Gismond took a moment to squint at her, as his wife would demand every detail of her attire when he returned home. But Gismond could see nothing extraordinary. She was tall and she appeared to be thin, though it was hard to tell, as she probably wore four or five petticoats. She stood out like a drop of blackness in the midst of glitter. Not being required to wear robes, peeresses tended to wear their fortunes instead; the benches reserved for them positively sparkled.

The Sergeant-at-Arms boomed a request for silence, and then they went through the formal ceremony that opened the proceedings (every moment of which thrilled Gismond's ceremonious soul). Finally, he himself knelt and handed the Lord Chancellor his staff of office.

The Lord Chancellor sat on the Woolsack, a backless chair with a vague resemblance to a throne, above the peers now settled in their crimson and gold on the red benches below him.

He rose. "Right honorable the Lords Spiritual and Temporal in Parliament assembled," his lordship said, his voice effortlessly filling the great hall. "We are gathered and convened with the charge of a solemn task: to determine whether or no the noble peer, your companion, the Earl of Islay, heir to the duchy of Ashbrook, should be declared lost at sea. We have assumed these medieval splendors of scarlet and ermine in his honor, in response to the 'Death in Absentia' petition submitted by his sorrowing heir, Mr. Cecil Pinkler-Ryburn, who quite fitly and rightly expresses his deepest sorrow at this tragic event."

There was a little rustle of approbation, and Mr. Pinkler-Ryburn shifted uneasily in the bench just below Gismond, who instinctively began to calculate the length of ermine needed to adorn the scarlet robes that would cover such a magnificent stomach once the man was a duke. But to do Pink (as everyone seemed to call the heir) credit, he hadn't the slightest air of triumph or joy about him.

"We will give our absent peer the title Duke of Ashbrook as a matter of courtesy," the Lord Chancellor continued, "since his honored father died after the young man's departure from England and indeed, likely after his only son had already succumbed to the waves. Consequently, the young Earl of Islay never assumed the titles and duties to which he was heir, and never took his seat among us, in the House of Lords." He paused for breath, and to allow the weight of his words to be felt.

"His wife was unable to grieve for him in his absence"—here he cast a paternal eye on the bent head of the countess—"and has been unable to assume the duties and responsibilities of a duchess, nor the freedom and protections of the widow. Moreover, the duchy itself has naturally suffered without the guiding hand of its master."

Gismond had heard the opposite; in fact, most people were aware of the countess's guiding hand in making Ryburn Weavers such a success. His own lady had reupholstered the drawing room in Ryburn fabrics, and they had cost a pretty penny.

The Lord Chancellor was now calling for discussion of the petition to declare the Duke of Ashbrook dead in absentia. As expected, the duke's heir, Mr. Cecil Pinkler-Ryburn, begged permission to speak to the assembled peerage. He climbed the steps and looked over the chamber, not speaking for a moment.

He had a strange dignity about him, for all he was portly and rather insignificant. "I am most deeply, and I may say with perfect truth, cruelly afflicted by the call to declare my beloved cousin lost to us in such a manner. I accede to this motion only on the request of Lady Islay. While I wish to avoid the duties and responsibilities of the duchy, *she,* of course, wishes to be free, as is only just, of the heavy burden she has carried in the absence of her husband."

Everyone in the room seemed to feel this was well put, and there was a happy murmur and a great many nodding plumes from the gallery housing the peeresses.

The assembly then heard from a representative

of the committee that had reviewed Mr. Pinkler-Ryburn's petition. He noted that, in all, twenty Bow Street Runners had been sent to the various parts of the globe once the young earl had been missing for some years, and the only news unearthed of him was of an equivocal nature.

Since there was nothing left to be said, the Lord Chancellor stepped forward again, holding in his right hand the scepter of his office. "We certainly appreciate the sentiments of Mr. Pinkler-Ryburn, for the heavy mantle of an English dukedom comes to a gentleman, as ever, with sorrow and mourning for his predecessor."

At this, an audible giggle rose spontaneously in several parts of the room; the spectators, it seemed, had witnessed more than one title assumed with delight rather than sorrow.

The Lord Chancellor ignored this lack of decorum. "The assembled might and force of all England cannot stop the march of time, any more than they can arrest the motion of the tides or the course of the planets."

The Countess of Manderbury wore high ostrich plumes that curled behind her and kept brushing across Lady Bury St. Edmonds's face. Gismond narrowed his eyes. Surely that metallic flash couldn't be a pair of embroidery scissors in Lady Bury St. Edmonds's hand?

Gismond resisted the impulse to check the timepiece he had discreetly placed under his sash of office, and let the powerful voice of his lordship—who had progressed from reference to the tides to the will of heaven—wash over him.

But at that moment something happened, an event about which Gismond never stopped talking for the rest of his days. It began with a commotion in the back of the chamber, where the Yeoman Warders were stationed in the event that some errant peer insisted on entering in a tardy fashion. (It was deplorable, yet known to happen.)

But the latecomer was surely not a peer. Striding up the aisle now was an interloper: a man wearing plain black breeches and coat, no gloves, and no wig.

The Lord Chancellor broke off in the midst of a sentence describing the arms of heaven embracing the lost nobleman.

Gismond moved forward a nervous step. He should, by all rights, throw the intruder out of the chamber. But he was not one for physical action; raising one hand, he looked to his Yeoman Warders at the back of the room. But they stood facing forward, their eyes lowered.

A little pulse of anger was followed by one of confusion: they had been properly trained and should assume that attitude *only* upon admission of a member of the peerage. Gismond felt himself turning pale. Could it be that a member of the journalist class had somehow dared to swindle his way past the guards and broach his doors?

He squared his shoulders and prepared to take action.

The man was at the front of the room now, and with one great step was on the very dais.

He was large, very large, but all the same, Sir Henry Gismond knew that this was a decisive moment in his life. He had to prove himself worthy of his position and save the ceremony from chaos. The very memory of the young earl depended upon it.

"I must beg you, sir, to leave this chamber," he said, pitting his voice against the babble that seemed to vibrate against the very walls of the room.

The man looked down at him, and Gismond involuntarily fell back a step. The intruder's hair barely touched his ears. His skin was brown as a nut, and below his right eye, he had the mark of a savage.

"By God, this is no place for a tribesman from the Americas," the Lord Chancellor roared. "Sirrah, return to whatever exhibit brought you to this country!"

With no other response than a rather grim smile showing a flash of white teeth, the man turned squarely to face the assembled peers. Still he remained silent. Gismond saw with one helpless glance that even the occupants of the Spectators' Gallery were on their feet, straining to see.

"Silence!" the Lord Chancellor bellowed. "If

you would please take your seats, we will discover the meaning of this disturbance."

The babble did not subside, but the peers began to settle back onto their benches.

And all the time the intruder merely stood before them, an odd grin quirking one side of his mouth. Gismond's mind raced. He'd heard tales of the Indian peoples of the Americas, of their strength and cunning. He'd even seen a tomahawk and shirt made of deerskin on display. Yet this specimen seemed to have no weapon. What on earth—

His speculation was interrupted. "Does no one recognize me?" the man asked. Gismond had never heard a voice like his: powerful, deep, a growl that quivered in the air like the howl of a bear.

Yet despite its roughness, it was unmistakably the voice of an English gentleman. There was no mistaking the vowels. Now there truly was dead silence in the chamber.

From the corner of his eye Gismond saw the Lord Chancellor twitch, caught between the exercise of his authority and a shock so profound that he—like everyone in the room—simply waited for whatever would come next.

"Given that you were so distressed to consign me to a watery grave," the man added, turning to the Lord Chancellor, "I quite thought I would be recognized."

His lordship made a noise like the squeal of a young pig. "Impossible!"

"Entirely possible," the intruder replied. He seemed to be enjoying himself. "The arms of heaven have not yet pulled me into their embrace, you see."

A wave of excited babble followed this observation. Gismond craned his neck to look at the countess, tucked into the gallery. It occurred to him that the lost duke—*if* it was indeed he—didn't realize that the peeresses were in attendance; he hadn't looked in their direction. But Gismond could catch only a glimpse of her face, white as parchment.

Then Mr. Pinkler-Ryburn came to his feet and once more climbed to the dais. Though the man claiming to be duke was by far the more ferocious figure, Mr. Pinkler-Ryburn had an odd dignity of his own.

"I do not recognize you, sir," he said. His voice was cautious and respectful, the sort of address one might give a lion that has suddenly expressed, in the King's English, a wish to eat you.

"We never knew each other very well," the man replied.

"If you are indeed the duke, your voice has altered beyond recognition."

"Having your throat cut tends to do that." The man tilted his head back. There was a little gasp in the room, as everyone saw the wicked scar that ran across his brown throat as neatly as a cravat.

Gismond had the impulse to clutch his own neck, but luckily he remembered the pristine beauty of his starched neck cloth in time.

"Where have you been during the last seven years?" Mr. Pinkler-Ryburn inquired.

"Spending my time with cutthroats."

Mr. Pinkler-Ryburn drew himself straight and squared his shoulders. "Then, if you would be so good as to answer a question, sir. By what name was I ridiculed in school, a name which you never yourself used?"

For the first time a smile softened that savage face. "Pink," the man said. "They bloody well called you Pink."

If there were any in the room who believed that Pink secretly wished to be duke, they knew at that moment that they were wrong, for he threw his arms around his cousin as if he had discovered his own long-lost brother.

It was such a mesmerizing sight that not everyone on the dais noticed immediately that Lady Islay—now the Duchess of Ashbrook—had fallen into a dead faint and toppled into her neighbor.

It was her own husband, the returned duke, for one had to assume that he had the right to the title now, who saw the furor, brushed off Pink's embrace, and leapt directly off the dais.

Gismond committed the impropriety of stepping

forward, the better to see. (As he told his wife sometime later, it was better than a play.)

The duchess lay, still and white, against Mrs. Pinkler-Ryburn. She didn't stir when the duke bent over her. A moment later His Grace straightened, holding his wife in his arms.

("A play," Gismond repeated that night. "Her head against his shoulder, if you take my meaning. All hero-like, except, of course, no hero looks like that." He couldn't explain himself. "It was his expression, maybe, not a patch of nervousness or even excitement. As if this sort of thing happened to him every day of the week.")

Wearing easy confidence like an ermine-trimmed cloak, the duke strode back to the dais and stood before it, holding his wife in his arms. He nodded up to the Lord Chancellor. "I do believe that my cousin, Mr. Pinkler-Ryburn, will withdraw his petition for declaration of my death."

"Yes!" Pinkler-Ryburn said immediately, his voice coming with a gasp. "Absolutely. The man's not dead. Not at all."

At that, the duke actually threw back his head and laughed. And even though it showed that terrible white scar again, Gismond almost found himself laughing as well. But he had never flouted ceremony in such a fashion in his life, and he did not intend to start now.

The peers, though . . . there was an eruption of

unrestrained laughter, the kind that follows and relieves pent-up tension.

("He's got a charming laugh," Gismond told his wife hours later. "Looks a proper savage, but when he laughed, it was an *English* laugh."

"What's an English laugh?" she asked skeptically. "And what was he doing, standing around talking to people while his poor wife was in a dead faint? I certainly hope and trust that *you* would never treat me so cavalierly, my dear."

Gismond manfully pushed away the thought that he would be utterly unable to pick up his wife—who outweighed him by more than a few stone—let alone carry her more than a step. "I shall not," he promised solemnly. "Never.")

Twenty-three

Theo's first thought was to flee. The savage, sunburned man on the dais could not, simply could not, be her James.

The way the man stood in front of all those lords, shoulders wider than anyone else's, the way his eyes calmly moved over the room, the color of his skin, his tattoo, and the way his hair didn't even touch the nape of his neck . . .

James didn't look like that, and he didn't act like that.

But, of course, she was wrong. It was actually the scar on James's neck that convinced her. She gasped at the sight, her heart gave one huge thump, and the room turned hazy.

She climbed back from a pool of darkness to find herself clasped in James's arms as he walked across the chamber. Something deep inside her instantly recollected the windy, outdoors smell of him, even though his voice was nothing like what she remembered.

As her head cleared, she became aware of a sardonic note of amusement in her husband's voice as he conversed with the peers on the dais. There wasn't even the faintest concern in his voice for her, for the woman—his *wife!*—in his arms.

She instantly decided not to open her eyes. The last thing she wanted was to meet the pitying gaze of those in the chamber, given that James could not have displayed his utter lack of concern for her any more flagrantly. It wasn't an experience that she would wish on her worst enemy.

One had to assume that her husband had been lurking around London for days, waiting for the moment when he could charge into the House of Lords like a marauding Visigoth and shock her into a swoon.

It wasn't that she would have expected him to throw himself into her arms if she'd known he was returning. They had parted in anger, after all. But they were *married.*

He could have halted this farce before it even

started. He could have pretended that he cared about her opinion, that he bothered about her enough to tell her he was alive before informing an assembly of nearly two hundred. Such a public shaming felt like a punishment. Her heart beat painfully in her ears. She hadn't felt this mortified since first glimpsing the "ugly duchess" etchings.

It made her feel unloved, unlovable, as if the very ground shifted under her feet, as if all the years of transforming herself into a swan had come to nothing, obliterated by the fact her husband hadn't even bothered to visit her when he returned to London.

All the anguish she had felt after James left, when everyone concluded that he couldn't bear to stay married to such an ugly woman, flooded back. Some of those etchings had depicted James fleeing with an arm thrown over his eyes. Theo had felt reduced to a cipher of a woman then, and she felt it again now.

She kept her eyes closed while James finished his conversation, walked through the chamber and out of the building, and gently deposited her on the seat of the carriage. He was so big that the vehicle actually swayed when he climbed through the door.

"You can wake up now," he said. There was that thread of laughter in his voice again. Laughter? He thought this was *amusing*—to make people who had loved him go through the agony of declaring him dead?

James had never been pitiless before. He had never been contemptuous.

She stopped pretending and sat upright with a jolt, eyes open. After all these years, her husband was across from her again. Yet everything had changed. James had become a *pirate*. A criminal. His eyes were dark and unreadable, yet they somehow still spoke of arrogance and power. She had no difficulty believing that he had forced people to walk down the plank.

Her fingers curled around the edge of the leather seat, holding on for dear life.

"Good Lord," she said, not quite under her breath. His skin was bronzed by the sun, and the dark blue flower under his right eye was arresting, up close. It was like some sort of alien word, in a language she didn't understand.

The sight of him filled her head with ridiculous comparisons. Englishmen weren't—they were white, lily white. With *white* skin. They didn't inscribe flowers on their skin.

Not James. He looked fifty times more alive than the white-skinned gentlemen they'd left behind in the House of Lords, and that tattoo . . .

It was a flower, but not a frivolous one. It was sinister. Frightening, even.

Her fingers gripped the seat more tightly. She would never in a million years have thought that she could fear her childhood friend. But now she did. Only an idiot wouldn't be uneasy in this man's presence.

"Good afternoon, Daisy," he said, as calm as if they had parted no more than a month or so ago.

She couldn't think what to say. Mr. Badger had described the tattoo as being worn by a ferocious pirate called Jack Hawk: should she mention the name? Then she met his eyes, and as quickly as it had come, her fear evaporated, and an incandescent rage took over. James was regarding her with amusement. There wasn't the faintest sign on his face that he acknowledged the gravity of the ceremony he had just interrupted.

And yet she had been genuinely moved by the formal declaration of his death. She had been struggling not to cry, thinking of the way the old duke would appear in Staffordshire every now and then and inquire whether she had heard anything from his son. That a son could treat his father with such indifference was contemptible.

Angry or not, her instincts warned her to remain calm. "Welcome to England," she said, finally. She reached up, unpinned her veil, and placed it on the seat beside her.

James merely nodded.

"May I ask what moved you to return?" she asked, quite as if he had been on a short trip to Wales.

"I nearly died after having my throat cut. It's a

trite commonplace, but having a brush with death does give a man to think."

"You certainly made a dramatic entrance." Theo was never more proud of herself than when her voice contained not even a drop of reproach. Exquisite self-control had got her through the humiliations of her past, and it would serve her now. She refused, absolutely *refused,* to let James know how much his nonchalant attitude wounded her.

"Yes. I should add that I had no idea you would attend the ceremony."

"Would it have made any difference to you?"

He tilted his head just slightly to the side, and for the first time she saw a mannerism that she recognized from the old James. "Yes."

"Where have you been staying in London while you waited for the ceremony?"

He frowned with what seemed to be genuine confusion. "My ship only docked last night. I went to the town house first to tell you I was alive; the butler was kind enough to inform me that I had better scurry over to Westminster or I might not arrive in time to save myself from dying, so to speak. As I calculated it, I would have been dead seven years on June sixteen. I thought I had several weeks to convince everyone that I was among the living."

"The paperwork would have cleared Chancery by your death date, thus ensuring that there was no delay between dukes."

"I was glad to see that Cecil showed no particular reluctance to lose the title he almost inherited."

"None. In fact, he wanted to wait another year or so."

"So it was my wife who wished to be freed on my seven-year anniversary." His voice was colorless.

She smiled at him as politely as any duchess at a musicale. "Only because I had no evidence of your continued existence, nor reason to assume it, I assure you. How did you find the house this morning?" Theo forced herself to relax her fingers, but she could not bring herself to fold them in her lap. Instead she reached for the strap by the window and hung on as if they were madly turning corners rather than sedately making their way toward Berkeley Square.

"I was there only for a matter of minutes. I dropped the baggage I brought with me and went directly to Lords."

She was unable to stop herself. "By 'baggage,' surely you mean *booty?*"

"So you know?" Perversely, he grinned at that.

She was so enraged that she felt her throat closing. But she schooled her voice again. "We had been told of a possible connection between you and a pirate called the Earl and another named Jack—Hawk, was it? Cecil and I were reluctant to believe that you had entered into that profession."

She left silent the obvious addition: *more the fools we.*

"Life is full of surprises," James replied, most unhelpfully.

It might have been the flare of her nostrils; his eyes narrowed and he seemed to grasp a hint of her feelings.

But what he said next did not reflect that. "The traffic around London has become appalling; it took so long to get to Lords that I actually thought I might be forced to play a resurrection scene."

The carriage was finally coming to a halt. "I am glad we were spared that," Theo remarked.

"Your butler told me that you left at seven this morning," he said, in a voice that carried an undertone of possessiveness. "The ceremony didn't begin for some time thereafter." James was missing for seven years, and now he thought to return home as the master of the household?

"I paid a visit to your father's grave," she replied, gathering up her reticule and veil as a groom opened the carriage door. "He often asked for you before he died. This morning, I wanted to tell him before I took the step of declaring you dead. A foolish gesture—in more than one way, it seems."

For the first time, he flinched; she saw a flash of deep pain in his eyes.

And she was glad. As she stepped from the carriage, Theo was truly shocked by just how glad she was. She felt as bloodthirsty as any pirate.

There was one more thing that she needed to clarify. Well, there were many, but this one would not wait. Once in the entrance, she nodded to Maydrop, and he instantly opened the door to the drawing room.

James followed her, and when she turned to face him he merely looked at her, waiting, an eyebrow raised. She remembered that look. Years ago, his raised eyebrow had evidenced the curiosity of a boy; now it clearly signaled the supreme arrogance of a man.

For a moment her heart quailed: what was she to do? She would *not* live with a pirate, with a scarred, uncivilized excuse for a duke. She was probably the most controlled—if you like, the most refined—woman of all her acquaintance, but now her heart was beating so fast it felt as if it might fly from her chest. Still, she pulled herself together.

"The Bow Street Runner who hypothesized that you were the Earl was quite certain that you couldn't be Jack Hawk," she said, stripping off her gloves so that she didn't have to look at him.

But she could see him through her lashes. He was lolling back against the wall as no gentleman would. "Your Runner was wrong there."

"One of his reasons for that conclusion was that Hawk had, if I caught his meaning correctly, left illegitimate children all over the East Indies." She did meet his eyes then, dropping all pretense of

246

civility and making sure that her own eyes expressed the contempt she felt for a man who had not bothered to return for years, not even to console his aging father; for a man who, given what she knew about pirates, not only stole for a living but had ordered people down a plank to a watery grave. For a man who had betrayed his marriage vows and then deserted his own children, uncivilized and illegitimate though they may be.

James was silent for a moment. The boy she remembered would have yielded to her glare, but the man just crossed his arms over his chest and looked at her thoughtfully. "You seem rather angry. When I left England you were in this state, and I had hoped that time had changed your displeasure."

"I was angry then because you married me under false pretenses. Our marriage has been irrelevant to me for many years, though not, it seems, as irrelevant as it was to you. Still, I can assure you that I no longer feel more than mild pique at your deceit with regard to our marriage. However, I will ask you again, Duke, did you indeed leave children behind? Or did you bring them home with you? Are your offspring the *baggage* that you mentioned?"

The silence that fell over the drawing room was like the crack of a whip: it had ferocity, as if the air had been sliced in half.

"Your Bow Street Runner was incorrect," James

repeated, just before Theo was about to go investigate the nursery herself. "I have no children, illegitimate or otherwise."

"Really?" she said coolly. "Are you quite certain? Am I to believe that you bothered to check on me nine months after you left England?"

"I sent a man to do so."

"A pity you didn't ask that man to assure the duke of your safety." Ashbrook's last thought had been of his long-lost son, though even in the deepest rage of her life, she did not say that. It would be too cruel.

"I did not think of my father as old. Stupidly, I never imagined that he might die before we managed to reconcile. It is one of my many regrets." But James said it lightly. "In fact, the news of his death transformed me from the Earl into Jack Hawk."

She waited, but he did not elaborate. Apparently he felt no obligation to explain anything more to her. She walked from the room and up the stairs without another word.

A half hour later, in her bath, Theo thought of the obvious solution to this unimaginable turn of events. She sat up so quickly that water sluiced from her shoulders and slopped onto the floor. "I need Boythorn," she said aloud.

"Beg pardon, Your Grace?" Amélie turned from where she was folding stockings.

"Please ask Maydrop to send for my solicitor, Mr. Boythorn," Theo said, standing up. "I should like him to attend me first thing in the morning." Of course one could dissolve a union if a spouse returns from a years-long absence with a reputation for walking people down the gangplank. In ordinary circumstances, it was difficult—nearly impossible—to obtain a divorce. This was not an ordinary circumstance.

In fact, she was quite certain her arguments would triumph. The Regent himself would dissolve the marriage, if no one else. He had done so for the wife of Lord Ferngast, after Ferngast joined the Family of Love and demanded that she share her bed with all and sundry. Lord Ferngast hadn't *killed* people.

London might be temporarily dazzled by the wholly unexpected return of the Duke of Ashbrook, but everyone knew what happened to captured pirates: they were hanged.

As she was contemplating that, the door opened and her maid turned around with a squeak. Theo turned more slowly.

But she turned, naked and wet as she was. James's absurdly large body filled the doorway. Infuriatingly, he took a leisurely look up and down at her.

"Amélie," she said a bit sharply, "may I have a towel, please?"

With something like a sob of excitement, her

maid pressed one into her hands and threw another around her shoulders.

James's eyes were still blue. But they were utterly expressionless, the eyes of a stranger.

"In civilized society," Theo said as she wrapped the towel around herself, "it is *de rigueur* to knock on the door of a shared chamber before entering."

Then she walked through the door that led into her bedchamber and closed it behind her.

Twenty-four

James walked down the stairs, his mind whirling like a windmill in a gale. He'd forgotten how pink and white Daisy was. Her skin was like the heart of a delicate English rose. He'd forgotten the curve of her hip and the length of her legs.

He'd forced himself to forget those things, but now they all crashed back into his mind, all the things he'd loved about her from the time he was a boy. Her exquisite bone structure . . . the arch of her bottom lip . . . the dark sweep of her lashes. His soul sang at the sight of her, and not just with carnal desire.

Damn.

Obviously, he had never truly forgotten.

There was one thing about her that made the breath catch in his chest. It was the look in her eyes when she saw him. There was surprise and anger; he had expected that. But there was also fear. *Fear?* From Daisy, his Daisy?

He'd thrown this fascinating woman away, sailing off to bask under a foreign sun. He reached the bottom of the stairs when he realized with utter certainty that he would—*could*—never sail away from Daisy ever again.

She was his heart, his other half. She filled all the empty places in his soul that he had desperately tried to paper over with pirate escapades and merry women.

And she feared him.

He'd been confident about his ability to overcome her rage. Now he felt as if the universe had given him a leveler. Daisy *knew* him. How could she possibly feel threatened by him?

His brain supplied the answer. Because he *had* hurt her, if only emotionally. Surely she didn't think he could ever hurt her physically. He felt undone at the thought and clenched his fists to stop his fingers from trembling.

Of course other people feared him: he was a pirate. He was big and tattooed and kept his head shaven—though his hair was now growing back. But it never crossed his mind that Daisy could fear him.

She was the only one who had always looked past the surface and loved him for himself. She had been the only person in his life who thought he was more than a pretty voice and a handsome face. Even his mother liked to parade him around the drawing room, cajole him to sing for her guests, and call him her "treasure."

He strode into the library, dimly registering that it looked different. How in the hell could he have let Daisy go? Where had his brain been the last seven years?

The days had been long, and filled with sometimes violent adventure, but somehow the years had been short.

He stood at the window, his heart pounding in a strange way that made him feel a bit sick. It couldn't be too late.

He could win her back.

He briefly imagined himself kneeling at her feet and just as quickly dismissed the idea. The one thing he would never do was beg. As a child, he had begged for affection, although his parents never seemed to notice. He had sung his heart out for his mother, hoping that she would do more than pat his cheek and smile at him.

A sound deep in his chest surprised him and he bared his teeth at his reflection in the window glass. He was being a sentimental ass. He could win Daisy back without prostrating himself. Women didn't want fools or weaklings. If she didn't respect him, she'd never take him back.

There was nothing to respect about a man who only had to look at his wife to find his entire body enflamed, the one thought in his mind a longing to lick every drop of water off her body. He'd like to carry her to bed, and . . .

And beg her to love him the way she once had.

His stomach lurched. He had a moment of clarity that sliced the world into two parts: one in which Daisy smiled at him, and the other in which she walked away, just as he had walked away from her.

The second was hell. And the first . . .

Her frightened expression came back to him like a blow.

True, he looked like a savage and he sounded like a dockworker. But he didn't have to act like either. In fact, he suddenly realized, what he should do is act like that damned worm Trevelyan. Daisy had always adored Trevelyan's sardonic manner, although it masked (if you asked James, though Daisy never did), a blistering lack of confidence. Perhaps even self-hatred.

A hard bark of laughter didn't make it from his throat. *He* was the one lacking self-confidence now. Still, as long as she never discovered his Achilles' heel—*her*—he could seduce her with carefully clever conversation. Then, once he managed to get her to bed, surely he could ignite the old affection she had for him.

But first she had to see him as the sort of man she wanted, not as an idiot begging for attention, let alone sexual attention. And not as a terrifying pirate, either. He had to be polished. Amused. Refined.

All the things he was not, but he shrugged that off. She could find out later what a primitive beast he really was underneath. He could play cultured for a while.

Probably.

He thought through his plan, elaborating it, considering contingencies, testing each phase in his mind as carefully as he had always done when they caught sight of a pirate sail. Thanks to the countless times Griffin and he found themselves in the company of royalty, he was in possession of all the clothing that Daisy would like.

She had certainly remade herself; she was like a polished silver bowl, every inch of her conveying classic elegance. And control. In fact, she bore an unnerving resemblance to a sensual general, if only women were allowed in His Majesty's army.

He preferred her without clothing. His mind skipped back to the image of her standing in her bath, and his body instantly hardened. Runnels of water had slid down her thighs. He wanted to fall at her feet and cherish those thighs . . . and everything between them.

But even more than that, he simply wanted to *be* with her, to be the first to share her brilliant ideas and fierce opinions. In all his travels, he never met anyone, not even Griffin, whom he enjoyed talking to as much as he enjoyed talking to Daisy.

Now that he'd seen her again, it was as if all those years on board ship had passed in a dream: reality was *here*. He wanted to grow old with her, or not grow old at all.

Bloody hell.

He was in serious trouble.

Twenty-five

The moment Theo closed the door, she pivoted, expecting James to open it and step through. He had blundered straight into the bathing chamber, after all. *Why* had she never divided that spacious room into two, one for each of the bedchambers? She'd had half a mind to do so for years. Instead, she'd installed the newest system of pumping water and a gorgeous ceramic bathtub made on their own estate.

She heard the sound of his feet retreating through his room and down the corridor. And told herself that she was glad. Perhaps he had forgotten that the bathing room was shared. From now on, he would respect her privacy.

She took her time dressing, not allowing herself to picture buxom island girls with curves her body would never achieve.

She had meant to remain at home that night to honor James's memory. But now there was no person to grieve, and, therefore, no reason to stay home. More importantly, she simply could not face the idea that she and James would have to sit opposite each other at supper. She desperately wanted to flee.

She sent Amélie to inform Maydrop that she would attend the theater, then she donned an evening dress made of a heavy, supple olive green silk that gleamed under candlelight. It fell from the bodice, but rather than belling out, the silk was cut on the bias and hugged every curve of her body.

The bodice was gathered under her breasts and trimmed with dark copper lace that glimmered with shiny black beads and widened into short sleeves. Her hair was pulled straight back from her forehead without even a wisp floating at her ears, and she waved away the ruby necklace Amélie offered. She wanted no distraction from her face.

She did, however, slide a sparkling ruby onto her right hand, a present she had given to herself when Ryburn Weavers made its first thousand guineas in profit.

How better to remember that milestone than to wear a sizable percentage of it on one's finger?

Finally, Amélie drew out a small brush and skillfully applied a few strategic dabs of face paint. The last thing Theo wanted was to try to look conventionally feminine, but she'd discovered that a thin line of kohl made her eyes look deep and mysterious.

After a final look in her glass, she felt her confidence settle back in place: confidence that had been hard won, as she coerced the estate back into solvency, as she conquered the French court, as she won the respect of the English *ton*.

Her husband's disregard for her—even expressed so openly, before the entire assembled body of peers—could not diminish her achievements.

Her butler waited at the newel post. "His Grace is in the library," he announced, concern written all over his face.

"Thank you," Theo replied. "I trust that you will reassure the household, Maydrop. The duke's return is unexpected, to say the least, but I am sure that he will make no changes in domestic arrangements."

He nodded. "His Grace did not bring a valet, so I have taken it upon myself to request the registry office send three suitable candidates tomorrow morning. I have put the duke's guest in—"

"Guest!" Theo interjected. She felt the blood draining from her face. Surely, no matter how savage he'd become, James had not brought back a woman from the West Indies?

"Sir Griffin Barry," Maydrop said quickly. "I gather that His Grace and Sir Griffin were partners in the last few years. I have placed Sir Griffin in the rose bedchamber."

"Excellent," Theo said, rather faintly.

She had an unnerving wish to run out the front

door as fast as she could. Her husband had not only returned, but he had also brought with him his companion in crime—and hadn't Mr. Badger said that Barry had a more invidious reputation than did James himself?

The constables would be pounding on their door by luncheon tomorrow. She hadn't missed her mother's support so keenly in years. Even the old duke would have been a welcome presence at her shoulder.

"Your Grace, I believe that you plan to attend the—"

But Theo raised her hand, and Maydrop's words broke off. "Later, if you please." She must confront James before she turned tail and ran.

She walked into the library before she could change her mind.

She had redecorated the room after James's father died. There was nothing left to remind her of the moment of humiliation that broke her marriage, when the old duke had met her eyes as she knelt before his son, performing a service that made her shudder to even consider now.

At that time the room had been all dark wood and crimson curtains, the only artwork portraits of long-deceased hunting dogs. These days, floor-to-ceiling bookshelves alternated with white paneling with periwinkle blue insets, each painted with a different set of fantastic images inspired by the discoveries at Pompeii.

The curtains, needless to say, were woven on Ryburn looms. They too were striped blue and white, with small flowers running down the blue.

Any remaining china shepherdesses that had escaped the former duke's fury had long since been banished to the attics; instead, one's eyes landed on Ashbrook ceramics, whose Greek and Roman themes provided a counterpoint to the grotesques painted on the wall.

Theo knew exactly what she was doing when she inspected the room rather than look at the man who occupied it: she was so seized by nerves that she was reassuring herself by cataloguing her own successes.

James was seated at the desk she used for her accounts, apparently writing a letter. He had tossed aside his coat and rolled up his shirtsleeves.

Theo took a deep breath. "Good evening, James," she said, walking forward.

As she spoke, he looked up from the sheet of foolscap before him and rose. Apparently he hadn't entirely abandoned the conduct of an English gentleman.

"Daisy," he said. He moved from behind the desk and kissed the hand she held out.

As he straightened she studied him closely, taking her time about it. "My name is Theo," she told him in a voice that brooked no misunderstanding. "Goodness, you've changed, James. No wonder I didn't recognize you this morning. May I offer you a glass of sherry?" She walked over to the cluster of decanters and removed the top of one.

"I rarely drink," James said at her shoulder. She jumped and dropped the glass stopper. His hand shot out and he caught it.

"May I?" he asked, taking the decanter from her hand and pouring her a glass of sherry. "I see you have three kinds of brandy, which suggests that you are as unlike other ladies in your taste for spirits as you are in other respects."

Theo wondered briefly if he was trying to discomfit her by obliquely alluding to her lack of English prettiness, but she shrugged off the thought, taking a heady sip of sherry and letting it warm her throat. "Your cousin Cecil is very fond of cognac and I keep it for him," she said, walking over to a couch that replaced the rococo sofa she had thrown away.

She sat down and watched as the stranger who called himself her husband poured himself a glass of port, then came to join her. As he approached, she tipped her head back the better to see his full height. "You've grown astonishly large."

"Yes." He sat beside her and she edged away from the heat of his thigh. "In my early twenties I suddenly sprouted a few more inches. My only explanation is the sea air."

Suddenly the sofa felt very small indeed. Theo took a comforting sip of wine, then leaned toward him and peered at his cheek. "I gather that is a poppy under your eye?"

He nodded.

Though she would die rather than admit it, the tattoo had a kind of primitive appeal. "Does Sir Griffin have the same emblem carved on his face?" Really, she was handling this tremendously well. How many women had the opportunity to speak to a pirate, let alone have two under their roof? And surely she must be the only English gentlewoman to find herself married to a man of this profession. It would all work out, she told herself. James would leave England—surely he would rather leave than be hanged—and her life would return to normal.

"He does," James replied, as casually as if she were inquiring about a cravat. Not that he was wearing a cravat. His neck emerged from his shirt as bare and brown as lads working in the fields.

"Are you concerned that your adopted profession might lead to some unpleasantness?" she asked.

"Of what nature?"

"Given the unorthodox, and I daresay, illegal nature of your activities, I would think that the constables will call on us. Or officers from the Royal Navy. Whoever it is who deals with pirates."

He settled back in the corner of the sofa and grinned at her over his wineglass. "What should I be worried about?"

"Dancing at the end of a rope? To the best of my knowledge, piracy is punishable by death." She took another sip of sherry.

"Yes," James said, sounding perfectly unconcerned. "I suppose that is the case. Under normal circumstances."

"And you are not worried?"

"Not in the least. How were the last seven years for you, Theo?"

"Wearying," she said, choosing candor over his evasive answers. "Life was quite difficult after you left the country. But you'll be happy to learn that Ryburn Weavers and Ashbrook Ceramics are now thriving concerns. Once I had both of them on an even keel, I moved to Paris, from whence I returned last year. I had thought—" She caught herself.

"You had thought to hand the estate over to Cecil," James said. "I cannot blame you for wanting to see the back of it. Shamefully, I planned never to return partly for that reason. In fact, it was one of the reasons I changed my name. I thought to ensure that no one ever put together the Earl and the Earl of Islay."

"How lucky for all of us that you changed your mind," she said, not trying very hard to sound enthusiastic.

He looked at her silently for a long moment. "Are you angry because I didn't inform you of my return before interrupting the proceedings at

Lords? My ship docked late at night, and I thought not to wake the household. I think of Lords as being men only, and it did not occur to me to look for women in the audience during the less-than-thrilling process of proving my identity."

"A wife is easily forgotten," she agreed.

He hesitated. Then: "I stopped thinking of you as my spouse some years ago, as I'm sure you did of me."

His words took Theo's breath away. Somehow she *hadn't* stopped thinking of James as her husband, though Lord knows, she wished she had.

Temper was rising up her spine again, but she hadn't reached the age of twenty-four for nothing. "I see," she said quietly. "If you are wondering whether I betrayed you in the years of your absence, I did not."

There was a flash of emotion deep in his eyes, but it was gone so quickly that she wasn't sure she saw it.

"My answer to that question would be the opposite," he said, as casually as if he were discussing the weather. "Two days of marriage failed to impress itself on me. I am fairly certain that most men would understand my lapse."

"Not everyone gives the same weight to marital vows," she replied.

"Our marriage was over, to quote your own words." His voice did not rise, but it took on a severe, rather chilling undertone. "You threw me out of this house and told me not to come back. I hardly see your command as honoring our mutual vow to stay together *as long as we both shall live.*"

"Am I to understand that my anger at being tricked into the marriage, the better to disguise the embezzlement of my dowry, became your excuse for committing adultery?"

The atmosphere in the library was so charged that she felt as if a dry spark might ignite the very air. Interestingly enough, James remained in obvious control of his temper. He truly *had* grown up.

"We have a great deal of hostility between us," he said, finally. "I had not thought that you would still hold a grudge. Frankly, our marriage feels like a different lifetime to me. I can hardly remember our last conversation—other than your insistence that our marriage was over—but in case I did not offer my apologies at the time, I am happy to do so now."

Theo felt a sudden wave of longing, not for the hard-faced man in front of her, but for the young man whose eyes fell when she screamed at him, who had loved her.

James apparently took her silence as encouragement. "I am truly sorry for having acceded to my father's request and married you under false pretenses. In years after, I realized that while the marriage may well have taken place anyway, our closeness undoubtedly made the sting of my betrayal more keen."

"Be that as it may, we scarcely know each other now," she said.

"The boy in me will always love you," he said, disarming her with a smile. "The man I am doesn't know you yet." And now there was a look in his eyes that she recognized, that resonated deep within her.

Instantly Theo quashed the feeling. She'd jump off a church steeple before she'd bed a man who cared so little for her that he had waited seven years to inform her whether he was alive. That was one lesson she had taken from her experience as an "ugly duchess": if she didn't value herself, no one would.

Except perhaps that boy whom James no longer resembled.

"You haven't been to bed with a man in seven years," he said softly. His eyes were frankly hungry now.

"That's true," she responded. "But that was before I realized that our vows had been dissolved, in practice, if not in the courts. Now I shall have to make up for lost time." And with that, she rose.

The desire in his face was instantly replaced by an unmistakable wave of fierce possessiveness.

Theo responded instinctively. "I am no longer your wife, James, and it seems you were my husband only as the Earl, for a matter of two or three years before you became Jack Hawk."

"How in the hell did you know that?"

"It's amazing what a good Bow Street Runner can discover. I take it that the Earl was mine, while Jack belonged to half the ladies of the West Indies and beyond."

"Rather an exaggeration," he murmured.

"Truly? Mr. Badger thought that you had illegitimate children sprinkled throughout the islands."

James's laugh was as rasping and deep as his voice. "I would rather father my first child on my wife."

"I'm afraid that's not an option," she said coolly. "I am confident that our marriage can be dissolved, and I would certainly hope that you have a thriving flock of children with your next wife."

"My *next* wife?"

"Our situation is clearly untenable." Theo didn't want to leave him with the least ambiguity. "I will petition for dissolution of the marriage as soon as possible; I've already contacted my solicitor. I have confidence that the Regent will accede to my request."

"No, you damn well won't." He bit the words out.

"I think we would both prefer to dispel the hostility between us," she said, ignoring his response.

"I see no reason for unpleasantness," he agreed.

But there was something about his tone—no matter how agreeable—that set her every nerve on edge. "My jointure is more than able to support my needs, and we own a house in Hennessey Street that the estate acquired five years ago for investment purposes. If you are agreeable, I will set up housekeeping there. I would be happy to buy the house from the estate, as it is, obviously, unentailed."

"I'll be *damned* if my wife will move out of my house, let alone buy another house from me!" His courteous tone slipped and his voice sounded more like a snarl.

It was unexpectedly attractive, which was absurd. Obviously, it was a tragedy that James had lost his exquisite tenor voice. It was absurd to think that the rumble that seemed to come straight from his chest was attractive. Though it was dark and deep and . . .

Theo pulled herself together. She hadn't even an iota of ambivalence about this decision, deep voice or no deep voice. James had enthralled her when she was a girl, but she was facing a stranger now, not her young husband. She could not live with a man like this.

"I'm afraid it is not a subject for negotiation," she said, smiling at him just as she had when a Wedgwood designer accused her of stealing customers. "I cannot imagine that you have any particular reason to keep me here, given your stated conviction that our marriage is over. If you prefer, I could live abroad."

"The marriage *was* over. But now I'm back."

"A marriage is not an object that you can throw away and retrieve whenever you wish." She paused, but he seemed to have nothing to say to that. "Do you intend to remain in London, or will you return to the sea?"

"I plan to remain in England."

He seemed to be utterly unmoved by the possibility of a charge of piracy. "I'm sure your continued presence will sway the *ton* in your favor," Theo said. "Of course there will be a scandal when our marriage is dissolved, but the title is such that you will obtain a new duchess in time. Now, if you'll excuse me, I plan to attend the theater this evening."

James took a step toward her. "Perhaps I will accompany you."

"There's no need." She glanced at his attire. He looked like a laborer, brown neck emerging from a white shirt, its sleeves rolled up to show arms solid with muscle. It was remarkable how civilizing clothes could be. "You will have to visit a tailor before you return to society. If you would join me for a moment, James, I'd like to introduce you to my butler."

He followed silently as she moved into the entry, talking faster than usual in an attempt to fill the charged silence. "Maydrop is an absolute treasure; he has done an inestimable job maintaining the household since Cramble's retirement. Maydrop, I know that you spoke to the duke earlier today, but I wanted to make sure that the two of you are properly introduced."

The butler bowed. James nodded.

"Perhaps you will introduce His Grace to the rest of the staff?" Theo suggested. "If I may have my pelisse, Maydrop."

"The carriage is waiting, Your Grace," he said with another bow. "However—"

James addressed himself to the butler. "You kept a carriage waiting even though you were aware that the duchess would be seeing her husband this evening for the first time in years?" His tone was not harsh but curious.

Maydrop bowed yet again. "Her Grace's maid informed me that her mistress would attend the theater tonight."

"So you didn't picture us having a cozy evening at home, renewing our vows?" James asked Theo, turning back to her as if the butler were invisible.

"No." Theo shrugged on her pelisse, a magnificent Parisian creation of silk brocade custom designed in the severe style she preferred.

"Who escorts you to the theater?"

"A long-married woman such as I need not worry about an escort. I have a standing invitation to join Lord Geoffrey Trevelyan—you do remember him, don't you?—in his box. He'll be surprised to see me, given the events of this afternoon, but I'm sure he won't mind. I am sorry that I haven't the time to greet Sir Griffin."

She gave James something that approached a genuine smile, though it came in response to the anger in his eyes, rather than from her heart. It seemed that her husband didn't like the information that Geoffrey and she remained friends. "Do give Sir Griffin my best, if you please."

She dropped a curtsy and waited a moment, thinking James would bow, but he didn't. So she turned toward the front door, which was flanked by two footmen who were not as skilled as Maydrop at concealing their fascination at this little marital drama.

Without the slightest warning, an arm caught her about the waist and twirled her so she stumbled back against a hard chest. James's blue eyes glared down into hers. "My wife does not curtsy to me," he said through clenched teeth.

Theo instinctively went as still as a rabbit in sight of a fox. "Unhand me, please," she said.

James raised his head. "Out!"

With a little scuffle, the footmen trotted around them and through the baize door.

"I said *out,*" James said, glaring at Maydrop. The hoarseness in his voice was particularly noticeable if he was annoyed, Theo noted.

Maydrop managed to strike a tone at once firm

and deferential. "If you'll forgive me, Your Grace, I am Her Grace's servant, and I would be loathe to leave her in any situation in which she might be uncomfortable."

Theo stood in James's embrace, trying to look unaffected by the muscled heat of his body. He seemed to believe she was desperate for a man, after all those years alone. It was a revolting thought. If there was one thing that had never tempted her, it was any sort of erotic encounter.

Or did he think that she had avoided adultery merely because no man wanted her, given her reputation for ugliness?

Only years of training herself to control emotion allowed her to maintain her poise. "I would be very grateful if you would free me," she said, her voice icy.

He stared down at her, having seemingly dismissed Maydrop from his attention. "You are my wife," he said, his voice low and rough. "At some point I'll have you again, Theo."

She refused to answer, though every cell in her body shrieked *no*. He must have seen it in her eyes, because he dropped a quick, hard kiss on her lips and let her free.

Theo ignored the way the touch of his lips weakened her knees. "Maydrop," she said, "please be so kind as to inform Amélie to pack my belongings, as we will be leaving the house tomorrow morning."

"The duchess is not going anywhere," James said, not even looking at the butler.

"Your Grace," Maydrop said, looking directly at Theo, "there is a situation outside of the house of which I must make you aware."

"Situation?" Theo was breathing quickly, her whole body trembling with the urge to dash for the door.

"The newspapers," Maydrop said, his tone distinctly anguished. "I'm afraid that the news of His Grace's return has titillated their interest. There are men surrounding the house, and even attempting to scale the garden walls. I've had to post grooms in the garden to keep them from peering in the windows."

"What a pity," James said with a wicked grin. "It looks as if you can't go to the theater tonight, Daisy."

Theo glared at him. "I most certainly can. Maydrop, if you would have one of the footmen escort me to the carriage, I would be grateful."

"Don't be foolish," James said. "They'll put out special editions just to discuss your cruelty in leaving me alone my first night in London. Not to mention the fact that they'll follow you to the theater like a flock of crows descending on a dead cow."

"A dead cow," Theo repeated.

"I must concur with His Grace's appraisal," Maydrop put in. "Any glimpse of either of you would exacerbate this unfortunate state of affairs.

I've had to post a footman in the attic to make certain that no one climbs down into the servants' quarters from the roof."

Theo swallowed. She suddenly felt as if it was all too much. To her intense dismay, tears welled in her eyes.

"Right," James said brusquely. Before she knew quite what was happening, he scooped her up in his arms and started tramping up the stairs.

Theo opened her mouth and then closed it again. There was something about being carried up the steps that felt very safe. "You mustn't think you can make a habit of this," she said about halfway up, deciding that she ought to protest.

"I will if I wish," James stated. He wasn't even breathing hard.

"I'm a *person,* not a possession," Theo said, her temper flaring into life again. "You will *what* if you want? Toss me around like a sack of flour? Stroll back into the house and act as if you left a week ago? What makes you think that you can treat me so cavalierly?"

He looked down at her with a steady, unreadable gaze.

"I'm your husband, Daisy."

"Theo," she snarled, feeling stupid.

He nodded. "Theo. May I just mention that I do not find it pleasurable to address my wife by a man's name?"

"No, you may not," she said. James pushed open

the door to her bedchamber with his shoulder, and then put her on her feet.

Then he backed up and gave her an easy smile. "Will you wear that gown to dinner?"

She narrowed her eyes. "Why?"

"You look ravishing." The compliment gave her an odd twist in her stomach. How could this man, who looked like a barbarian, be so *urbane?*

She hated it.

But she might wear the dress to dinner.

Twenty-six

James walked downstairs, but he couldn't make himself return to the library. He didn't want to write letters; he wanted to throw his wife onto the bed and slide a hand under the shimmering green thing she was wearing and . . .

He shook his head and readjusted his breeches. All things considered, he'd managed a decent imitation of Trevelyan, especially considering that he felt like a ragingly possessive pirate without a shred of sophistication to his name.

Since he couldn't go out the front, he walked out the back of the house, making his way though the garden to the small door that led directly into the mews.

He remembered the stables as dusty and crowded, smelling pleasantly of straw and horses. Now the walls were whitewashed, and the floor

274

looked clean enough to sleep on, if not eat on. His wife liked it to be immaculate, or so a groom told him a minute later.

He watched as boys swept out straw from the stall of a dappled gray. It was the second bedding change of the day, they told him. Meanwhile, the mare was being groomed for the third time. James shrugged, and then strolled down the central passageway. It seemed that he owned two precisely matched grays, two black geldings without the slightest spangle of white, and a matched set of four bays.

The stablemaster, Rosloe, was a cheerful sort who maintained order with an easy authority. But by the time James wandered back to the garden door, he'd heard "This is the way her ladyship wants it done" so many times that he found his lips moving along with the phrase. Rosloe caught him at it and burst out laughing. "Her ladyship has a way of thinking through the best way to do things," he explained. "They're not all her ideas either; even if one of the youngest lads has an idea about a better way to organize the tack, she'll listen. She's fair about it too, though of course she makes the final decision."

Obviously, Theo would have made a brilliant sea captain.

He and Griffin had survived years together—but they'd had two separate ships and two separate crews. How on earth was a household supposed to run with two captains within the same walls?

Back inside, he allowed Maydrop to introduce him to the housekeeper, Mrs. Eltis, and then to the chef, Monsieur Fableau, a Frenchman so small that he barely reached the ovens. Every surface in the kitchen evidenced strict organization. There were two turning spits, for example: "One is reserved for poultry," Fableau explained, "and the other for cuts of meat."

The pantry was lined with row after gleaming row of conserves. "Surely the household doesn't eat all this in one year," James exclaimed, realizing that the shelves covered four walls.

"Oh no," Mrs. Eltis replied with more than a trace of pride. "When the conserves are sent up from the country in the fall, I mark each jar and place it to the left, and then use those on the right. When the year comes to a close, I give any that haven't been eaten to an orphanage. That's the way her ladyship wants it done." The house-keeper's beaming smile spoke for itself.

Aboard ship, the captain was the absolute ruler of his particular world. James hadn't failed to get his own way in years; a crewmember would no more think of disobeying him than of jumping into a shark-filled bathtub.

He climbed the stairs thinking how interesting it was that he had no sooner entered England than he was led to understand, in no uncertain terms, that he was not the master of this particular world. In fact, it could be that here, at least, Daisy was the captain and he a mere visitor. It was disconcerting.

Griffin was in the rose bedchamber, Maydrop had said. Not that James knew which one that was. Everything had changed in the house. He remembered a dimly lit corridor at the top of the staircase, but Theo had knocked out the wall that faced the front of the house. Now the staircase led up in a sweep to an open passage, fronted with a satinwood balcony. He liked the way the railing felt like the rail of a ship in his hand.

He eventually succeeded in locating Griffin, only to find him in a temper; his response to James's entrance was a string of curses—and when a pirate captain is in a rage, the breadth of his vocabulary is truly astonishing.

"I've had a delightful reunion with my wife," James said, dropping into a chair and pretending he hadn't heard Griffin's blistering welcome.

Griffin perked up at that. "Kicked you in the arse, did she?"

"I would say she hit a more tender area. She's bent on moving out. The only thing keeping her under my roof is the fact that the house is besieged by journalists."

"Wait until my wife gets the news that I'm back in London," Griffin said, shifting his weight from one side to the other side with a grunt. He was still recovering from the slash to his leg that had endangered his life—and his manhood. James had

277

had a relatively uncomplicated recovery, given his injury, but Griffin had succumbed to infection and was still recuperating. "She'll be in the hills of Scotland by next week."

"I commanded Daisy to stay," James said, stretching out his legs. "In case you're wondering, I used the same tone I employ with the crew."

Griffin let out a bark of laughter. "I gather that Her Grace did not appreciate it?"

"Even the butler knew I didn't have a snowball's chance in hell. I caught a gleam of sympathy in his eyes."

"Turned into a hellion, has she?" Griffin grunted, shifting onto his right hip again.

"She's angry," James replied. "She's got a right to it, I suppose. I had hoped for . . ."

"Instant reconciliation?"

"At least a cessation of hostilities. She's changed."

"So have you. Remember that fresh young lad who greeted me by tossing his wig overboard? That's who she remembers. Now she's faced with a burly, scarred pirate with a tattoo under his eye. No wonder she's leaving."

"She has changed as well," James objected, feeling foolish.

Griffin snorted. "Did you think it was easy for her after you left? You're lucky she hasn't turned into a virago."

"That goes for your wife as well," James retorted, but without much force.

His old friend, guilt, was at his side. Yes, he had been furious when he left England all those years ago. He hadn't given much thought to Daisy's predicament. He was a thoughtless bastard, no matter how you looked at it. "She's turned to an icicle. She's . . . she used to be bubbly and funny."

The corner of Griffin's mouth twitched, but he said nothing.

"Damn it," James said heavily. "I've bungled every damn thing in my life. I've ruined her, Griffin. Now she's like one of those ice sculptures we saw in Halifax. Beautiful but frozen. She wasn't like that before I married her. She's furious that I didn't keep my beef in my breeches."

Griffin grunted. "Got a right to that, I suppose."

"When she threw me out of the house, she said the marriage was over, and I believed her. Was I supposed to remain faithful for the rest of my born days?"

"Apparently so." Griffin was obviously enjoying himself.

James gave him a sour look. "Sometimes I wish that knife had slashed you just an inch or two higher. Men are a good deal more compassionate when they're minus their dangling bits."

"Who has a 'bit'?" Griffin retorted. He gave himself a pat in the front. "I have an oak tree, I'll have you know."

"Reminding yourself that it's still there?"

"How would you feel if a sword whistled past

your best feature? I'm still having nightmares about it. I would have made a bitter *castrato*, I'll tell you." He gave his inner thigh a rough rub. "The scar itches like the devil's arse, so it must be finally healing." Griffin pulled himself to his feet and began walking around the chamber. "How soon do you think those pardons will come through? I've been in this room for only half the day and I'm about to rip down the curtains."

The procedure for receiving a royal pardon for two privateers (*not* pirates), who had spent their careers protecting the seas from the incursions of rogues and criminals, had been put in motion two months ago.

"It's only a matter of the Regent's signature, at this point. I gave McGill that ruby we took from the *Dreadnaught* to give to His Royal Highness as a gesture of our gratitude."

"How can the Regent not sign, when a virtuous privateer turns out to be one of his own dukes?" Griffin drawled. "Not that I mean to imply that a ruby as large as the royal toe would sway his decision. Did you have any trouble taking up your title, by the way, or had they already sung a dirge for you?"

"I was still alive when I entered the chambers."

"Do you suppose your wife had another candidate all set to go? Must be deuced disappointing for him now that you've turned up."

"Oh, I'm fairly sure she does," James said

280

grimly. "Before we married she was infatuated with a jack-a-dandy named Trevelyan. I couldn't stand him when we were in school together, and I'm damned sure I can't stand him now. She was planning to join him at the theater before she discovered that we're trapped in the house."

"I wonder if Poppy has someone lined up. Not that she thinks I'm dead, the way yours did."

"Why don't you go see your wife? I'll send the pardon after you."

"I can't say I'm overeager. We were complete strangers up to the moment when I was supposed to bed her, and I couldn't get a rise to save my life," Griffin said, a thread of amusement lightening his voice. "She was three years older than I was, you see, and when you're seventeen, the difference between a lad and a girl of twenty feels like a century."

"Seventeen is young."

"You weren't much older," Griffin retorted. "I failed to consummate my marriage and fled from humiliation. I got drunk, ended up in a pub, and next thing I knew I was bundled onto a ship and turned into a sailor. At the next port, I jumped ship and joined another crew, only to find out too late that it was a pirate vessel. 'Twas the beginning of a lurid career."

"On my wedding night the room was so dark that I don't think either of us had any idea what we were doing."

"Were you afraid that you'd be put off if you lit a candle?"

"Theo is beautiful," James said, admitting no arguments. "You'll see her tomorrow, if you get yourself downstairs before she leaves. Unless I miss my bet, she'll have herself and her maid out of the house not long after dawn."

"A far cry from the way those women used to flock to the docks when the *Poppy*s hove into view, isn't it? If my wife looks at me, all she's going to see is a crippled man with a bum leg. If your wife looks at you, she'll see the man who tricked her into marriage and is keeping her from this Trevelyan fellow."

"If I can persuade a woman who thinks I married her for her money that I want to take her back, surely you can convince your wife that you're not the limp lily she remembers?"

"You lied to her the first time around," Griffin said. "She'll never believe a thing you say from now on."

"My problem is not as great as yours," James replied, nettled. "Daisy used to love me, after all. *You* have to convince a reluctant stranger to give you another shot at intimacy."

"Neither one of us looks the part of the elegant wooer," Griffin said with a shout of laughter. "Want a bet on which of us gets his wife to bed faster?"

James found himself grinning back at Griffin. "*Not* the action of gentlemen."

"It's too late to claim that particular status. You can play the duke all you like, but a gentleman? No. You're no gentleman."

"If I take your bet, you'll have to take yourself off to Bath and actually talk to your wife."

"I might do it, just to beat you."

James was so restless that he couldn't sit still. He got up and walked to the window. "Damned if there aren't journalists perched on the garden wall!"

Griffin joined him just as two very large grooms strolled down the paved path, carelessly swinging mallets. The so-called reporters disappeared in a hurry.

"We're trapped here," James said slowly. The germ of an idea had just occurred to him.

Griffin pivoted. "I'll leave directly. The last thing I want is for my wife to learn from the *London Chronicle* that I've made my way back to England." He frowned, squinty-eyed, at James. "What in the hell are you grinning about?"

"Nothing! I'm off to talk to the butler. He has to do something about the crowd out in front of the house."

"Why don't you step out and play the big, bad buccaneer? That'll show them that pirates can't be caged."

"Not unless we choose to be," James said, knowing his grin had a calculating edge. "Not unless we choose to be."

Twenty-seven

Theo decided to go to supper wearing the green gown and the ruby ring. After a moment's thought she added a ruby necklace as well.

It rather amused her to think that she was dressed like a pirate's queen. Or would that be empress? Even her heeled slippers twinkled, as well they should, given their trim of diamond chips. Theo narrowed her eyes at her reflection. Surely the consort of a pirate glittered from head to toe.

She had the suspicion that pirates didn't have empresses. They had doxies. But one glance showed her that no one could possibly mistake her for a woman of the night. She looked regal, perhaps a bit too stern. As if she didn't laugh enough.

Theo frowned at herself again. Of course she laughed. All the time.

But as she descended the stairs, she couldn't remember when. Probably the last time she saw Geoffrey; he always made her laugh. Most likely he had a group around him at this very moment, and he was driving them into fits of laughter by describing the way the "savage" had waltzed into the House of Lords almost in time for his own funeral.

There was something remarkably tasteless about Geoffrey; the more she came to know him, the clearer it seemed. She didn't want to make fun of James; she just wanted to be free of him. In fact, she didn't want anyone else to ridicule him, either.

She was still thinking of Geoffrey's probable mockery of James when she entered the drawing room.

"Her Grace," Maydrop announced and closed the door behind her. For a moment her eyes met those of James, and then she saw his attire. Her lips parted in astonishment, and she came to a halt.

James was wearing one of the most extraordinary costumes that she had ever seen, in Paris or out. His coat was made of dull gold silk with a lustrous sheen. Under it he wore a waistcoat embroidered with roses, and fastened with azure blue buttons. His neck cloth was a glorious Indian silk dyed in colors that shifted from orange to rose. The final touch? Breeches that clung to every inch of his muscled thighs, tied with small rose-colored bows just below his knees.

Those bows were the most incongruous thing of all. Slowly, she looked back up his body. The costume was so beautiful as to be unmanly. The fabrics were exotic, and the tailoring Parisian: the collar was edged with deep cuts and much wider than worn in London. His breeches were tighter than Englishmen chose to wear them.

Yet no one could glance at the unmistakable aura of tightly controlled power that hung around

James like a cloak and ever, *ever* think of him as unmanly.

It was the first time in over a year that Theo found herself riveted by a bolt of pure sartorial lust. "Your coat," she said finally, "was made by Monsieur Bréval, was it not?"

James strolled toward her holding a glass of champagne. "That sounds familiar," he said amiably. "A round little man with very small feet and a propensity for gilt?"

"His waiting list is two years long," Theo observed, accepting the glass.

"Every man has his price, and, if I remember correctly, Bréval found himself dazzled by a garnet set in silver. If I had realized he was so sought after, I would have been less abusive when he wanted to decorate this coat with tassels."

Theo laughed and sipped her wine. A wash of relief hit her, so strong it made her feel a bit unsteady. James no longer resembled a pirate. His neck cloth fell in an expertly tied cascade; his short hair was tousled into a Brutus. True, he was large, but as always, in the right clothes, a man took on his best self. He looked every inch a duke.

"What exquisite silk," she said, running her fingers down his sleeve. It was only stupidity that had her noticing the contained power beneath the silk.

"How awkward," James said, after a tiny pause. "It's difficult to know where to begin with a spouse one hasn't seen in seven years. The weather doesn't seem an appropriate subject for conversation, somehow."

Theo walked away from him and sat down on a small settee. For a moment she thought he would take the spot beside her; there was something intense, almost lit-from-within, in his eyes. But instead he sat, most appropriately, in a chair opposite her.

"Will Sir Griffin join us for supper?"

"No. He had meant to leave in the morning to join his wife in Bath, but journalists crawling through the back garden changed his mind. He has already left, and asked me to give his apologies for not thanking you personally for your hospitality."

"His wife!" Theo exclaimed, distracted by the thought that there was another gentlewoman in her position. "Did *she* know he was a pirate? And that he was alive?"

"She knew he was alive," James said. "I'm not sure about the piracy."

"Well." She pushed away the fact that Sir Griffin Barry didn't leave his wife in the dark about his safety. Presumably they had not parted on such unpleasant terms as she and James had. "I would like to hear about the life of a pirate," she said, taking another sip of the champagne, and then putting it aside. She preferred not to drink overmuch.

"Ah, the life of a pirate," James said musingly. He put down his glass as well, permitting Theo to glimpse a narrow starched ruffle at his wrist, trimmed with metallic gold thread.

"Oh!" she cried, interrupting him. "Your ruffle is superb!"

He held out his arm, staring at it. "You don't think it's a trifle overdone? I thought so, but then a princess on the island of Cascara shared your enthusiasm."

From his smile, Theo surmised that James had pleasant memories of the princess. She straightened her back.

"She was quite bent on assuring me that my galleon would always have a warm welcome in her harbor," he went on. "Not that I chose to dock my ship in that port."

"Why ever not?" Theo said coolly. "Too fatiguing for a man of your years?"

"Too crowded," he replied, his eyes shining with wicked humor. "Pirates prefer to find an island so small that no man has walked her sand. We like to find a small haven that lies dreaming in the sun. Waiting."

Despite herself, she felt a smile tugging at the corner of her lips. James had loved punning nonsense when he was a boy. He used to make her laugh until her ribs ached. Perhaps he hadn't changed *that* much.

"So you'd like to know about the life of a

pirate," James said, stretching out his legs.

Theo jerked her eyes away from his thighs and looked at his face instead. When he was a young boy, James's face looked as if a master sculptor such as Donatello had carved it. She was never surprised that his mother considered him angelic: he had looked and sounded like a cherub, the kind who would spend his life singing hymns so joyful that birds would weep with envy.

No longer. His face had broadened along with the rest of him, and what had been elegant cheekbones had become more spare and brutal. His nose had clearly been broken in some conflict. And there was the tattoo, of course.

"What did you enjoy so much about that life?" she asked and held her breath. Despite herself, there was a silent addendum in the air: *so much more than you liked me.* Damn it, this was no time for vulnerable Daisy to make an appearance.

Yet it *hurt* to be hurt.

Twice, she had felt as if her heart was torn from her chest: when she realized that James had lied about his reasons for marriage, and when her mother died. The memory steadied her.

"You know what I'm like," James said lazily, ignoring, or not catching, the question she didn't ask. "As a boy, I was forever dashing out of the house, trying to calm myself by tearing around the garden. The first three or four years, I stayed in motion. Every day, all day. Sailing is hard work; taking down pirate ships is even harder."

"I can only imagine," Theo said. She got up and walked to the bell cord. She couldn't take much more of this intimacy. It would be better to be in the dining room, where she would have something to do with her hands and be flanked by footmen. "And what did you see?" she asked, seated once again.

He told her about huge fish that leapt from the water to smile at them, the long arms of an octopus, the dawn breaking over the ocean when all around there was nothing to be seen but blue water, bending gently to hug the curve of the earth.

When they moved to the dining room, James dismissed the footmen behind their chairs with a jerk of his head. Theo was about to protest that her household ran smoothly because . . . and realized it wasn't *her* household any longer.

But then he asked a question about the weavers, and it was such a pleasure to talk to someone interested—to whom she didn't pay a salary.

The candles guttered, and still they talked, on and on. A few times she reiterated that she would leave the house in the morning. But James seemed entirely reasonable in response, not at all like the ferocious brute who had snatched her in the hallway earlier that day.

In point of fact, he escorted her up the stairs and

ushered her into her bedchamber, bowed like a perfect gentleman, and withdrew.

It wasn't until Amélie had put her in bed that she realized that she felt a little sad. Flying fish had been enough to keep him from her?

She had been such a fool. Somehow she had preserved the idea of her childhood friend. And now, even as a grown-up version of that friend smiled across the table, urbane and charming, she wanted more. She wanted him to adore her, the way she remembered.

Obviously, he had changed.

In the end, she lay for hours staring into the dark, feeling a little maudlin from a surfeit of champagne. For all James said that he didn't sail into that princess's harbor, he probably did. And judging from his smile, the harbor had been seductive.

Curved, no doubt.

Theo could be charming, perhaps . . . but seductive, never. Her old ragged hurts presented themselves, and in the middle of the night, she decided that no matter how beautiful the silks and satins in which she draped herself, she still felt ugly. No need to refer to waterfowl of any variety.

Just *ugly.*

Not to mention sorry for herself.

It was all very depressing.

The next morning she woke feeling angry— mostly at herself, though she reserved a bit for

James as well. Couldn't he have simply stayed away and lived his life out with those golden island maidens with their hidden coves and all the rest of it?

She would have been a happy widow. She would have found a man with intelligent eyes and a thin face. He would have been strong, but lean. And very gentle. After a moment's hesitation she gave him a slightly longish chin. She didn't want beauty.

Every once in a while she would think about how amiably James had regarded her from across the table the previous night, and how kindly he had asked her questions—precisely as if he were a well-meaning uncle whom she'd somehow mislaid—and another little ember of irritation would light in her stomach.

When she finally came downstairs for luncheon, Maydrop met her at the newel post. "The situation has only grown worse outside the house," he told her, keeping pace as she walked to the dining room. She had taken only a cup of hot chocolate for breakfast and she was ravenous.

"Worse?" she asked, hardly listening. She didn't wait for him to open the door to the dining room but opened it herself.

James was sitting at the table, eating what looked to be half a roasted pig and reading a newspaper. Theo took a deep breath. He looked up and rose to his feet. "Forgive me for having started the meal. I erroneously believed you were not joining me for luncheon. I thought you were eating in your chamber."

"I *never* eat in my chamber," Theo said, keeping her voice level with an effort.

James's eyebrow shot up and he looked at Maydrop. "That would suggest you didn't have breakfast. Does no one in the household understand that you turn into a whirling dervish if you don't eat frequently?"

A footman held out a chair, and Theo dropped onto it. By the time she'd eaten a piece of trout, delicatedly cooked with just a touch of butter, she was feeling better.

James hadn't said another word. And he hadn't stopped reading the paper, either. If this was what married life was like, she wanted none of it. Courtesy was what made life tolerable. If people read newspapers when they should be engaged in civil conversation, they might as well just squat before a fireplace and gnaw on charred hunks of meat like savages.

Maydrop offered three different desserts, each presented by a footman who advanced one step, at precisely the same time. At least not everything in her household had fallen to pieces. She nodded at the pear cake.

Across the table, James drawled, "I'll have a piece of that as well."

Maydrop paced around the table, followed by the footmen.

"I saw what Her Grace was offered," James said impatiently. "There's no need to come around here." He pointed at the cake with his fork.

The air in Theo's chest felt heated, as if she'd walked into a smithy. But she began eating her pear cake, trying to ignore the fact that James was still reading. *And* chuckling as he read, but without bothering to share what amused him so.

"This is absurd," he finally said, raising his head. His eyes were brimming with laughter. "I've never seen this sort of paper before." He held up a page. "They don't name anyone except by an initial."

"Gossip rags. I don't have twaddle of that nature delivered to this house," Theo said. "Where on earth did you get it?"

"Maydrop sent a footman out for all the papers," James replied, turning back to his newspaper. "I wanted to see how my entry into Lords was described. Vulgar curiosity, I admit."

"And?" She took a last bite of pear cake, which was truly delicious.

"Her Grace will try the blackberry tart," James said, pointing his fork at the appropriate footman.

"I make such decisions for myself!" Theo flashed. She made it a practice not to overindulge in sweets. But the footman had already placed a slice of the tart in front of her. It smelled wonderful and she took a bite despite herself.

"Most of these descriptions are surprisingly

unimaginative and simply paint me as a savage," James said, a hint of complaint in his voice. "*Town Twaddle* is the best of the bunch; at least they put a little effort into it."

Theo was definitely feeling better. "Brute? Monster?"

"Neptune himself!" James said triumphantly. "Wait a moment." He rummaged in a stack of newsprint he had apparently dropped on the floor beside his chair.

Theo closed her eyes for a second. Of course she couldn't order Maydrop to clean up that mess immediately. A piece of loose newsprint drifted onto her foot and she kicked it away.

" 'He appeared from the sea like an ancient god,' " James read aloud, " 'his shoulders broad enough to carry the woes of a kingdom.' "

Theo snorted.

"What? You don't want to hear the part about how I tamed the waves?" James tossed the sheet across to her. It settled on top of the plate sticky with blackberry tart.

She automatically looked down and read the description of James. "You brought home a treasure trove?"

"Well, that's true enough," James said. "I had Maydrop stow it in the attics until you wanted to take a look."

Theo's eyes had moved automatically to the paragraph beneath, the one that described a "baffled world" waiting to see whether a certain duke would realize his wife was no more than Aesop's jay decked in borrowed plumes. They predicted he would choose to retreat, like Orpheus, to the land of the dead.

She didn't hear James move, but the paper disappeared from before her. With a curse she'd never heard before, he tore the pages to shreds and tossed them aside.

Theo looked up. "It's not that bad," she said, managing to smile. "I've got quite used to being compared to fowl of one variety or another."

James *growled*. He sounded for all the world like a crazed beast merely pretending to be a man. Scraps of newsprint were sticking to the butter, and a piece had fallen into her water glass.

"Maydrop," she said, "if you would summon the carriage, I shall be departing in the next hour or so."

A look of agony crossed the butler's face. "Your Grace, I would judge that to be impossible."

"I disagree," she said, her voice welcoming no further assessments.

The butler actually wrung his hands, a gesture Theo had never seen him do before. "The house is under siege, Your Grace!"

A voice at her side said, "Maydrop, I will convince the duchess." The butler and his footmen withdrew without another word as James drew her to her feet. Theo's head whirled. How dare he order her servants about? Except they weren't *her* servants; they were his.

"Come here." James pulled her over to the window and set the curtain aside with one finger. "Look."

Not only were people crowding the pavement, but they were thronging the street as well—and more looked to be arriving every moment. "Impossible!" Theo gasped.

"It's the same in the back. We cannot leave the house until this dies down, Daisy."

Theo considered snarling at him for not using her chosen name, but she managed to stop herself. She couldn't relinquish all civility simply because a foolish journalist had compared her to a jay. Jay, duckling, swan . . . no difference.

For a moment they merely stood there, James's body warm behind hers as they peeked through the curtain at the crowd excitedly milling about.

"I just don't see what's so interesting about our situation," she stated, watching as a group of young boys rounded the corner and joined the throng.

"Let's give the scribblers something to write about," James said.

Before she could answer, he jerked open the curtain, pulled her into his arms, and slammed his mouth down onto hers. Dimly, she heard a rising storm of voices, but she wasn't listening.

She had missed kissing. Not the bedding, but kissing.

He was hot and possessive and—

Protective. She jerked her head away. Pushing against him was like trying to move a block of marble. "I don't need you to defend me," she hissed.

James glanced at the window. Out in the street, people were jumping up and down, trying to see better. He raised his hand and waved at them.

"Oh God," Theo groaned.

Then he raised her chin with one hand and dropped another kiss on her lips, while with the other he jerked the curtains closed.

They stared at each other for a moment. The urbane sophistication of last night? Peeled away. That was *lust* starkly written on his face.

Pure, shameless lust.

A wave of panic hit Theo, and she stepped back.

"Daisy," James said sharply. "Daisy, you're not *afraid* of me, are you?"

She couldn't tell him the truth. Of course she wasn't afraid of him.

She was afraid of herself.

So she ran for the safety of her bedchamber.

Twenty-eight

For years, Theo's life had been beautifully organized. She knew each book on her bookshelves, each ribbon in her drawer, each gown in her wardrobe. She surrounded herself with beauty. Not one of her possessions was less than exquisite.

James used to have that glowing perfection.

But now—notwithstanding his extraordinary costume the night before—he was more brutal than beautiful. All his edgy energy was still there, but the excess had been converted into physical power. There was no question in her mind but that he would want to resume the undisciplined erotic relations they had briefly shared.

She would never do that with him again. *Never.*

Still, other than royalty, there was no more powerful man in England than a duke. If James wanted to keep her, he would keep her. And he would make sure she was in his bed.

Her heart started beating in her throat again in a desperate rhythm, and she suddenly felt as if the room was as hot as the inside of an oven. James would probably walk straight into her chamber this very night and demand his marital rights. The way he had walked into the bathing room.

He had the right. He had the right under English law.

She stood up jerkily and pulled her morning gown over her head, followed by her chemise. She'd wear sackcloth to dinner. She crawled into bed wearing no more than her drawers, curling into a ball as small and tight as she could.

Perhaps if she napped, she would wake to find

that this day had never happened. Perhaps she was in a fever dream.

After all, the fairy story was supposed to end when the Ugly Duckling became a swan. Everyone knew that swans got everything they wanted. Beautiful people always did.

She fell asleep thinking about beauty and dreamed that she was circling a ballroom on the arm of a man who was, quite literally, radiant. She squinted, trying to see whether his skin was actually incandescent.

"Yes," he said to her, his voice gentle. "I am one of the blessed."

The old, familiar sense of being a lesser being descended on her like a blanket. It didn't matter how she dressed, she would never be able to *glow,* for goodness' sake.

He whirled her faster and faster . . . and she woke with a tear sliding down her cheek. Theo had never been good at lying to herself. She didn't feel like a swan. She felt like one of those china shepherdesses that the old duke prized at such a low rate.

She felt like an empty vase, a useless woman whose husband ignored her existence for seven years. The kind of woman stupid enough to marry a man who had inherited a capacity for criminality.

The first tear was followed by another, and another.

She was just getting control of the heaving sobs when she heard the door to the room open. "Amélie," she called, her voice scratchy. "Bring me a handkerchief, if you would."

There was no use trying to hide a fit of sobbing from one's maid. Amélie knew everything about Theo's life, and she always would.

So she remained curled up, as tight as a dormouse, and when she heard footsteps, she held out her hand. Sure enough, a soft handkerchief was pushed into her waiting fingers.

"I find myself rather demoralized," she said, wiping up a last tear. She'd cried so hard that her hair was wet under her cheek. Her eyes and throat burned. "Would you be so kind as to have a pot of tea sent up, please?"

But instead of Amélie's soft footsteps stealing away, the bed swayed as someone sat down beside her. Someone who weighed a good nine or ten stone more than Amélie.

"Oh *bollocks*," she whispered, closing her eyes.

"Is that your strongest oath?" James asked curiously.

"I have a better one," she said between gritted teeth. "I'm reserving it for direct address. Would you please go away?"

There was a moment of silence, almost as if he was pretending to think about her request. "No."

She should sit up, confront him. But she was too miserable, too beaten down, too sorry for herself,

301

if the truth be told. So she pulled the sheet higher around her ears and shut her eyes a little tighter.

"Did I tell you what pirates do after a hard day's work?"

"Other than walk spare personnel down the plank?" she snapped.

"After that," he said, agreeably enough. "A pirate captain can't afford to lower his guard. So Griffin and I never joined the crew's celebrations."

Theo was trying to breathe quietly, but a shuddering hiccup surprised her.

"I wash in hot water. Then I wrap myself in a blanket and go to sleep." He stood up, and his footsteps receded into the bathing room. A moment later she heard the squeak of the pump, and the rush of water into the bathtub. Grief and exhaustion seemed to have slowed her thoughts to treacle.

She even fell back asleep for a moment or two, listening to the rush of water. But she woke the moment she felt herself being plucked from the bed. She held onto the sheet as tightly as she could—which meant it came with her. "Stop," she said, clearing her throat when her voice emerged in a thread of a whisper. "Put me down!"

"In a moment."

From her position in James's arms, she could clearly see the scar that traversed his neck. It made her feel quite odd. She rather hoped that he had managed to kill the pirate who had done that to him.

But then he set her on her feet and towered over her, huge and male. Air played over her skin—and she was suddenly aware that her sheet had disappeared, leaving her naked but for her drawers.

The sound that emerged from her throat was like the screech of the peacocks that strolled the grounds of Buckingham Palace. "What in the devil do you think you're doing?"

She reached out and snatched the sheet back before James could reply. He lost his balance and toppled against the wall. "Get out of here!" she cried, her voice breaking. "What are you doing here? Where is my maid? Why can't you simply leave me alone?"

"I came instead of your maid," he said, righting himself.

"Leave!" Theo flashed, feeling better now that she had covered herself again. Her eyes burned and were swollen, and her voice was jagged. Her entire body ached with a terrible, withering exhaustion that she hadn't felt since her mother died.

She took a deep breath. "I must ask that you give me some privacy. I realize that you are likely not used to such on board ship, but I need to be alone."

In his eyes she thought she saw the dim shadow of the old James, her childhood companion. "You should get in the bath," he said. "You'll feel better. I can tell you've been crying."

"Brilliant deduction," she said flatly. "When I take baths, I take them alone. Good-bye."

"Why are your drawers so plain?"

"What?"

"Your drawers. I remember them as confections of French lace, ribbons, and silk. I spent a good deal of time thinking about them on board ship."

She frowned. "My drawers are plain because I put away childish things."

"I liked them."

"So much you didn't want me to wear them!" The sentence hurtled out of her mouth without conscious volition.

"That was just erotic play," he said, shrugging.

"Those garments were frivolous," she said, rather coldly. And they reminded her too much of that dreadful afternoon: since then, she had never worn anything next to her skin but unadorned, austere linen.

His hand twitched and she narrowed her eyes. "Don't think of snatching my sheet again or I'll put a knee where it will hurt most."

There was something in his face . . . he looked *sorry* for her. Or was it *pity?* Theo swallowed. That was the topping to a truly wonderful day. "Could you please leave the bathing chamber? If not from common courtesy, then simply because you respected me once? *Please?*"

His eyes were shuttered, and she couldn't tell what he was thinking. But rather than leaving the room, he sat down on the maid's stool in the corner. "No," he said.

"Then I will leave," Theo said, turning. "Thank you for pumping the water for my bath."

He sprang up and caught her wrist before she could take more than a step.

"What are you doing?" she gasped. Then her eyes flew to his. "You—you didn't ever *force* women, did you, James? Not that?" Despite herself, tears sprang to her eyes again.

A low growl erupted from his chest. "How can you say that to me?"

"Because you're a pirate. Because you—you . . ." Her voice choked at the look in his eyes. It wasn't angry as much as hurt.

"Are you afraid that I would do such a thing to you?" His voice was raw, with a dark edge.

Theo swallowed. His eyes had taken on the bruised blue of the sky before a storm. "Of course not." She didn't succeed in making the statement quite convincing. The worst of it was that she wasn't entirely certain that she would resist.

"I have *never* forced a woman," he said, his growl a sudden reminder of his voice's pure beauty. Before.

"But you have killed people," she said, biting her lip.

"Only when I had to. And never an innocent: under my command the *Poppy Two* attacked only pirate ships flying the skull and crossbones, as did the *Flying Poppy* from the moment Griffin and I joined forces."

"No walking the plank?" she asked, despising the pathetic note of hopefulness in her voice.

"No." His eyes held steady on hers, and although so much had changed about him—his very body was different, and his voice was gone, and his face had matured—his eyes were the same. Prideful and honest.

Honest?

Another wave of exhaustion hit her. James wasn't honest. He had tricked her into marriage, lied during his vows in front of God and man. She turned on suddenly unsteady legs and collapsed on the stool he had just deserted.

Then she made sure the sheet was decently covering her, folded her hands in her lap, and looked down at her toes. "This will not work," she told him. "Ever."

"Why not?" He sounded reassuringly calm.

"I've changed. I'm not easy anymore. I prefer my life to have order in it. I prefer to be respected and honored in my own household." She waved her hand in the steamy air. "Let's be honest with each other, shall we? I loved you once. I believe you loved me too, although you didn't feel it strongly enough to thwart your father. Still, before your father forced the issue, I had no idea that I loved you—at least, not in that way."

The memory of their intimacies presented itself, and she flinched.

"What?" he asked, instantly.

"In retrospect, there were some very disturbing aspects to our relationship, in particular to our marital relations," she said, adding: "I was quite angry at you, but I gave that up several years ago."

"Until I made you angry again by appearing at the House of Lords."

She looked back at her feet. "I do not offer this as an excuse, but it was difficult being known as a woman so ugly that her husband could not tolerate living in the same country with her. I am perhaps overly sensitive to slights as a result."

"You didn't reveal the truth about why I left because any explanation would implicate my father and his financial dealings," James said slowly. He sat down on the edge of the ceramic bathtub.

She didn't reply.

"They truly believed I fled the country because I thought you were ugly?" He sounded stunned, which was gratifying. After her mother, James had always been her blindest supporter.

"It took me a few years to stop listening," she continued. "But once I made the estate profitable again, I went to Paris, and when I returned to London last year, I wore a cape of swansdown to Cecil's ball."

He didn't even smile.

"I was a success," she insisted, leaning back against the wall.

"You are gorgeous no matter what you wear," he said flatly. There was no compassion in his eyes; as he had never accepted that she was less than beautiful, he couldn't celebrate her triumph as a swan.

"My point is that when you appeared so suddenly in Lords, it played into my rather overwrought sensibilities, and I did become angry. I do accept that you attempted to contact me in the morning, but the fact that I had no idea you were alive until the moment you identified yourself will confirm the impression that you couldn't bear to live with such an ugly woman. Still, I'm not angry about that anymore," she added, striving for a bright tone and not succeeding in the least.

"That is absurd." His face was utterly expressionless.

"I'll move to France," she said with sudden urgency. "I'll move anywhere, James. Just please, let me be who I am now. I can't pretend that the girl you married will ever come back. I can't—I could not go to bed with you." Despite herself, a drop of liquid disgust curdled in her voice.

His shoulders tightened. After a moment, he said, "Because you despise me for leaving or because of the way I have changed?"

"*I* told you to leave. Believe it or not, I accepted blame for my rash statement long ago."

"I had no intention of slighting you in front of the House of Lords."

"So you said, and I believe you," she said, ladling on reassurance. "So I think—I hope—we can simply be honest with each other, like the friends we once were, and with respect to the affection we once shared."

He muttered something.

"I'm sorry?"

"It was love, not affection," he said, raising his head.

"Of course," she said lightly. "I've come to think of our marriage as being very like Juliet and Romeo's in its brief intensity. I expect it was a good thing that we were never tested by life. Our love was too passionate, like a summer storm that quickly dies down."

"I disagree. I think we would have had children by now," he said evenly. "We would have fallen more deeply in love. I would have confessed why I married you, at some point, and you would have forgiven me, because that's what people in love do."

There was a fierce, intense spark in his eye that made a shiver streak down Theo's spine. "It might have happened that way. My point is that we can't pretend that those emotions can be reawakened. They cannot. I truly think that the courts would be willing to grant us a divorce, even if they rarely grant divorce. They do so in extraordinary cases."

"The extraordinary case being my career as a pirate."

Her voice came out a little apologetic. "Even if you never walked anyone down the plank."

"Or forced any women."

"Yes, even though. You see, it's enough that they *think* it is so."

She didn't care for the tight control he kept over himself, she realized. It was almost better when he used to lose his temper and shout. Now the very air around his head seemed to shimmer with feeling, and yet he didn't raise his voice an iota.

"You want me to pretend to be a rapist and murderer so that our marriage can be dissolved." He said it flatly.

"No!" She half-shouted that.

He didn't reply.

"Of course I don't want anyone to think that you are—that you are those things. Indeed, I'm so relieved that you are not. I think just the fact that you . . . well, you look quite different than you used to, James. You're so large. And you're tattooed. Your voice . . ." Her own voice trailed off and she gestured aimlessly. "We don't belong together."

"Why not?"

She almost laughed. "I would be willing to wager that I am the most organized woman in all London. That's how I managed the estate and built the ceramics and fabric concerns. I make lists.

No"—she corrected herself—"I make lists within lists. Life is so much more pleasant and efficient when everything has a proper place."

"I do not understand why your abilities as an estate manager preclude marriage to me."

It was not said aggressively, so she tried to explain. "I take a great many baths, and I like them to be precisely the right temperature. I had the pump in the bathing room installed so that the servants didn't have to haul water up the stairs; this way it comes straight from the copper in the scullery. My baths are scented with three drops of primrose oil. Not just any oil, but a particular fragrance that's made for me on the Staffordshire estate."

James didn't look impressed.

"Life is easier, much easier," Theo told him, "if you eliminate questions that other people dither about. My bath is scented with elderflowers throughout the winter, but I switch to primrose on April first."

"You're rigid as a picket fence," he stated. It wasn't the first time something like that had been said to her.

"I suppose I am," she said, nodding. "I prefer to think of myself as logical. I know precisely what I want to put on for any type of occasion. I don't own more gowns than I can use, and I wear them exactly the same number of times before I give them to my maid. I never have to worry about finding myself in a gown that's out-of-date or showing wear."

He tilted his head slightly, and she felt a tiny pang of sorrow for the young James of her memories. That was one mannerism he'd had since boyhood.

"Is such a level of rigidity necessary?"

"No one is harmed by it. My household runs like clockwork. I am comfortable and happy. My employees know precisely what is expected of them, but in return, I don't ask more than they can achieve."

He still didn't appear to have been won over.

"My system allows me to be far more productive than most women—or indeed men," she pointed out. "Generally speaking, gentlewomen are required to do little more than run a household."

"I apologize for leaving you with the responsibilities of the estate," James said quietly.

Theo smiled, quick and sweet, and suddenly his own Daisy was there again, if only for a moment. He had a sudden feeling of vertigo, as if the world had tilted slightly to the side.

"I liked being left with the estate," she admitted a bit sheepishly. "My mother told me before she died that I had no right to whine over the end of our marriage, and she was right. I am happy telling people what to do. I probably never would have made a very good wife, but I do make a good duke."

James thought about that for a moment or two. One had to assume that there was room for only one duke in any given duchy. "I am very sorry about the death of your mother," he said at length. "When did that happen?"

Theo's face clouded, and she looked back at her feet. "A few years ago. I still miss her."

"I miss my father." He said it conversationally, but he couldn't bring himself to look at her, so he turned and put his fingers in the water. It had turned cold, so he began pumping again.

"I am so sorry about his death," Theo said. "He was quite confused when they brought him home after his heart seized, but he didn't seem to be in pain. He simply drifted away during the night."

James swallowed. The water was throwing up steam into his face. He could feel it beading on his eyelashes. "Well. One of my many errors. I should have liked to have been with him."

There was nothing she could say to that.

"And I would like to avoid another error and remain married to you," he stated. He stopped pumping, still not looking at her. Annoyingly, his voice was not as even as it could be.

She didn't answer, so he glanced at her and thought he saw pity in her eyes. He straightened and wiped away the drops of water that clung to his skin.

"You are my friend," he said, rising and walking to the side of the room farthest from her. "I would

313

like to be married to a friend. You knew my father, all the bad and good sides of him. I would like to be able to be honest with my wife, to have her understand that it is possible to love someone and hate him at the same time. Even though he's dead."

She gave a little huff of laughter. "You changed while you were gone, James."

"There's not much to do on board ship but read and think. I fell into the habit of reading philosophy."

"But you were a *pirate!* Pirates don't read philosophy. And I thought you hated reading."

"We were not pirates. We were privateers who attacked pirates. We spent a great deal of time lurking in navigational routes, pretending to be innocent vessels, flying the flag of the kingdom of Sicily, waiting for a bunch of cutthroats to hoist the Jolly Roger, as their flag is called. Most of the time life at sea is rather boring; I chose to occupy that time with reading."

"But you always hated being bored," she said.

She looked a bit better. Her eyes weren't as red, and her mouth was curving in a little smile. When Daisy smiled, she was the prettiest thing he'd ever seen.

With an effort, James reminded himself of his plan. Trevelyan would never lunge across the room and kiss away a smile. She hadn't taken well to his kiss in the breakfast room. The kiss that had sent him reeling merely seemed to throw her into a panic.

"I had to learn to control myself," he said. "On board ship, you can dive from the railing and swim beside the ship if you feel restless. That sort of frequent physical exertion was very beneficial to me."

Her eyes drifted over his chest and she nodded. "I see that."

"I am not so large," he said, a little defensively.

"I didn't mean to imply it. I think we're talking at cross-purposes, James. I would also like to be friends with my husband. But I know you too well. You do not really want to be merely friends with your wife. You want more."

"I do want children."

She nodded. "Yes, and more than that." She held her body so still that it might have been carved from wood. "You want all that heat and passion, and I cannot do it."

"Why not?" He involuntarily snapped the question, so he took a breath. "I realize my appearance has changed, but you might become used to it. Or is it because I was not faithful?"

"No." She had begun pleating and repleating her sheet, which pleased him because it showed *some* sort of reaction to what he was saying.

"No to infidelity, or no to my horrific appearance? And voice," he added, remembering how she loved to be sung to. If he sang to her now, it would probably frighten her out of a good night's sleep.

"Neither. That is, none of the three. You're as James-like as you ever were, I can see that now."

He could feel the corner of his mouth curling. Many women had called him beautiful; he preferred *James-like*. "In that case, why won't you consider bedding me?"

She gave a little shudder, and to his shock, he realized that what he had seen was a genuine sensation of distaste. Disgust, even.

"I can't do that again. My feelings partly stem from the shock of what happened with your father. But I would have come to this realization even so," she said more confidently.

"Come to what realization?"

"I am simply not that sort of person. All those things you asked me to do—not wear drawers under my gowns, leave my hair down although the servants would surely see—those sorts of things are abhorrent to me." She was being utterly truthful. He could see it in her eyes. "I can't imagine what came over me to acquiesce in something so distasteful. Although I don't want you to think that I am being critical of you and your needs. I am not." She sounded very earnest. "It's just not for me."

He cleared his throat. It was a shock to realize that the world could give you guilt of so many

316

kinds, some that pierced the heart, others likely to fade. The fact that he had somehow been party to killing Daisy's joy in intimacy, the delight with which she had welcomed his touch and found pleasure in their bed . . . that guilt didn't seem likely to fade, the way his response to his father's death had.

On the other hand, he was no nineteen-year-old, crippled by his own remorse. He could change her mind. Even if it took him fifty years. He couldn't do anything about his father, but he could try to mend this.

"I think you're wrong," he said, keeping his voice gentle.

"I know myself." She said it with utter assurance, the confidence of someone who had had no one but herself to rely on for years. "You and I always were opposites in that respect."

"I am comfortable with my body," he said.

"You always were." Her face was drawn and too severe, but for just one moment he caught sight of the dimple in her right cheek again. She had always had only one dimple, as if a pair would be too exuberant. "If your tutors had simply driven you around the stables like a horse that needed breaking, in between Greek lessons, you would have been a happier student."

"I got in a lot of fights at Eton, and that helped."

The dimple again. "Piracy, I suppose, was just an extension of the schoolyard and its squabbles."

317

"Piracy played to the recklessness that I inherited from my father."

She nodded. "That makes sense."

"Unfortunately, danger is not as exciting as it looks. I learned that exercising the mind can be as interesting as exercising the body."

She nodded.

He chose his next words very carefully. "It seems to me that you responded to the unfortunate end of our marriage by going entirely in the other direction. I threw myself into danger, you surrounded yourself with sterility."

"Sterility is not a very nice word, but I see what you mean. I am quite happy without demeaning myself on an intimate level," she explained, again with that air of utter confidence. "That is why we should dissolve our marriage, James. I know you want a woman who will submit to you. And again, I do not mean to be critical. I will never be that woman, and I cannot be that woman. I would hope that neither of us would want the other to be in a perpetually unhappy arrangement."

"No." But he found himself in the grip of one of the fiercest emotions of his life: he wanted Daisy back. Not Theo—or rather, because he admired Theo, he wanted parts of Theo. But he didn't want to be responsible for having snuffed out Daisy's joy. He couldn't bear it.

And he *needed* her. Without her, he might as

well walk the plank himself. Not that they ever did that to a man. He'd be the first.

She smiled at him obliviously. "You will find a woman who likes your sort of intimate play. And I may find a man who is more akin to my temperament. Or not." She shrugged. "I would like to have children, but I am quite happy by myself."

From what he had seen of her so far, Daisy was probably the most lonely person he'd seen in years. After he had left England, Griffin had become his right arm, his boon companion, his blood brother.

But Daisy had remained alone.

If he agreed to her tomfool plan—not that he ever would, because the mere suggestion made him want to smash his fist into the wall—she would marry Geoffrey Trevelyan or someone of his ilk. Trevelyan was completely uninterested in sensuality. If they ever had children, it would practically be a miracle.

If there was one thing he was sure of, it was that he would die before he allowed Daisy to make love to anyone except himself. Ever.

"Is something wrong?"

"I don't want to marry the sort of woman you're talking about," he said bluntly. "And you might think that you want to wed Trevelyan, but you would find bedding him to be incredibly distasteful. Even worse than you seem to imagine bedding me."

"Perhaps," she said. "But—though I would point out that I never said anything about Geoffrey as a possible consort—he would understand my disinclination to submit to the sort of feverish embraces that you prefer. I would actually guess," she said thoughtfully, "that Geoffrey would find marital congress as objectionable as I."

" 'Marital congress?' "

She ignored his interjection. "Geoffrey and I are both adults. Distasteful or not, we would engage in carnality as required in order to procreate. Actually, I would say that Geoffrey and I are alike in that. I'm not so much disinclined to bedding sports as I think I am incapable of responding in the way that you desire. I cannot stay married to you, James. I think it would tear me apart."

James was thinking as quickly as he ever did in the heat of battle. None of his reading on board ship—in Machiavelli, in the arts of war, in the philosophy of the ancient Greeks—was helping him in this most crucial moment of his entire life. He could have bellowed with pent-up fear and rage, but instead, he closed his eyes, ignoring Theo for the moment.

Then he tried to sort through the tendrils of shame, guilt, rage, and—yes—love that bound them together. There was a reason he could speak of his father only to Daisy. There was a reason he was able to express his own self-loathing and regret to her, and feel cleansed and forgiven by a glimpse of her dimple.

They were bound together, and probably had been from the summer when he was blind and she became his eyes.

He couldn't imagine how he had lived without her for seven years. She was like sunlight. Like food and drink.

He walked toward her, every bit of his body concentrated on her. She was *his*. She was all that he wanted, all that he had ever wanted, even though he had lost track of that truth for a while.

"James," she said, a slight warning in her tone.

He closed his hands around her slender waist and plucked her to standing, careful not to disturb her sheet.

"I want you," he said. For the first time, his altered voice sounded just right. He *should* be growling at the wife who didn't want him, who thought she never wanted to be in bed with him again. The sound was fitting.

He didn't want her to speak more of those words that caged her as surely as iron bars, so he bent his head to her lips. They were lush and sweet as he remembered—and he did remember, even all these years later. He had never forgotten their first kiss.

He almost lost his head, but he caught himself. He had to make her comfortable with him, in essence, to act like the castrated male she thought she wanted. Griffin would think it was the stupidest thing he'd ever heard of. But Griffin wasn't a woman who had experienced precisely two days of married life, seven years ago.

Griffin wasn't his adorable, controlled, rigid Daisy.

She pushed him away, and he stepped back instantly, remembering to smile.

Twenty-nine

"There's something I must tell you that you don't understand," James said.

His expression made Theo fidget. She wound her sheet more tightly around her breasts. "What I don't understand is why Amélie, my maid, hasn't appeared. I rang for her long ago."

"I told her to go home; it's her mother's birthday."

"But—" she said, and stopped. She hadn't known it was Amélie's mother's birthday, but if it had truly mattered, Amélie would have asked for the day off. Theo prided herself on never being unreasonable to any staff request stemming from personal life.

"I suspect she didn't want to upset your routine."

"There would be no upset," she explained. "When Amélie takes her half-day, Mary helps me. She's very well trained."

"I sent Mary home as well."

Theo frowned at him. "One of them is always with me. My gowns are not like gentlemen's clothing. I generally don't bother with corsets, but if I had worn one under my morning gown, I would still be in it now."

"You have no need for a corset," James remarked, his gaze frankly admiring.

"Yes, well," she told him. "I can't expect you to understand. I'll just have to fetch one of the other maids."

He shook his head.

"You didn't!" She dropped back onto the stool.

"I thought it was a perfect moment to give the staff a treat. I want them to like me, you see. And it's very unpleasant for them being in a house under siege."

"They will always like you as long as you continue to pay their wages. You didn't let them *all* go home, did you?"

"Everyone except for Maydrop and his footmen, who are guarding the house."

"Are you mad? Who will bring us food? Who will . . ." She looked around wildly.

He smiled at her. "Maydrop had the staff leave in several carriages, confusing the gossip-mongers."

"How will we dress for calls tomorrow morning?" she demanded. "You cannot think that I will traipse down to the drawing room in a state of disarray?"

"Any visits we receive would be from people thirsting for a close look at my tattoo. I'm not receiving callers, and neither are you. In fact, I had Maydrop remove the knocker. I'm hoping that between the confusion caused by the staff leaving in different carriages and the missing knocker, the hordes of hacks will come to the conclusion that we managed to give them the slip and flee to the country."

She had forgotten how avid the *ton* would be to get a close look at the pirate duke. Strangely enough, he looked more and more like the old James to her all the time.

"Well, perhaps it is better that we remain here," she said, somewhat reluctantly. The next day or so would be a trial, but it was better than playing host to inquisitive crowds. "You were right," she said, giving credit where it was due. "It would have been a dreadful crush once people began to pay calls."

"Yes." He was lounging against the wall in a way no gentleman would, looking slightly amused by the whole situation.

"If you'll excuse me," Theo said, changing the subject, "I would like some privacy to take a bath."

"As we are virtually alone in the house," he responded, "I wanted to clarify one mistake that you're making. You believe that I am the same young man whom you made love to seven years ago, with the same needs and desires as I had then."

She started to speak, and he held up his hand. "Back in '09, we made love because we were in love."

Theo nodded. All this steam was dampening her hair and causing strands to fall over her eyes. She remembered how much he had loved her curls, and quickly sleeked it back from her forehead.

"In the interim, you have changed," James said.

"Obviously," she said, pushing away the image of herself hanging over him like a streetwalker, teasing him with her hair. She must have been out of her mind.

"What I've been trying to tell you is that you have not allowed for the possibility that I have changed as well. I assure you that I have. I'm no longer a young lad."

"You are not yet thirty."

"With age came control." His smile was a bit smug, though she didn't think it would be polite to point that out. "I was angry several times today, but I did not lose my temper."

"I noticed that; it's a remarkable achievement, given your family background," she offered.

"For every good, there is a darker side." He sighed. If she didn't know better, she would think that he was being melodramatic. Yet James didn't have a melodramatic bone in his body.

Her bottom had begun to ache from the stool's

hard little seat, and she stood up. Amélie often sat there sewing while waiting for Theo to finish her baths. The stool would be much more comfortable with a padded seat. She made a mental note.

"We'll practically live like savages in the next few days," she said, changing the subject, "but new experiences are always worthy of note."

James gave a bark of laughter, and before she could stop him, he walked across the room, put a hand under her knees, and scooped her up against his chest again.

"You really must stop this!" she cried. But he was pushing open the door to her bedchamber with his foot. It was very peculiar, being in his arms. She hadn't really noticed before, but his forearms were corded with muscles. Or perhaps she had noticed.

"Daisy," he said, his voice managing to be severe and amused at once. "Do you truly think that we will live like savages, given the splendor of your bedchamber, not to mention the rest of this house?"

Of course the room was very luxuriously appointed. The Venetian silk drapery was a particularly elegant touch. "We have no servants," she said, pointing out the obvious. "Life without servants is terribly uncomfortable. Will you please put me down, James?"

"Not yet," he said. "I like holding you." Then he

did the oddest thing: he bent his head and dropped a kiss on her nose.

It was as soft as the touch of a butterfly and just as fleeting. And yet somehow it jolted down her entire body.

She saw two of him for a moment: the sleek, young husband of seven years ago, and the huge pirate of now.

Any moment he would probably get that hungry look in his eyes. She began to struggle in earnest. "Put me *down!*"

He did.

"Here's what I'm trying to tell you," he said very rapidly, before she could speak. "I'm not as young as I was, Daisy. I don't have that same sort of uncontrollable desire anymore. Yes, I would like to make love to my wife. I want to have children. But do you want to know precisely how many women Jack Hawk made love to?"

She scowled at him. "No."

"Three," he said. "Three. And there were many months, as many as eight, between the days when I saw one of my mistresses. That's what they were: not lovers, but mistresses. In the last year, I slept with no one. In fact," he said thoughtfully, "it's been about sixteen months. Griffin and I went to China, and then we were on our way to India when we were attacked. It took months to recover from the wound to my throat."

Theo glanced at his scar and shuddered.

"Did you hear what I said, Daisy?"

"You are not the womanizer that the Bow Street Runner described," she said obediently.

"Along with control of anger comes control of desire. You cannot do one without the other."

"Why not?"

He shrugged. "All I can say is that I don't have any particular wish for the sort of fervent encounters that we shared when first married. I certainly do not want to make love in the drawing room, or indeed, anywhere other than in complete privacy, under the covers of a comfortable bed."

"I don't care to make love at all," she said, squinting at him in an effort to see whether he appeared truthful.

"As I said, I want to have children. And I want you by my side, Daisy. I am completely in control of my appetites, and in case you're wondering, I will not be unfaithful to you ever again. I will never take a mistress."

Despite herself, a little flare of hope lit in Theo's heart. It would be so nice to have James back if she didn't have to worry about those bedroom activities.

But she didn't quite believe him. "I'm certain that I saw something in your face earlier."

"When?" His voice sounded sleepy, tranquil, and he seemed utterly relaxed.

Maybe she was wrong. Maybe what he really meant was that he preferred the lush rounded bodies of those mistresses of his. He would have control around her because he was used to such beautiful women.

She bit her lip.

"I can prove it to you," he said.

"You can?"

"Take your bath, and I will act as your maid."

"No!"

"Why not? You *know* that I would never force you to do anything, Theo. You must know that." His eyes caught hers. "I may have married you under false pretenses, but I never said anything to you that I didn't mean. When we made love, I told you everything I was thinking."

"I suppose that's true."

"I sang to you."

Theo broke into a crack of laughter. The horror in his voice was so *James.* If he truly didn't want to rekindle all that erotic nonsense, then she would quite like to be married to him, tattoo and all.

"Will you grow your hair again?"

He frowned. "If you wish. But no singing. I can't sing anymore."

"I can hear that." It made her sad, but he was grinning, so she was the only one who cared.

"I would like your children," he repeated, and again she could see the honesty in his eyes. "Even though you've become as rigid as a picket fence, you're still my closest friend and the person I admire most in the world. And who knows? Maybe you will learn to relax."

"No, I won't," she said. "You'll understand if you live with me for a while. I take the time to think out the best way to do things, because that way, I needn't think about that specific problem ever again."

He shrugged again. "I'll take your word for it." He pulled off his coat.

"What on earth are you doing?"

"Naked, you can tell whether I'm telling the truth or not," he said, sounding reasonable, but insane.

"You can't simply take your clothes off . . . oh my God. Is that another scar?" She took a step toward him. This one ran from his right shoulder over his stomach. It was white and taut against skin that was the color of dark honey.

"Bayonet," James said cheerfully. He bent over to remove his boots, and suddenly she was presented with a swell of shoulder leading down to a powerful male back. He was beautiful. That is, he was still beautiful. His body was like a powerful machine. Muscles moved smoothly under his skin in a way that made her fingers itch to touch him.

"There's another one!" she gasped, seeing a white slash halfway around his waist.

"Saber slash," James said, tossing off his second boot, followed by his stockings. "The souvenir of

330

a foolish Frenchman who fancied he was fighting a duel. I shot him."

"How many times did you nearly die?" Theo asked, hearing the faintness in her own voice.

"Only the once," he said cheerfully. He put his hands on his breeches.

"Wait!" she said, but somehow her voice came out breathy rather than decisive, and he pulled down his breeches and smalls without hesitation.

And there he was. He was bigger—all over. Surely he wasn't that big seven years ago. No.

She pulled her gaze away. "I thought you were in control of your lust," she said accusingly. The very sight of him had her on her toes, ready to bolt to the other room. There was a key in the library door. There—

But his gaze was still tranquil, impassive. "I am."

"Then why?" She nodded sharply toward his groin.

"Oh this?" He gave himself a careless pat. "Don't you remember this?"

"I do. And it should be . . . it should be down."

"Down?" He cocked an eyebrow. "Do you remember me ever being down?"

Theo scowled at him. "Perhaps not. But I'm sure that it's supposed to be down."

"Not mine," he said, giving himself another pat. "I'm up all the time." He had already turned away from her and was walking back toward the bathing chamber.

She stared after him, utterly nonplussed. His buttocks were the same honey brown as his arms. How was that possible? She remembered distinctly that his bottom had been pearly white. Now it was more defined, and a different color. As if he'd been in the sun without clothing. Curiosity drove her after him.

James was pumping hot water into the bathtub for the third time and testing the temperature with his finger. "How did you say that you like the water?"

"Not too warm," she said cautiously. Really, his body was so strange. Any one of those wounds could have killed him if he'd caught an infection.

"Were your wounds ever infected?" she asked.

"A couple," he said, not turning around. A chill crept down her back. She knew infection. She lost one of her scullery maids when the girl cut her finger. One of the ceramics workers died after accidentally burning himself.

"You could have died," she stated. And then, because she needed to get his attention and make him understand, she walked over to stand beside him. She was a tall woman, but next to James, she felt small. Almost delicate, which was a joke because no one could ever call her delicate.

He straightened up and smiled down at her. Smiling made the poppy under his eye shift slightly, as if it were a real flower stirred by a light breeze. "I suppose I could have, but I didn't. I seem to have the constitution of an ox. How's the water?"

She leaned over and put in a finger. It was perfect.

"May I take your sheet, Your Grace?"

She looked again, suspiciously, at his tool. It was straight upright, the way it always was, if he was to be believed. And when she looked back into his face, he gazed back at her limpidly, with an expression that seemed almost bored.

"All right," she muttered.

Everyone knew that men were compulsively lustful. A man couldn't avoid a surge of desire if he merely glimpsed a woman's breasts.

Though perhaps if the woman's breasts were very small . . . if the woman was lean and had no curves . . .

Theo sighed and dropped her sheet. She refused to be humiliated by her own appearance anymore. She had learned that if she pretended to be a swan, she could fool the majority.

Though perhaps not without clothing.

Without further ado, she removed her drawers, stepped into the bathtub, and sat herself down. Before she asked, a huge male hand held out a bar of soap.

It was the vervaine that she used in every bath, and she took it. But just as she was about to start soaping, he took it away again.

Startled, Theo looked up. James was much

closer to her than she had thought, kneeling beside the bathtub. "You needn't," she began.

But he said, "How else will you see how calm and unaffected I am? There's no reason to be afraid of me, Daisy. I'm in perfect control."

Theo swallowed. It didn't feel like the best thing in the world to learn how very unaffected her husband was by the sight, not to mention the shape, of her body. But that was life, wasn't it?

At least she wouldn't have to do those freakishly odd things he had asked of her back when he was attracted to her. Back before he met dusky island maidens with curves like one of Titian's women.

"All right," she said. She stole another glance between his legs. Goodness, his tool was large. And red. It looked painful to her, so rigid that it seemed like to burst. But presumably that was just the way it was for a man.

She automatically held out her arm, because Amélie bathed her upper body (though not her breasts, of course), and then, while Amélie washed her hair, Theo washed her lower parts herself.

James was quite methodical while washing her arms. It felt good to be touched. Since her mother died, no one had touched her for any reason, except Amélie.

After all, she was a countess. People didn't hug a countess, or do more than touch her gloved hand in the briefest of kisses. She missed . . .

Well, she missed simple touches.

So she let her head fall forward and didn't talk, just enjoyed a touch that seemed so undemanding and yet so pleasurable. It was all right to enjoy James's touch, whereas it was pathetic to be comforted by Amélie's. She *paid* Amélie.

He soaped up one arm and across her shoulders. "Compared to yours, my back is terribly skinny," she said, feeling a little awkward. "You have so much muscle there."

"I suppose."

"Does your throat hurt, if you don't mind my asking?"

"No. Why do you ask?"

"It sounded so rough just now. As if it hurt. So I'm glad it doesn't," she added quickly.

His hands were so large that they spanned her entire back, and his soapy fingers made her feel exquisitely sensitive, as if every touch left a little kiss in its wake. She never felt this with Amélie, thank goodness.

She bent forward slightly, hunching so that he wouldn't realize that her nipples were hard. He truly wasn't affected by her nakedness; he was breathing just as regularly as he was before.

That was one thing she remembered quite clearly from their bed play together. When he was aroused, his breath came fast and his chest heaved. His eyes had been bright like fire, and his fingers had trembled. She glanced down. He was soaping her left wrist with hands as steady as they could be. A little sigh escaped her.

That was life.

If she'd learned anything since the day her life fell apart, it was that her life didn't fall apart. One can survive a missing husband, and a dead mother, and being known throughout the British Isles as ugly. It was all survivable.

Difficult and demoralizing, but endurable.

"Your leg, please," James said. His voice still sounded painfully hoarse, but she wasn't going to mention it again.

Amélie never touched her below the waist, but Theo straightened one leg and put her ankle in his hand anyway. After all, her legs were her best feature: slender, with lovely round kneecaps and delicately curved ankles. It was a stupid thing to hold onto, but when one doesn't have much to celebrate in the way of physical attributes, ankles matter.

James began soaping one rather slowly. He'd told her once that she had beautiful ankles.

"I like my ankles," she said, wanting him to notice again. He drew a finger down the sole of her foot and made her squeal. It was very playful.

Theo had to swallow hard, because this wouldn't have been so silly years ago.

"It's hot in here," James said. He wiped his face with his forearm. He did look rather red.

"I can do the rest," Theo said, pulling her foot

from his hand. "You've proved your point, James. I can see it."

"See what?"

"That you're not attracted to me. So just give me the soap."

She reached out for it, but he held it away from her. "You're not taking this seriously."

"I most certainly am," she snapped. She'd taken it about as seriously as she could without bursting into a howl of aggrieved femininity.

James rolled his eyes. "If I don't wash all of you, Theo, you will always have questions in your mind. I want us to remain married." He reached out with a soapy hand and caught her chin. "Our children will probably be informed precisely the time at which they are allowed to wet their diapers, but I still want you to be their mother."

She could feel a crooked smile on her mouth. "Oh. Thank you." He had used twice as much soap as Amélie, and bubbles slid down her chest as she bent toward him.

They both looked down at the same moment. Bubbles were flowing down the slope of Theo's breasts.

"Yes, well," James said, and then he moved around behind her and she heard a stifled noise, almost a groan.

"Are you all right?"

"I'm not used to kneeling on a tiled floor," he confessed, and she heard a thread of amusement in

337

his voice again. "I would be a terrible grumbler if I were a lady's maid."

"Amélie doesn't clamber around my tub on her knees," Theo said. "So what—" She broke off. James's hands made a slow slide over her shoulders and down her front. His touch lit a fire in her stomach, even before he touched her breasts.

"I don't think that is necessary," she said, catching her breath on a gasp. He had a breast in each hand now.

"Breasts are just breasts," he said. "Of course, your breasts . . ." His voice trailed off.

Her nipples looked like pale rosebuds peeking through his brown fingers. She thought they looked quite nice. Then he slowly rubbed a thumb across each one, and it felt so amazing that she sucked in her breath and forgot to wonder about whether or not James was aroused, because *she* was. In fact, her head fell back against his arm, eyes closed, because he was doing something with his thumbs that had nothing to do with cleanliness.

It was as if lightning jolted through her, electrifying parts that hadn't been touched for seven years. Even the private place between her legs suddenly tingled, as if to tell her that it was still there.

The moment she realized *that,* her hands clapped over his. "What are you doing?"

"You said I'm not attracted to you, Daisy." His lips brushed her ear. "You're wrong. I've *always* been driven mad by your breasts, and you know it." At the moment she could only think about what a simple touch of his lips had done to her. "Don't you remember?" he murmured, kissing her ear again.

"Yes," she said weakly. "At the dining room table."

"I used to sit there and dream about touching you like this," he said, his voice like a caress. "I would watch you talking and think about how beautiful and intelligent you were, but to be honest, my eyes just kept going back to your breasts. There were times when I thought I might lose control, right there in the dining room."

Theo kept her hands over his, but she did lean back against him again. "Surely not."

His laugh was ragged, but somehow just as sensual as it had been. Perhaps even more so. "I promise you that was the case. I was capable of fantasizing about you through four courses. After the dessert, I would hobble from the room." Under her hands, his thumbs moved gently across her nipples again.

Her toes were curling, and she was having trouble remembering her name, let alone what James looked like as a hungry youngster on the other side of the table from her.

"Are you saying that you might have trouble straightening up?" she said, finally managing to come up with some sort of sentence. She seemed to be losing strength in her limbs, which would explain why her hands fell away from his, letting him play with her breasts all he wanted.

There was a moment of silence, and then he said, "I told you I'm in control these days, Daisy. But you have to let me prove it to you."

She was starting to feel feverish, and even though she knew it was muddled thinking, she let herself pretend that what he was saying made sense. "Prove it how?" she whispered.

One of James's hands skated across her stomach on a film of soap, slipped under the water, drifted between her legs, the place where she felt open and vulnerable and soft. "Like this." His voice had slipped from ragged to guttural. The very sound of it made her feel like a smoldering log, about to burst into flame.

"May I touch you?" James asked. He didn't wait for an answer, but did something intimate with his fingers. Her answer was lost in a gasp.

"Just so I can prove my self-control," he added.

She could have pointed out that she wasn't demented. That she knew an excuse when she heard it. But her mind had turned black and ravenous, and the groan in her chest turned to a little sob. She pushed against his fingers, thinking, *Harder, there, please, there!* And as if he could hear her, one broad finger pressed down sharply, and another did something else, invaded her in just the right way.

Just like that, Theo broke, with a little shriek and a shock to her body that made her arch up and half out of the water. She only dimly heard soapy water splashing onto the floor, because everything in her was focused on the hot ripples spreading through her body.

Then James's fingers slipped away and he pulled her a bit more firmly back against his arm. While she was still reeling, he leaned down and whispered in her ear, "If Amélie performs that service for you, I'm dismissing her tomorrow."

A giggle broke from Theo's lips. "Don't be absurd." Her body was limp, and she felt swollen and hot between her legs.

"In fact, no one can touch you like that but me," he added, and now his voice sounded not casual, but hotly possessive. Before she could answer, he rose to his feet, bent over, and scooped her into his arms.

It felt different now that they were both naked. His skin burned against hers.

"I must be heavy," she murmured, stealing a glance up at his face. Against all common sense, she wanted to see arousal there.

She saw none.

Rather than answer, he set her on her feet and rubbed her briskly with a towel. Even the touch of the rough fabric gave her a wanton pulse of pleasure.

James's jaw seemed taut, but then he looked at

341

her and smiled. She reached out and took her wrapper off the hook, pulling it around herself and knotting it tightly.

Tossing the towel aside, James picked her up again, as if she couldn't walk to her own bed.

"Don't smile at me anymore," she said tiredly, turning her face to his chest and closing her eyes. "I learned my lesson."

"Lesson?" He sounded puzzled.

"You're in no danger to succumbing to lust. I understand." It wasn't overly painful to acknowledge it aloud.

He dropped her on the bed and frowned at her. "That's what you want."

She rolled off, coming to her feet, and flapped her hand at him. "It's not important. I need you to help me make the bed. I cannot rest in a bed with rumpled sheets, and of course, the top sheet isn't even here any longer."

He blinked at her. "What are you talking about?"

"We have to remake the bed," she said painstakingly. "I would ring for a maid, but you sent them away."

"Right. If you'll excuse me, I have something to do." Theo's eyes dropped and she saw that he had a hand cupped over his privates, as if he was in pain. He brushed past her and into the bathroom without another word. *That* wasn't very polite.

She had no idea how to make the bed, but surely

she was capable of it. She pulled all the remaining bedding off, and then made certain that the bottom sheet hung off all sides by precisely the same amount: she judged four and a half inches, though of course it was hard to tell without a way to measure it.

She tucked the sheet in at the head of the bed. That was rather awkward, as she had to reach toward the middle of the bed. She could hear water running into the bathtub again, which was distracting, but it didn't bother her much. James's "personal" service, for lack of a better word, had left her feeling quite happy.

She moved around to the side and managed to get the sheet tucked in precisely the correct amount.

She had just started the other side when the door opened again. She was bent over the bed, trying to make sure that the sheet didn't form wrinkles as she tucked.

"Oh good," she said, looking over her shoulder. James's tool was down, the way she had thought it was supposed to be. With a mental shrug, she said, "Will you please help me? This is impossible to do on one's own. I can't imagine how the house-maids manage it." She moved to the foot of the bed and bent over again, trying to smooth the sheets so there were no wrinkles.

There was a funny noise, like a deep groan, but when she looked back at James he was obediently walking toward her. His tool was straight up in the air again. So he was telling the truth about that being his normal state.

She kept thinking about it all the time that they worked on the bed, making sure the top sheet was smooth before they replaced the rest of the bedding.

Every once in a while she would steal a glance at James. She felt terribly self-conscious wearing a wrapper with no drawers and no chemise, but he seemed unmoved.

When the bed was finished, she slipped between the sheets, still wearing her wrapper because she couldn't bear the idea of being naked in front of him again.

He stood beside the bed, that irritating smile on his face. "Are you hungry? I'll have Maydrop send up a hamper with one of the footmen. I think if we eat here, it will be easier for him, given the lack of kitchen staff."

"I never eat in bed." But she was ravenous.

The amusement on his face vanished. "You will tonight. You're not to even think about leaving that bed. I'm not touching those damned sheets again." Annoyingly, he seemed to be showing more emotion over the bed than anything else. Such as the almost naked woman lying between the sheets.

The emotions in Theo's chest were so turbulent that she didn't even frown at his blasphemy and the set of his jaw. There was a naked man in her room. Staring at her belligerently over his folded arms.

She started that train of thought over. There was a naked *pirate* in her room, and she wasn't frightened by him in the least. What's more, she let her eyes drift over his scarred, muscled body and didn't shy away from the fact that the sight of him made her own body feel needy. For some reason, every scar sent a little thrill to her toes. She glanced at his scandalous tattoo. It made her feel a melting rush of desire.

James—make that Jack Hawk—was glaring at her as if she were no more than a pirate's captive. Theo found that a little smile was curling her lips at the thought. She had been a prisoner, of a sort. Not to James, but to her own fear.

She ran over that old memory of the library again, testing it with the detachment of seven years. It *was* embarrassing. But all of a sudden, she remembered the utter beauty of James's young, lean body. The way he had thrown back his head in utter bliss. The groans that broke from his lips when she caressed him.

"Well?" he demanded.

Her husband was a pirate. But he was also a man who had loved her deeply. Who had pleasured her, and then happily succumbed to *her* seduction.

"Well, what?" she asked, unable to remember what he was talking about. Her mind was reeling. For a moment, she remembered the pain of being called ugly, and then it melted away like soap washing down a drain. She had told herself a hundred times that she could be humiliated only if she allowed it: now she needed to believe it.

The same was true for intimacy . . . for marriage. She *had* been a prisoner, but not to a pirate. She had been trapped by her own fear. In fact, she'd been something of a coward.

Without a second thought, Theo shrugged off her wrapper, taking her time since the sheet slipped below her breasts in the process.

James watched her, his face impassive, but she thought she caught a glimpse of something deep in those blue eyes: shock, perhaps, and a touch of hopefulness.

She handed the wrapper to him with her sweetest smile. "You wouldn't mind hanging this up, would you? Since there's no one else here to do it for me?"

The sound he made might have been a growl. It made Theo feel a little better, even more so when he took one look at her sitting up in bed with the sheet barely covering her nipples, and then stalked out of the room.

"Put on some clothes," she called. "I don't want you to horrify Maydrop with all those scars."

The only answer was a soft thump as the door pulled firmly shut. She instantly hopped out of bed and brushed her teeth. Then she combed out her hair.

When she heard footsteps walking up the stairs, she got back into her bed, dismissing the unease she felt about crawling into a rumpled bed. Who would have thought that making a bed was so much work? James entered with a hamper and set it on her dressing table. Then he grabbed the bottle of wine and took a swig straight out of the bottle.

Theo would have liked a drink, but she could hardly say so now.

He poured her a glass straight from the same bottle. "I couldn't," she said politely.

"It's been a hell of a day," James said, pushing the glass into her hand. Then he narrowed his eyes. "You're saying no because I drank from the bottle, aren't you?"

"We all have different standards of hygiene," she said, sounding prim even to her own ears.

"Are you afraid of my mouth? Of my *spit?*"

"It's just—"

He leaned over, fast, put a hand behind her neck, and pulled her toward him. Theo closed her eyes reflexively when his mouth met hers. But the kiss wasn't what interested him: his tongue thrust into her mouth, warm and wet and aggressive.

She couldn't summon any interest in the lesson he was doling out about spit and wine bottles. She wanted him to look at her with eyes that glittered, the way they used to, years ago, so she wound her arms around his neck and kissed him back. She was chasing the promise of his tongue, the way it reminded her whole body of deep pleasure.

A while later, she took a deep, shuddering breath. James straightened, seemingly reluctantly, and turned away. His back was to her, so she savored the curve of his buttocks and the thick muscled weight of his thigh. And the fact that he was shaking slightly.

By the time he turned around again, he clearly had himself in check.

"Well," he said genially, "how about a piece of chicken?"

Theo eyed the wine bottle and thought about how satisfying it would be to knock him on the side of the head with it and chase away that maddeningly amiable expression. Instead, she did something that was as foreign to her character as throwing a ruby overboard would be to a pirate.

She reached over, grabbed the bottle, and brought it to her mouth. The wine was wonderful. It tasted of peaches and summer and the sharp smell of crushed flowers.

It was probably the best wine she'd ever had in her life. She had lost her grip on the sheet during their kiss, and when she lay back, she felt her breasts slip free. She didn't bother to pull the sheet back up. Instead, she lolled against the pillows and took another swallow of the ambrosial wine. With her eyes closed.

For once, she didn't have to watch her guests, waiting to see if the vintage would be pleasurably received. She didn't have to analyze the flavor to ascertain whether it agreed with the course before them.

Instead, she drank for no other reason than delight. The cold wine slid down her throat as if it had been pressed from fallen stars.

Thirty

James had experienced pain, of course, but he couldn't remember ever being in as much agony as he was at this moment. Theo was lolling back against a mound of pillows, her gorgeous, pink-tipped breasts beckoning to him like the finest sweetmeats heaven could offer, and he had to stay on his side of the bed. He had to.

This was a siege, a long-term battle. He made himself think about how long it had taken to put on those damned sheets; his desire cooled an infinitesimal amount. Though, of course, his cock-stand was going nowhere, and his balls would probably fall off by tomorrow morning.

After a while he reached over and pulled the bottle away from her. Her eyes were a bit glazed. He suspected that she hadn't had more than a sip of wine in years. If that much.

"Chicken," he said, pushing a piece into her hand. "Eat this."

Watching her lush lips close around the chicken leg like a sailor gulping fresh water after months at sea, he reached down and gave himself a hard flick. The flare of pain at least kept his self-control somewhere within grasp.

"Doesn't it hurt to do that?" she asked. She was ogling him from top to bottom, and he made sure he was lying on one side, like one of those decadent Romans in a bath. He felt like an idiot, but if she liked what she saw, it was worth it.

She would find her desire again. He knew she would find her desire. It couldn't have permanently disappeared, not the huge well of sweetness and joy that had filled both of them when they made love years ago.

"Not really," he replied.

"Tell me more about being a pirate," Theo said. Chicken leg demolished, she now reached for a ham tartlet.

James swallowed hard. He had to stop thinking about her breasts and the color of her lips and how unbearably desirable she was with her hair slicked back like that, all cheekbones, plump mouth, and silky eyelashes.

"I told you I was never was a pirate," he said, almost apologetically. "That's why I'm not worried about an arrest. When we recovered items from royal treasuries, we gave them back, and in so doing were granted documents which permitted us to fly Spanish, Dutch, and Sicilian flags."

"Isn't it twice as dangerous to attack hardened pirates?" She had finished the ham tart and was making progress on another. He'd forgotten what an appetite she had: the way she was able to eat a grown man under the table and not gain an ounce.

"It was rather like being a member of the navy." He dragged his eyes away from her glossy lips. "Once we identified the target, generally because they made themselves known by putting up the skull and crossbones, we took them down."

"A navy of two ships," Theo said musingly. "What were the most difficult ships to defeat?"

"Slave ships," he said without hesitation.

"*Slave ships?* Pirates are *slave dealers?*" Her mouth formed a perfect circle.

This was never going to work. Sooner or later he'd find himself begging her to do that thing she never wanted to do again.

"Pirates take over slave ships," he said, taking a deep breath. "Because the booty is human, they don't simply transfer the slaves to their own ship. Instead they transfer some crew over to the slave ship, who sail it to a port where the cargo can be converted into cash. We attacked any vessel we could identify as a known slave ship, pirate or no."

Theo's mouth was a thin, hard line now, and she put down her half-eaten tart. "Absolutely reprehensible. Revolting. I hate the whole business. It's a crime that so many countries have hesitated to follow England in abolishing the trade."

"I agree."

Her eyes lit with amusement. "I'm glad to hear that, because the Duke of Ashbrook, or rather his estate, has supported efforts to make the owning of slaves illegal, not just trading in them. Sad to say, it has cost us hundreds of pounds in bribes."

James nodded. But there was something he had been wanting to say. "Theo"—he used that name deliberately—"I can see how well you've run this household. But can you tell me how in God's name you managed to get that sorry excuse for an estate to the point where we could spare hundreds of pounds even for the best of all causes?"

"I began with the weavers," she said, smiling. "Do you remember that I had the idea of asking them to reproduce cloth from the Renaissance, the old figured fabrics that are so hard to find these days?"

"Yes, but as I recall Reede was unsure that the looms would be able to create such complicated patterns."

"One of the first things I did was let Reede go," Theo said, without apology. "And it was only partially because of that mess with your father and my dowry. He simply didn't have the guts for it, James. He didn't."

"What kind of guts do you mean?"

"We had to take risks in the beginning." Theo picked up her tart again, and began telling him the story of how she discovered that the weavers at Ryburn Weavers were all women, but the managers were all men. "I was always having to talk to the weavers about colors, you understand, James. Florentine blue is a very hard color to achieve, for example. If we wanted to create proper copies of Medici fabrics, we had to create it. Reede couldn't stomach it."

"Couldn't stomach what?"

"I finally let the men go," Theo said, a spark of mischief in her eyes. "Instead, I put one of the weavers, a redoubtable woman by the name of Mrs. Alcorn, in charge. It was one of the smartest things I ever did, but it nearly gave Reede apoplexy."

"What was so wonderful about Mrs. Alcorn?"

"Well, for one thing, she arranged for a loom to be smuggled from Lyons."

"Smuggled?"

"We were unable to make shot silk. It turned out she had a cousin, who had a friend, who had a French brother . . . before I knew it, we had just the right loom."

James laughed suddenly. "So neither of us made our money entirely on the side of the law."

"Ryburn Weavers are far from being *pirates*," Theo said loftily.

"What about the ceramics company? How on earth did you get that off the ground? Did you steal someone from Wedgwood, the way Reede suggested?"

"Oh no. There was no need for theft."

James leaned forward, loving the combative look in her eyes and the smugness in her voice. "Tell me."

"I offered them a proper wage," Theo said with a grin. "They came to me with no need for stealing or bribes. I'm afraid that some people at Wedgwood were *dreadfully* upset, but really, I had nothing to do with it. It was a decision made entirely by the men in question. I didn't contact a single soul at Wedgwood. But if their workers discovered what I was paying, and shared that information with their friends, it was hardly something to blame me for."

James burst into laughter.

"From the very beginning, I had the best crafts-men working on our kilns," she said, finishing her tart. "I decided that we should specialize in ceramics with Greek and Roman patterns, and luckily those pieces have proved very popular in London."

"It's not far from your idea for the weavers," James said, fascinated. "Renaissance fabrics, Greek ceramics . . ."

Theo hopped out of bed and ran across the room. James instantly forgot the subject of conversation. Theo from the back was a revelation: long graceful legs, a sweet, tight rear, shoulders that were as elegant as the rest of her.

Lust swept up his body as if he were nothing more than a bundle of twigs hit by a forest fire. He could feel his eyes glazing as she climbed back onto the bed, clutching a large leather folio.

She curled her slender legs to the side, twitching the sheet over herself, and opened the book. "Here are the fabric samples from Ryburn Weavers this year," she said. "See this?" She pointed to a fabric and he made an effort to pay attention. It was a black cloth. Just beyond the edge of the book the sheet had slipped and he could see her thigh and a patch of skin so sweet and delicate that he longed to lick it.

"It's a pattern of birds in flight," Theo told him. "You can't see the repeat unless you look very, very closely."

"Lovely," James managed.

"One of my weavers lost her baby," Theo said softly. "She designed this because she wanted to think that her daughter flew to a better place."

"Truly lovely," James said. And this time he meant it.

"We sold thirteen bolts in one week after the Prime Minister was shot," Theo said, her voice reverting to brisk practicality.

"He was?" James raised an eyebrow. "What was his name? When?"

"Spencer Perceval," Theo replied, looking surprised. "He was assassinated in '13. Didn't you get any news while abroad, James?"

"Very little. I'm looking forward to reading the newspapers every day."

"It shows a grim side of owning a business concern," Theo said, "but the truth is that the poor man had thirteen children, and his widow loved this design. Suddenly everyone was wearing our fabric. I felt sad and triumphant, all at the same time." She hesitated. "You must have felt the same at times, James."

He nodded. "The slave ships were heartrending, not because of the fight, but because of what we'd find on the ships once we'd overtaken them."

"I've read about it. Filthy stinking holds crowded with humans, dead and alive, none of them fed properly or given light or even ventilation. Despicable!"

Her voice shook, and he loved her more in that moment than he had realized possible. His Daisy may be rigid, but she was ethical to the very core of her being.

The same second, it came to him that he might take advantage of that decency. "We would dispatch the slaver dealers during battle and then give the men and women on board the choice to sail their ship back where they came from—along with a good amount of gold coin—or continue with us, and we'd drop them at our next harbor, again with all the treasure we'd found on board the pirate ship." He gave her a pious look and then held his breath, hoping.

Sure enough, Theo leaned over and put her lips to his, in a little girl's version of a kiss. In response, James carefully rolled onto his back and, equally carefully, pulled her on top.

She looked down at him in surprise, but he opened his mouth and welcomed her in. Her velvet tongue tangled shyly with his. Though James felt as if his body was blazing, he managed to keep the kiss relaxed and easy.

"I like kissing you," she whispered, some time later. Her lips had turned ruby red.

"Not as much as I love kissing you," he said honestly.

She ran a finger along his eyebrow. "If that were true, you would never have stayed away for seven years."

"I was on the verge of coming back after two or three years. I had a heap of fabric for you in my cabin that I'd confiscated from pirates. I couldn't stop dreaming about you. I kept rethinking what I should have said after you overheard that conversation with my father. Most of my solutions involved locking the bedchamber and making love to you until we were both senseless."

A smile trembled on the curl of her lips. "That wouldn't have worked at the time."

"But would it have worked if I had returned two or three years later?"

She was silent a moment, the brush of her finger unbearably tender as she traced the shape of his tattoo. "It might have. Why didn't you return?"

"Father died, and I wasn't with him."

"Oh, I see." She dropped a kiss where her finger had touched.

"I fell off some sort of cliff," James said with a grimace. "I know my father was a fool and a swindler. I spent my boyhood dodging flying objects he'd launched at me, and trying to ignore his outlandish schemes. When I left England, I thought it would be blissful never to see him again. He had traded my happiness for stolen money, as I saw it."

"But?"

"I would guess that he died grieving, because he didn't know whether I was dead or alive. In his own way, he loved me."

Her eyes fell.

"Did he die asking for me?" His voice scraped like iron on iron.

Theo ran a hand down his cheek. "He was confused. He did ask for you, so I told him that you had stepped out for a moment but you would be there when he woke. He fell asleep with a smile on his face. And he didn't wake up."

At this, James waited a second until he had control of himself again. "Father was a criminal, and a fool, and all the rest of it. But he loved me. I was his only child, and his only tie to my mother. He loved her too, for all he said it was merely a prudent marriage."

Theo nodded, then bent her head and dropped another kiss very precisely onto his tattoo.

"I don't know what happened to me," James said. His hands instinctively rounded her bottom, settling her more snugly into the cradle of his legs. "I think I lost my mind. I shaved my head. I took a mistress, and then two more, because to my mind, I was such a worthless person that it was better to betray you than return to England."

Her next kiss dropped onto his lips.

"I killed James Ryburn," he said flatly. "I became Jack Hawk, and I swore I would never return."

"Until your throat was cut."

"Yes." He looked at her and hesitated, the truth on the tip of his tongue. But she wasn't ready yet. "When I survived against all probability, I realized that I wanted to come home. Of course, by then Griffin and I were very successful privateers. I do have a pirate's treasure in the attic, and even more in various banks around the world. But I wanted to come back to England and not be in danger every single day."

"To sum up your career at sea," Theo said, smiling at him, "the British government is more likely to knight you for services to the empire than they are to arrest you for piracy."

"Yes." A great peacefulness was descending onto James's heart.

"You could have been killed rescuing slaves," Theo told him, her face taking on that queer seriousness that came so easily to her. "I'm proud to be your wife."

He preferred her dimple, so he pulled her head down and gave her a hard kiss. It wasn't until they were both gasping that he said, "Daisy, making love needn't include the parts that you don't like. Because there are parts that you do like."

She bit her lip.

"You liked it when I touched you in the bath," he pointed out, gentling his voice.

Surprisingly, she grinned at him. "Only an idiot would dislike that."

"And you like kissing—"

"May I say again, I'm no idiot?"

"I would never again ask you to walk around the house without drawers."

"*Why* did you ask that?" She looked genuinely curious.

"I was mad with lust for you. And I was drunk on the fact that you were responding. I had some sort of inchoate idea that I would make love to you everywhere in our house, on the stairs, in the butler's pantry, on the window seats, and that it would be easier without drawers because I could simply pull up your skirts. It was stupid. But it was the kind of thing a young man dreams about."

Her finger was tracing his tattoo again. He liked it. But at the same time he was starting to feel unhinged. Her soft body against his was driving him around the bend. He tried again to rein in his lust. If he gave her the faintest idea of how it was raging through him, she'd be out the door.

Instead, he carefully put on the sleepy, amused expression that covered up everything else.

"I suppose," she said. But there was discontent in her tone.

"And I wanted to kiss you in your sweet spot," he said, succumbing to the truth. "Hell, I wanted to kiss Bella there, but she never permitted it. I love that part of a woman, especially yours. You're all soft and pink and you taste so good, Daisy."

"Theo." But her voice was gentle.

"You must remember that I was only nineteen. I had no idea what married couples did or didn't do until my father blurted it out. Men don't talk about that sort of thing. And I wasn't the sort to form close friendships with other boys."

She nodded.

"I always had you." He watched her closely, cataloguing her every blink. "I would *never* have asked for something you might feel demeaned by. When you offered to kiss me in the library, it was the most sensual thing that had ever happened to me. It never occurred to me to say no. I would have stripped myself in Kensington Square if you had asked me to. I was in love with you, but I was also overwhelmed by love of your body and fascinating with making love to you."

"So it was all new and raw to you as well?"

He nodded. "Bella had been my mistress for around a month, I believe. She would allow me to have some time with each breast, and then it was time to do what I paid her for. And that was that."

"Dear me."

"I didn't even like her breasts; they made me feel as if I might drown in all that flesh, whereas yours . . . You know how I feel about *your* breasts."

He liked the smile in her eyes. He liked it so much that he would spend his whole life just trying to get her to smile at him like that. But there was one thing that was bothering him, and he knew he had to confess before they could make love.

"I must tell you something you won't like."

"Oh?" The bleakness in her eyes replaced her smile as fast as summer lightning.

"I bet Griffin that I could get my wife into bed before he got his wife into bed."

She pushed away from him, tumbling onto her knees. *"What?"*

"I bet Griffin—"

"I heard you. Why on earth would you do such a thing?"

She looked down at him, eyes sharp and disapproving. But not horrified. He saw that. Not horrified.

"Because I'm an idiot. I made up a reason to woo you. But the truth is that I just wanted you back, Daisy. I came home for you."

It was all so complicated. James said he wanted

her, but then he placed bets about whether she would let him into her bed. Theo wrapped her arms around her knees, realizing with a shock that the sheet had slipped, and she had been naked for some time without even noticing.

The actions that had seemed utterly demeaning and horrible a day ago didn't feel that way now. Of course, she knew what had happened. She had fallen as stupidly and helplessly back into love as any mouse into a trap.

James was still talking. "I can help run the estate now, you'll be glad to know. I managed all Griffin's and my finances."

"Those bank accounts?"

"Gold," he said, sitting up and leaning back the headboard. "Jewels. Five bank accounts in various countries. A scepter. That sort of thing."

Theo uncurled her legs and climbed down from the bed. "This is a mess," she said, surveying the remains of their picnic, hands on the curve of her waist.

It wasn't possible for James to be any harder, but he managed it just looking at her.

"Are you still hungry?" she asked.

"Yes," he said, not really listening.

"For *food*," she clarified.

"No."

"Good." She reached over, collected the plates, and put them neatly on her dressing table. She then collected the wine bottle and glasses, the napkins, and the little cakes they hadn't touched, and added all of it to the pile on the table. "You need to move," she informed him.

James rolled off the bed, telling himself that he was probably going to spend a good deal of his life being told what to do. And making beds. It didn't matter. He wouldn't trade one of her commands for a moment of piratical freedom.

"Now we're going to tidy this sheet," she announced.

He eyed her. "I think we should go to that island we own and live in a hut with no well, only one stream, and no sheets at all."

"I think not," she said. "If you stand on that side, we can get this nice and tidy again."

He obeyed. "And then?"

"And then we will put the coverlet back as well."

"And?"

She looked up at him, and the expression in her eyes sent a bolt of heat straight to his groin. "Then we're going to make love the way respectable married couples do."

"We will?" His voice came out in a groan and he snapped the coverlet over the bed as if a tornado had entered the room. "What way is that?"

"Under the covers," Theo told him. "In the dark."

"Right." He cared neither where nor how it took place as long as she would consider letting him back inside her delectable body.

A few minutes later he learned that when his wife said "dark," she really meant it. Theo snuffed the candles and turned the Argand lamp down to a dim glow, and then had to feel her way in the dark back to the bed.

He heard a thump and a "drat" that made him grin. For his part, his eyes adjusted quickly; he was used to stealing aboard ships in the dead of night.

By the time she made her way under the covers, James was shaking all over with less-than-altogether-controlled desire.

But he had one last thing to tell her first.

"I love you." He whispered it into the darkness, running his hands through her sleek hair. "You're too elegant for me, and too beautiful, and far too smart, but I *still* love you, even given those drawbacks."

She snorted, but then she turned her head and kissed his wrist. He'd take it.

James was sure of one thing. He would keep the sheets over their heads, if that's what she wanted. He didn't need light. All he needed was her warm, sweet-smelling body twisting under his hands.

He gloried in the way she arched toward him with a sigh of relief when his lips found hers, and her squeak of pleasure when he ran his fingers up her inside thigh, her moan when those fingers moved on to warmer and wetter areas.

Every time their movements disarranged the

sheet, he pulled it back into place. No words were exchanged, until he was kissing his way down her stomach.

"Are you . . . you aren't going to do *that,* are you?"

Her voice came with a little pant, it gratified him to notice.

"Yes," he said, trying to keep his voice mild and detached—and failing. "I am. I must, Daisy. You never said *this* was distasteful."

He thought she muttered something, but it wasn't in a *Theo* tone of voice, so he took it as a yes. Surely she would be Daisy for him, now and then? Between the sheets?

She tasted like the sweetest nectar a god could wish for. He licked and played and did all the things he spent seven years dreaming of doing. He eased her legs apart to give himself more room and kept exploring until he could feel tension building in her body. When she was strung tight as a wire, her breath escaping in tiny gasps, he slowed down and practiced torment.

And when he could feel that she was on the very edge of breaking, he raised his head and said, from under the tented sheet, "I don't think we should have babies, Daisy."

He heard a mumbled expletive, followed by a sharp "Don't stop!"

"But I have something to say," he persisted. "As I said, I don't think we should have babies. I've

366

changed my mind." He blew on her, very gently, and ran his thumb down all that silky skin.

She trembled under his hands and then the sheet was snatched off and tossed to the side, and she cried, *"What did you say?"*

"No babies," he said, easing his finger into a passage so tight and wet and hot that he nearly came on the bed, in a way he hadn't since he was sixteen. He stifled a groan and dropped his hand down to readjust himself.

"Why?" she asked in a husky whisper.

"I'll never be able to love anyone the way I love you. I don't think I ever have, in fact. I'm a limited person. I wouldn't want to make a child feel unloved." It was a trifle manipulative, but at the same time, it was true. He couldn't imagine having any love left for a baby.

He slid a second finger inside her. She gave a little shriek.

"Hadn't you better pull up the sheet?" he asked, raising his head again.

"You!" she said, and the command thrilled him to his bones. *"Don't stop."* He obeyed her command.

When she was sobbing and shaking, he crawled back up her body and whispered, "Would you be more comfortable if I were to lie on my back?"

She didn't seem to be thinking clearly, so he rolled over, lifted her into the air, and put her gently in position.

"Might I ask you to lower yourself a little?" he

367

asked politely. He kept his hands loose on her arms, though he wanted nothing more than to pull her down and thrust up into her wet warmth.

"Yes, of course," she said. She sounded a bit odd.

"I won't last very long," he said, gasping as she slid lower.

She stopped.

"Daisy?" James's hands were shaking, so he made himself let go of her arms and grip the sheet instead. He couldn't frighten her. He couldn't provoke a disgust for him.

Damn, she was pulling away. He gave a silent groan: this was agonizing.

"I want a lamp," she said, stumbling away from the bed. A gentleman probably would have risen to help, but James didn't feel like a gentleman. He felt like a bloodthirsty ex-pirate with blue balls. An ex-pirate who was on the verge of losing every claim to control he had, because it had been too long.

She managed to find the Argand lamp across the room, and turned it all the way up. The light spilled over her body, making her limbs shine like alabaster. When she didn't immediately return to bed, he sat up, groaning a little; his body did not want to bend in that precise fashion at this moment.

"Aren't you coming back?" It emerged as a harsh growl.

Theo was standing by the mantelpiece, her hands once more on her hips. "What's the matter?" he asked, choking back *"now."*

"This," she said, with a wave of her hand. She seemed to be waving toward him. Or possibly the bed. "It's not the same." Her eyes pooled in the soft light like darkness itself. Her lips were plump and luscious. "Doesn't it all seem different to you?"

"Well, you're much more beautiful than you were as a mere girl," he said, schooling his impatience. "And I'm more battered."

She opened her mouth, and then stopped. "Right." She paused and then said, "No. We must get this right."

"I'll do anything," he said instantly. "I shouldn't have—or rather, I *should* have—let you—"

"Don't!" She shouted it at him.

"What?"

"Don't *be* like this!"

James cleared his throat. For the first time, he wasn't sure he could be the man she needed or wanted. Which meant he wasn't sure he could stay married to her.

In that moment a stroke of fury lit his entire body, fueled by an hours-long erection that was driving him around the bend. In one stride he was beside her, hands on her arms. "You *are* my wife!" he growled.

She tipped her head back to see his face, baring

the long clean line of her neck. He wanted to bite it. He wanted to bite her all over, to sweat on her, and plunge into her, and lick her head to foot. He wanted to use her body. He wanted his own to be used.

"You liked the way we made love. No: you *loved* it. I can't become some sort of tame spaniel just so you'll go to bed with me!" The last declaration came out in a shout worthy of his father.

She didn't seem to mind. An expression that looked a great deal like relief spread over her face and she looped her arms around his neck and tried to pull his mouth down to her lips.

James didn't let her. Instead, he picked her up and half threw her onto the bed, then crawled on top of her, acutely conscious of his bulk and muscle looming over her. "I'm tattooed and scarred, and bigger than hell," he reminded her, when she said nothing.

The smile that curled on her lips was pure greed. He felt a germ of hope. "I see that," she purred. She gave up trying to pull his head to hers and ran her fingers up his arms instead.

"Are you afraid?"

She laughed, and something in his gut eased, but he had more to say.

"I don't give a twopenny damn what you wear under your skirts, but if you wear drawers, I might rip them off you in the pantry. I want you so damn much right now that I feel as if I've lost my mind. I've never really wanted any woman but you." He took a deep breath. "My mistresses were just signs of how dead I was. Dead to you, dead to the world. Dead to myself."

Her eyes softened, and she cupped his cheek with her hand. "You're back now."

"I am. I'm back. But I didn't come back a lapdog, Daisy. I can't pretend to be some sort of lily-livered, bloodless version of myself anymore. I can't be Trevelyan."

"I don't want you to be."

"I need you to come back, too." He had to be very clear about this. Everything depended on it.

Her brows drew together.

"I need you to find the courage you had when you were my Daisy." He chose his words as precisely as he could. "I died to myself—and to you—for a few years, but part of you died as well. You won't allow yourself to feel joy."

"I feel joy," she objected. "At times."

"Life is messy. It's messy and smelly and embarrassing. And desire is messy and smelly and embarrassing, too. There is nothing about your body that is distasteful to me. And I don't give a damn what society thinks we should or shouldn't be doing in our marriage bed."

Her lips were trembling, and he didn't know whether that was bad or good, but he kept going. "You can make love to me any way you please, and I will never, ever deny you. For my part, I want to kiss you everywhere. I always did, and it hasn't gone away. It's even stronger. We'll be at dinner with the Regent himself, and I'm going to be looking at you and planning where and how I will kiss you."

Her eyes shone with tears.

"Here," he said, running a finger over her lower lip. "Here." He shifted to the side and wrapped a possessive hand about one of her breasts. It plumped in his hand and a little sound broke from his lips. But he wasn't finished. "Here." Holding her gaze, he ran his fingers, fast and rough, over her belly and into the little tuft of amber hair between her legs. She was wet and warm and open.

But he didn't stop.

"Here," he said, his fingers sliding back to caress the most private place of all.

She gasped, but he could see a faint shadow of pleasure on her face even as she squirmed away from his touch.

"There is no place on your body that I don't want to kiss, Daisy. That I don't lust after. Because this is the most beautiful breast in the world." He bent his head and gave her nipple a kiss and a warm lick. "And this is the most—"

He started to head south, but she was laughing through her tears, and she pulled him back up.

But he wasn't finished, still wasn't finished.

"I'll kiss you in the Regent's own dining room if you'll let me. You're the only one for me. I came back from the dead for you, Daisy. Twice."

"I'm so glad you came back for me," she whispered. A tear like liquid crystal ran down her cheek and disappeared into her hair.

"I never should have left you."

More tears. He caressed her wet cheek with his thumb, pulling her tight against his chest.

"I love you," he said, telling her hair because she had buried her face against him. "You haven't told me the same," he continued, "so I'll say it for you. You love me too." Then, because there are limits to how long even the most self-collected man can wait, and because he had reached his furthest limit, he reared over her, and said, "I shall now have my way with my duchess. Speak now, or hereafter hold your peace."

He saw a kindling of pleasure in her eyes, which he took as her reply, so he pushed her knees farther apart and thrust.

She arched against him with a gasp, hands clenched on his forearms. "*Again,* please, James. Please."

He gave her one more.

"Oh, that feels so good!"

He took a deep breath and fought for control. "I cannot be a proper gentleman all the time," he growled, needing to make one last point. "I'm not tame like that. I can't *be* tamed like that. I felt like an ass trying to be amused all the time, the way Trevelyan is." His jaw clenched even saying the name.

Theo looked up at her husband and felt as if her heart was going to burst. James *wasn't* at all like Geoffrey, but powerful and fierce and domineering. He had a tattoo under one eye, and he would never be at home in a drawing room. He was disorganized and untidy, and he threw newspapers on the floor. He wasn't much good at making beds. He would always make fun of her Rules, even as he respected her. He meant to kiss her in all the wrong places.

He would not be delicate or, sometimes, even courteous.

Sure enough, at that moment he grabbed her hips and thrust forward deep and hard.

Her scream came from somewhere so hidden within her body that she hadn't known it existed. His only response was to bend down, his nose to hers, and declare, "I have my *cock* buried in you, Daisy. That's a word ladies don't like, but you like it. Don't you?"

Theo nodded. And then he flexed his hips, again. She did. Scream again.

"This is not *amorous congress* or *carnal intercourse*," James told her, his jaw clenched as he fought to regain control (though he never quite did). "This is the Act of Shame. And. We. Are. Not. Ashamed."

After that the duke proceeded to demonstrate for his duchess almost all of the terms he knew for the sport of Venus. He was a pirate. He knew a lot.

That night, they pounded the bed and danced in the sheets. They boffed and boinked and did the dirty deed. After a while they started making up their own descriptions for the sweaty, messy, joyful games they were playing.

Her Grace proved to have a knack for coming up with phrases all of her own, and they played the blanket hornpipe until they collapsed. The sheet had long ago migrated to the floor, but neither noticed.

They each did each other personal services of one kind or another, taking turns gulping air, crying out, and losing control, utterly. Sometimes they did it at the same moment.

As it turned out, the Duke and Duchess of Ashbrook did not leave that bedchamber for four days. They spent a good deal of their time in the bed. But they also made love in the bathtub, on the little stool, and on the floor.

One morning a chambermaid almost caught her master and mistress making love when she came to light the fire; His Grace threw a sheet over his wife, who was giggling so uncontrollably that the whole bed shook.

At some point the duke decided to make a point about just how beautiful his wife was, and before she could stop him, he tossed a Parisian-designed cape worth a small fortune out the window, where it fell into the garden and became stuck on a hedge, rosy silk lining shining in the sunshine.

"Just like it was before," one of the footmen told Maydrop. "Her wedding dress went out that same window seven years ago." Neither of them could make head nor tail of that.

Maydrop summoned back the staff, and the duke told him—*sotto voce*—that he could pay off all those extra men he'd bribed to act as journalists.

By the end of the week, the duchess was almost used to being disheveled and imperfectly groomed, at least part of the time. She had resigned herself to the fact that her husband stubbornly considered her to be just as beautiful now as she was at seventeen, as well as to the fact that James would never really understand what clothing did for a woman—or a man. Though he was an expert on the lack of clothing.

She was very, very happy.

She was still married.

A Rather Long Epilogue

The Regent's Ball
May 1817

As every married couple in the history of married couples has discovered, married life is not always a bed of roses.

It was the afternoon on the day the Regent was to bestow the Order of the Bath on James. Hours earlier, Theo had screamed at him because he'd knocked over a jasperware fish, which had been delicately balanced on its tail in a positive marvel of Ashbrook Ceramics craftsmanship.

James had shouted back that positioning a slender marble column next to the library door was a daft thing to do, because someone might easily enter the room and then move to the side as he had done, with calamitous consequences. "My life was a damn sight easier when the only fish in view had scales!"

"Fine," Theo had shouted in return. "Feel free to join your fishy friends once again!"

At the sound of raised voices, Maydrop had whisked his staff away from the library door. Experience had taught him that the duke and duchess sometimes required privacy outside the matrimonial bedchambers.

Sure enough, when the duchess had emerged an

hour or so later, her hair was tousled rather than sleek, and the clasp of her necklace was hanging over her bosom. She didn't emerge on her own two feet, either.

The duke loved to carry his wife about. "Putting those muscles of his to good use," the maids whispered to each other, giggling madly.

Marriage was not easy, but neither was it unrewarding. In fact, James had grinned all afternoon following the demise of the china fish, even though he was dreading the evening. He was to receive a commendation for meritorious duties to the Crown in the unfortunate matter of the slave trade, and the ceremony was to be followed by a ball. He loathed that sort of occasion, but if putting on a sash and wearing an absurd costume for one evening would help him win the upcoming vote on abolishing slavery (rather than just the slave trade) throughout the British empire, it was the least he could do. At least they'd waived the ritual purification by bathing; that was something for which to be grateful.

Besides, Theo wanted him to accept it. And what Theo wanted, James gave her, to the best of his power. Even when it meant he felt as ridiculous as a peacock draped in a velvet stole.

Thus, he was now standing in his bedchamber while his valet, Gosffens, fussed over him. He had already put James in a doublet sewn all over with pearls, and then a surcoat of red tartarin, lined and edged with white sarcenet. That was followed by a white sash, which was bad enough, but now Gosffens had brought out boots adorned with huge golden spurs, practically as large as wagon wheels.

James peered down at them with distaste. "Where did that vulgar rubbish come from?"

"Specially made for the Knights of the Bath," his valet stated.

James jammed his feet into the boots.

"And now the Mantle of the Order," Gosffens said in a hushed voice. He reverently shook out a mantle of the same color as the surcoat and tied it around James's neck with a length of white lace.

James glared at the mirror as if daring it to crack in two. "White lace, Gosffens? White *lace?* I look like a horse's arse."

Gosffens was lifting the lid from yet another box. James glanced over—and realized his valet was removing a red bonnet. *A bonnet?*

He put up with a lot in the area of dress. His wife had decided opinions, and she loved nothing more than to dress him in velvet and silk, in colors not generally seen on men and sometimes embroidered with flowers; she said that the more extravagant his clothing, the more piratical he appeared. Once James discovered just how seductive his duchess found that piratical look, he had even been known to wear a coat in a subtle shade of pink.

But a bonnet was going too far. James held out his hand without a word. Gosffens handed it to him, and then watched with a tragic expression as James ripped it straight down the middle and tossed it out the window.

"Your ceremonial bonnet," the valet wailed.

"I'll let you put on a wig," James said, by way of compromise.

Gosffens came at him next with a stickpin topped with a diamond the size of a large grape.

"Where did that monstrosity come from?" James said, waving it away.

His valet gave him a smug smile. "It is a gift from Her Grace, in honor of your investiture as a Knight of the Bath."

James sighed, and Gosffens stabbed it into the crimson mantle. "After all, you are the pirate duke," his man said. "We must not disappoint your followers."

For his part, James would be perfectly happy to disappoint anyone stupid enough to give a hang about what he was wearing. "I suppose the duchess will be particularly magnificent this evening?"

"I believe they began the dressing process at one o'clock," Gosffens affirmed. James's valet received a good deal of his sense of self-worth from the fact that he lived under the roof of the most stylish woman in London. One o'clock was three hours ago, and James thought it likely that Daisy wouldn't be ready for another hour.

• • •

In the end, the ceremony wasn't too intolerable. The Regent was mercifully brief in bestowing the Order of the Bath. At the ball that followed, James accepted the congratulations of eleven fatuous knights who were convinced that the twelve of them were the cream of the kingdom. Successfully suppressing the impulse to laugh aloud, he used his new knightly influence to push Sir Flanner (knighted for service in the war) toward support of his anti-slavery bill, so that was a night's—or *knight's*—work well done.

By then James had long since lost track of his duchess. Theo was in high demand among the *ton*. The papers described her every opinion and new gown; he himself never seemed to be able to leave his own front door without brushing up against members of the penny press waiting to see his wife.

Far too often for his own taste, a bored reporter would amuse himself by writing up another description of the pirate duke, with his "brutal" tattoo. Those articles invariably ended with some variation on the same theme: no one could understand how the most elegant woman in London tolerated marriage to the most uncouth man in the peerage.

But at the same time, no one could argue with the fact Her Grace obviously adored her husband.

The duchess didn't smile often, but she smiled for the duke.

Personally, James thought her face in repose was lovely, but when she smiled—especially at him—it was extraordinary.

Thinking of that, he began to look for her with more purpose. They'd been here at least two and a half hours, and he and Theo had negotiated a three-hour limit for social occasions involving more than ten persons. (The duchess may have abandoned her Rules in the bedchamber, but she was still given to them in other aspects of her life. One of these days he was going to stop dropping the newspapers on the breakfast room floor.)

He poked his head into the drawing room, but there was no sign of his wife. He looked in the card rooms, and the ballroom, and she didn't seem to be there, either. There was nothing for it but to extend his search to the floor above.

He was dawdling in the long gallery, looking at the portraits of pompous royalty, when he heard Geoffrey Trevelyan's drawling voice around the corner. For all James despised the man, Theo insisted on dancing with him now and then. James was of the considered opinion that she did it because she knew that it drove him mad.

Just as he turned on his spurred heel to head in the other direction—he took the avoidance of Sir Geoffrey to the level of art—he made out what

Trevelyan was saying in that arrogant manner of his.

"The Ugly Duchess might as well be wearing the Emperor's new clothes." This, with a snigger. "All the fine clothing in the world can't give her the figure of a woman, *or* the profile of one. I really think that she might be a man. You know the reputation that pirates—"

At that precise moment James rounded the corner. Trevelyan, aghast, snapped his mouth shut.

Just because a man has learned to control his temper doesn't mean that he isn't capable of losing it when circumstances demand. James twisted his former schoolmate's cravat around his hand, hoisted him into the air, and slammed him against the wall, bellowing at the top of his lungs. "How *dare* you say such a thing about my wife? You foul, malicious piece of garbage. You cur, unfit to be in her presence."

Trevelyan's face was turning an interesting color of plum, and he seemed disinclined to answer, possibly because the cravat was cutting off his air supply. That was all right: James's question was rhetorical.

He slammed Trevelyan against the wall again. "She is the most beautiful"—*slam!*—"exquisite"—*slam!*—"woman in all of London."

By now James could hear people rushing up the stairs, but he didn't care. "I never saw a woman more beautiful, not in China,"—*slam!*—"not in the Indies,"—*slam!*—"and certainly not in the British Isles. Even more important, she is incredibly kind. Witness the time she wastes talking to you, you spiteful, shriveled worm." *Slam, slam, slam!*

A hand touched his sleeve, and he turned, teeth bared. It was Theo.

"Dear heart," she said, and with just those two words, the rage drained from him and he dropped Trevelyan like a piece of discarded laundry.

The spiteful worm instantly began to crawl away. *"You!"* James said, in precisely the same voice with which he used to roar some version of *"Time to die!"* as he leapt over a ship's rail.

Trevelyan heard and understood; he froze.

"If you ever utter a word about my wife that is less than complimentary, I will not slam you against the wall again. I will instead send you through a window. And not on the ground floor, either."

James didn't wait for an answer; who expects garbage to answer back? Instead, he held out his arm to his wife.

When they turned, they saw that the gallery was now crammed with people.

"My duchess," James stated, his eyes sweeping the crowd with the air of a man who has ruled the waves. "She is not a swan, because that would imply she had once been an ugly duckling."

He glanced down at Theo. Her eyes were

painted with an exotic tilt at the corners. Her cheekbones were regal and her bottom lip was colored a perfect red that made it more kissable than it already was. Small but lush breasts, skin the color of clear moonlight, rose above a waist the size of a man's hand.

But none of that mattered compared to the innate kindness in her eyes, the joyful turn of her lip, the wild intelligence with which she greeted every day.

That was beautiful.

Without another word, they walked down the long gallery, Theo's fingers poised on his sleeve, the crowd parting like the Red Sea as they approached. James saw approval on their faces, and then someone began to clap. It may even have been the Regent himself.

Two hands clapping became several, and then more, and finally they descended the stairs to the sound of a ballroom full of peers applauding.

Safe in the carriage while being driven home, Theo managed to stop herself from crying. James asked her if she was all right, but words were so bundled in her heart that she couldn't utter them, and she just nodded and held his hand very, very tightly.

Once inside the house, she handed her cape to Maydrop, caught James's hand before he had removed his greatcoat, and wordlessly led him to the foot of the staircase. He followed her up, his coat still on, with a bellow of laughter.

She remained silent when they were in her bedchamber, and the door was closed behind them. For a precious moment she allowed herself to just look at her pirate. James's elegant features were still there. His tattoo only emphasized the sweep of his lashes, the curve of his lip, the arch of his cheekbones.

As he shrugged off his greatcoat, she reached up to pull off his wig, then tossed it aside. He was huge, and beautiful, with a contained power about him that had made a shipful of pirates—and a crowded room of lords—acquiesce to whatever he proposed.

He was *hers*.

"Are you angry that I slammed Trevelyan about a bit?" James asked, even though in this one matter he obviously didn't give a damn what she thought, and would do it again in a heartbeat.

She took a moment to find the right words. "You told the whole world that I was beautiful to you."

"You are," he said simply. "Not just to me, either."

Tears threatened to fall again, but again she willed them away. James was lounging back against the door like the pirate king he was, his expression wicked and tender, both at once.

"I always thought," she said haltingly, "that you started loving me when you were blind, when you were twelve. Because you couldn't see me."

His eyebrow shot up. "Rubbish. I loved you long before."

"You did?"

"The year before, when my mother died. You came to me that night. Don't you remember? You were still in a small bed in the nursery, and I had graduated to a larger bed next door. You came to my room without a word, after Nurse retired for the night, and you crawled in bed with me. I started crying then, and I sobbed until I didn't have another tear in me."

"I'd forgotten that," Theo said, remembering now.

"But do you know *why* I fell in love with you?"

There was a shining glint of impious laughter in his eyes. She shook her head.

"Because you brought eight handkerchiefs to my bed with you. Eight. And precisely eight starched handkerchiefs later, I felt able to live another day."

She couldn't stop her smile. "I like to be prepared."

"You *knew* me." His eyes were naked and vulnerable. "All through my life, you've been my lodestone, the key to my heart. I lost you for a while, Daisy." He straightened and went to her. "I couldn't bear it if I lost you again."

"You won't," she whispered, pulling his head down to hers.

One of the moments that Theo—or Daisy, as her

husband persisted in calling her—remembered throughout her entire life came later that night.

They were sprawled on the bed. As usual, one of the sheets trailed on the floor. The duchess's hair was standing up on one side. The duke was complaining that he'd pulled a muscle in his left hip and it was her fault, because "no man was meant to bend in that fashion."

Theo gave her husband a kiss, and told him a secret that she had kept nestled in her heart, waiting until she was absolutely certain. "And *you,*" she stated, "will be the most wonderful father this baby could possibly have had."

James couldn't seem to find any words. He stared at her for a moment, then sat back against the headboard and gently eased her between his legs, spreading his huge hands on her belly.

As she relaxed happily against his shoulder, to her utter astonishment, he began to sing. His voice was nothing like the clear tenor he'd once had. It was the voice of a man who'd been to sea; it sounded like brandy and sin.

"Dance with me," he sang, "to the end of life."

He paused after that line and whispered in her ear. "That means that you and I will dance down the days of this life together, and perhaps even beyond." He dropped a kiss on her nose and sang on, his hands tenderly resting on her still-flat stomach. "Dance me to our children, who are waiting to be born."

Theo swallowed her tears and raised her voice to sing with him, her clear soprano entwining with his imperfect—but oh, so beautiful—bass.

"Dance with me," they sang together, "to the end of life."

It was the first of many songs that James sang for their firstborn, and their second born, and for the third and fourth, who came as a matched set. The children knew that their father didn't like to sing. But they also knew that if their mother asked him . . . well, Papa never could say no to her.

So together the family danced and sang—a pirate and a duchess, a duke and an artist, a man and a woman—down the many days and byways of a long and happy life.

Historical Note

All my novels have drawn inspiration from a combination of literary fiction, historical facts, and elements of my own life (my husband would be the first to point out that Theo's wish to catalog her ribbons is duplicated in my own shelves). *The Ugly Duchess* obviously follows that pattern, in that its greatest debt is to the story "The Ugly Duckling," written by the Danish poet and storyteller Hans Christian Andersen. Andersen's fairytale was published in 1843, making use of it here anachronistic, for which I beg forgiveness. I wanted to place my story in the Regency, and more precisely, I wanted Theo to be in Paris after the 1814 Treaty of Fontainebleau.

At the same time, this novel is my first to have received inspiration from a living person outside my own family (I don't count Sir Justin Fiebvre, in *The Duke Is Mine*; while Justin Bieber is obviously inspirational to many, Sir Justin was a minor character). Some time ago, my attention was caught by an article describing the "Rules" created by the fascinating, eclectic, and altogether magnificent Iris Apfel. Theo came up with rules suited to her own time and place, but Iris's ("Visit the animal kingdom") served as a jumping-off point. Another source of fashion advice was Genevieve Antoine Dariaux's *A Guide to Elegance:*

For Every Woman Who Wants to be Well and Properly Dressed on all Occasions. Elegance, Dariaux announces, is harmony, a lesson that Theo took to heart.

I want to add that the chapter set in the House of Lords owes much to a similar scene depicted in Dorothy Sayers's *Clouds of Witness* (1926). And finally, Sir Griffin Barry is modeled on a real life pirate from the Renaissance, a young reprobate who was a playwright and a gentleman, as well as a pirate.

Center Point Large Print
600 Brooks Road / PO Box 1
Thorndike ME 04986-0001 USA

(207) 568-3717

US & Canada:
1 800 929-9108
www.centerpointlargeprint.com